I0733227

This Calamitous Sea

Darren John Wilson

First Edition Published in the United Kingdom
in 2022 by aSys Publishing

eBook Edition First Published in the United Kingdom
in 2022 by aSys Publishing

Copyright © Darren John Wilson 2022

Darren John Wilson has asserted his rights under 'the Copyright Designs and Patents Act 1988' to be identified as the author of this work.

All rights reserved.

No part of this book may be reproduced or transmitted in any form or by any means, electronic, mechanical, photocopying, recording, or otherwise, without prior written permission from the Author.

Disclaimer

This is a work of fiction. Names, characters, businesses, places, events and incidents are either the products of the author's imagination or used in a fictitious manner. Any resemblance to actual persons, living or dead, or actual events is purely coincidental.

ISBN: 978-1-913438-58-6
aSys Publishing 2022

ONE

I often found myself drinking in the middle of the afternoon. For me, standing in front of an Oxford public house, daring myself not to enter, was a semi-illicit thrill. I was like an erotomaniac standing outside a brothel. I was not a hardened drinker and certainly not an alcoholic. One drink was often enough, and two drinks were never too many, and what I drank was beer, ale, not spirits. Though I enjoyed human society when drinking, I was content to drink alone. Drinking with company often turned me into a bore. I would sound off about how youngsters today didn't know they were born, or give my hapless interlocutor chapter and verse on the Winter of Discontent and its attendant ravages. "All women become like their mothers. That's their tragedy. No man does. That's his." So said Oscar Wilde. I felt entitled to conclude from that delightful epigram that all men became like their fathers, so that, when talking in public, I sounded like my father would have sounded, had he lived to be forty. I supposed that it was one way of getting to know Albert James Winter, three decades after his death. As often as not, in any case, I found companionship in pubs, owing to my ability to attract the kind of people that sensible folk crossed the road to avoid. Then I would be regaled with tales of a thousand winters of discontent told by someone several soiled sheets to the wind.

***

Two pints of Tribute later, I stumbled out of the King's Arms feeling yet more melancholy than when I'd entered. That had less to do with the beer and more to do with the weather: as a pluviophile, I'd stepped into the pub, with the January wind and rain blowing in my face, feeling content in my melancholy, but had emerged onto streets still windswept but now bathed in low winter sunlight, a sight which depressed me somewhat. Kendal had often called me a vampire: she was always marching around the flat, opening the curtains, while I took refuge behind anything which shielded me from the daylight pouring in through the windows.

Wondering which way to go, I looked left, towards Radcliffe Square, and decided that, apart from the possibility of again admiring a collection of fine-looking buildings, I had no reason to venture in that direction. Then I looked right, down Parks Road, and told myself that I had *every* reason to take that particular highway, for it would take me home, via my new office. In the event, I walked straight ahead, towards Broad Street, keen to while away half-an-hour or so in Blackwell's, a bibliophile's paradise if ever there was one.

In the King's Arms, I'd supped my beer alone, wondering what *should* go through a man's mind when he's drinking alone. What did I normally think about when drinking alone? Nothing much. I simply allowed thoughts to drift into my mind and to leave before they'd had a chance to get a hearing. Inasmuch as I'd thought of anything, I'd thought of Roseanne. Five months after discovering her whereabouts, I'd still not been to see her. It wasn't that I didn't want to see her. It's just that I'd no idea what to say. After all, what on earth does a middle-aged man say to a woman, his mother, who'd left him when he was a boy of eight? Laura, my sister, was angry with me for being so disposed to keeping my distance, but rare was the time when she wasn't upbraiding me for one misdemeanour or another. It was like being related to a spitting cobra. I lived in hope that she would lighten up one day. That said, I lived in hope of meeting the great John Thaw, and he'd been dead four years.

What other thoughts had chanced upon me as I imbibed Cornwall's finest ale in Oxford's finest hostelry? Well, it had occurred to me how impossibly young the staff looked: as I sat at the bar, on the Holywell Street side of the establishment, I'd realised that I was being served by people barely old enough to be in a pub without falling foul of the law. I was used to feeling old in the King's Arms, given that students used the place like a common room — sometimes, even as a study room, where they researched and wrote their essays — but the staff there today had made me feel like a certified ancient monument. Perhaps I was at that age when police officers started looking young. That's when you knew you were getting old.

Before crossing the threshold of Blackwell's, I toyed with the idea of treating myself to a swift couple of halves in the White Horse. You got a nice drop of fluid in there. Very cosy it was too. Good sense prevailed. I'd had enough to drink already that day, and I couldn't be sure that I would get through the rest of the day successfully resisting the blandishments of the Dew Drop, my North Oxford local. There was always an excuse for another drink. If ever I failed to conjure an excuse, circumstances would step in and provide one. I *would* have another drink, in Blackwell's, a coffee, in the shop's sumptuously upholstered café. If I could get a seat, that was, for the café was enormously popular, and not just because of the coffee: people came from miles around to partake of its carrot cake, which was so rich and stodgy that only the best coffee in town could wash it down.

Blackwell's welcomed me with open arms.

***

"Hello, Daniel!"

I'd been roused from my literary reverie by the exquisite voice of Helena Johnson-Roffey. My eyes lit up at the sight of her. She was stunning as ever. For a woman of her standing, she was underdressed in jeans, sweatshirt and fleece jacket, but there was no mistaking her class. Her accent was so cut-glass that it homed in on the book I was holding and nearly sliced it in two. The book that I was clutching was none other than my very own attempt to leave a mark on literary posterity: *Crystal.* Blackwell's had done me a favour by agreeing to stock the book, though I was bound to wonder why there was only ever one copy on display, possibly the same unsold copy, the copy doomed never to sell.

"Hello, Duchess," I replied, once I'd digested the woman's beauty in all its magnificence.

"Duchess?" she said. "Is that another of your working-class affectations?"

"My working-class credentials are impeccable."

"Aren't you from Lancing?"

"Yes, but don't be fooled into thinking that Lancing College has anything to do with Lancing."

Helena and I often bantered in this way. An onlooker might have mistaken it for flirtation. If that's what it was then it had no chance of consummation.

The lady looked me up and down with disapproval written all over her sublimely crafted features.

"I shall have to take you shopping, Daniel."

"Well, if you're paying..."

"You're always dressed in black."

"Perhaps I'm in a perpetual state of mourning."

"You make the Grim Reaper look cheerful in all that black."

More often than not, charm was mightily disarming. It had served me well in the past. It was about to do me proud once again.

"May I say how lovely you look today, as always, Helena?"

She shot me with a look of outright suspicion. She looked like a duchess studying a diamond, trying to convince herself that it wasn't a fake.

"Interesting," she said, "that you should pay me a compliment after all this time."

"All this time?" I returned with mock indignation. "I've only known you six months."

"And, in all that time, you've never thought to compliment me."

"I was waiting for the right moment."

"What are you up to, you proletarian scoundrel?"

"You sound like a well-heeled character from an Agatha Christie novel."

We both laughed at that.

"Am I not allowed to tell a friend how delightful she looks today?"

I was laying on the flattery with a trowel now, and I had little or no idea why I was doing it. Perhaps I was just telling her the truth. Perhaps it was the beer talking. Perhaps the beer was eliciting the truth. Perhaps, reprehensibly, I was just amusing myself at her expense.

"You always look so distinguished, Helena, even when so casually dressed as you are now."

"Are you saying I'm scruffy?"

"On the contrary. I'm saying that class speaks for itself. It doesn't have to try. There's no hiding it."

"Have you been drinking?"

"I'm the working-class blackguard," I declared theatrically. "You can take the boy out of the council estate, but you can't take the council estate out of the man. You simply can't polish a turd."

Helena winced at that last sentence of my little speech.

"But, by the same token," I went on with a flourish, "you can't unpolish a diamond."

"Give me that book!" Helena said by way of dismissing my flannel. "I keep meaning to buy that book of yours." *Crystal* was snatched from my grasp. Even that was done elegantly. I felt like renaming the book *Diamond*, just for her.

"But it's the last copy," I protested, playfully, as I chased Helena to the till. "All the other copies have been remaindered," I said to the sales assistant, winking, daring her to recognise me as the author of the book being paid for.

"Let's talk about your book over a coffee," Helena suggested.

"Okay," I agreed. Talking over a cappuccino represented a definite step up in our relationship. "But *I'm* paying."

"Agreed!" The word was uttered as Helena received her penny change from a ten-pound note. "Ridiculously over-priced, some of these books," she proclaimed with a wry smirk at me, and a wink at the lady behind the counter, who must have been wondering why customers kept taking her into cheeky private confidences. Anyway, she played along by smiling.

I nursed the insult all the way up two flights of creaking stairs to the coffee shop.

TWO

The coffee was first-class and the company even better. Until that moment, I hadn't realised quite how much I liked Helena Johnson-Roffey. As if it were remotely possible, her conversation was yet more sparkling than her appearance. I found myself fully cognisant of the fact that I was flirting with her, and she with me.

"Thanks for this," she said as she gazed wonderingly at the large cup of the frothiest cappuccino ever crafted. She poked around the froth with her teaspoon as if to check that there was some coffee underneath the ethereal topping. Once she was satisfied that she would eventually encounter something substantial, she looked at me with a smile so radiant that it almost blinded me.

I smiled at her in turn, mindful that my smile was about as radiant as a wet Tuesday afternoon in Bognor Regis. "I felt that I owed you one after all those compliments," I joked.

"You're ever the enigma," she said.

"Me? Enigmatic?" I replied. "I'm an open book."

Helena shook her head and her mane of blonde hair moved with it. "I can't make you out."

"You're right," I said. "I'm complicated. My life has been one long complication. There were so many complications when I was born that the midwife feared that my mother would give birth to a Milan Kundera novel."

Helena thought about laughing. She contended herself with another radiant smile.

"Weren't you born *before* Milan Kundera's first novel was published?"

The question was posed with a knavish impudence and had to be answered in kind.

"How old do you think I am?"

"Oh, about forty, give or take…"

"*Take*, if you don't mind," I lied.

Though my words were addressing her directly, my eyes were fixed on her flowing golden locks, and the scrutiny was not going unnoticed.

"Why do you keep looking at my hair?"

"I'm looking for clues."

"Clues about what?"

"Your age…"

"I don't dye my hair, if that's what you mean."

"That was never in doubt."

"If you want clues as to my age then take a look at my world-weary, careworn features."

Her modesty was as false as a duchess's dropped aitches. All the same, I played along with it.

"I don't see a single wrinkle," I demurred.

"Look closer."

"Actually, you might be right."

Helena glared at me.

"Close your eyes," I said.

Her obedience was quite endearing.

"There are two large wrinkles just above your nose."

"You're such a comedian!"

Her rejoinder was accompanied by a kick at my shin. Her shiny black boot was a near-lethal weapon, and her aim was perfect. Who would have thought that coffee with a duchess would have ended with grievous bodily harm, and she the perpetrator?

"Sorry, did I hurt you?"

"Not at all," I gasped. "Please kick the other shin," I urged her with a grimace. "I'm OCD and I hate imbalance."

"So, you want a matching bruise on the other shin, do you?"

"I insist." Tears were making of my eyes two conspicuous harbingers of pain.

"I really hurt you, didn't I?"

"Don't worry, I'm a masochist."

"I'm so sorry."

Now, I've been called many things in my time, one of them being opportunistic, and it was a fundamental principle of mine never to miss an opportunity to live up to my reputation. So, I told her that she could make it up to me by agreeing to dine with me at a time and place of her choosing.

"Lovely!" she replied with unexpected relish. "How about ..."

"How about tomorrow evening, at seven o'clock, at your place?"

"You've got a nerve!"

"Would you like some carrot cake?"

She pondered the question for a second. "No, let's save our appetites for tomorrow."

Our cups were drained of coffee. I for one could not remember having taken a single sip, such was my absorption in my companion and her multifarious charms. I did recall several times having had to pull my chair in to let people pass. They certainly crammed people into that little space.

Outside, Helena offered me a lift back to Summertown. I declined, saying that I needed a walk and some fresh air. What I meant was that I wanted a pint of ale in the White Horse.

As we went our separate ways, as I stepped eagerly towards another of Oxford's irresistible watering holes, I was made to reflect upon what Helena had said over the remnants of two large cups of cappuccino.

"Let's save our appetites for tomorrow."

Whatever had she meant by that?

THREE

Two pints of Brakspear went down a treat. I walked home. When I reached the gates of the University Parks, I found them closed, which was a shame because I had an urgent need to relieve myself. I fancied that I would take advantage of the dark by doing the deed behind a tree, but my brain—addled more by the prospect of romance than by the booze—had failed to compute that the park was closed *because* it was dark. So, I walked home wondering if it were possible to walk with my legs crossed, and finding that it wasn't. I'd wanted to go to the toilet in the White Horse, but the pub was tiny, and it was so busy that the path to the toilets was blocked. So, I hadn't troubled myself with the effort. Now I was paying the price for my laziness with a bladder ready to burst.

I arrived back at the office just in time to avoid being mistaken for an incontinent tramp.

"Where the hell have you been?" Kendal asked me as I dashed for the lavatory.

"There and back to see how far it is," was my childish reply.

"If I want to see and hear Niagara Falls, I'll take a plane to Africa."

Kendal had got up from her seat at the desk. She kicked the toilet door shut in a fit of teenaged pique. She really was getting far too big for her boots.

I was not so absorbed in blissful relief that I was unable to correct the jumped-up little tyrant.

"Niagara Falls are in North America," I said, barely able to hear my own voice.

Kendal was still staying at my flat. She'd been there nearly six months now, though she'd made one or two forays back to her house in Jericho, there to argue with Rosie, her mother, a woman who held me in barely concealed contempt.

"Niagara Falls *are* in Africa," Kendal told me as I came out of the lavatory and stood over her.

"You're thinking of *Victoria* Falls," I said.

"Whatever…"

"What are you doing on the laptop?" I asked.

"Typing up your case notes…"

"I didn't know I'd made any case notes."

"You haven't. *I've* made some. I'm recording your cases, Daniel."

"Are you the Doctor Watson to my Sherlock Holmes?"

"It's important that you document your cases, Daniel."

"I do…up here." I tapped my forehead with a finger.

Anyway, I agreed, and I thanked her for being so helpful and conscientious. I even suggested that she was making herself indispensable, to which she replied that she'd made herself just so before I'd taken my second case. There was no point in arguing with her. She was more stubborn than a mule and self-doubt did not exist in her universe. If ever I got the better of Kendal Waterhouse in an argument, that is an event that I *would* record.

"Talking of cases," I said, "I've had your mum on my case again."

"What does she want now?"

"What she always wants…"

"She's not going to report you to social services, Daniel."

"That's easy for you to sit there and say."

"Mum knows that she and I cannot possibly live together, so you're doing her a favour by letting me live with you."

"I'm letting you *stay* with me."

"What's the difference?"

"There's a *huge* difference."

Kendal shook her head as if the slightest motion of her imperious cranium settled the matter.

"Mum threatens to set the dogs on you because she wants to get back at you for dumping her."

"I didn't dump her, because we were *never* an item."

"Whatever you say, Daniel…"

"Unbelievable!"

"Make yourself a coffee and calm down," she ordered, "and make me one while you're at it."

Pleased that there was something in my domain over which I had some control, I went over to the kettle and regarded it gratefully. I almost kissed it for not answering me back.

"How many calls have we had?" I posed the question more in hope than expectation.

"Lots!"

"Great," I said. "Things are looking up."

"But only one call was for us."

I shook my head in despair. "Not more bloody calls from tenants of Greetwell Housing Trust?"

Kendal nodded. "You name it, they've called about it: broken boilers, blocked toilets, leaking taps, smashed windows, and more broken boilers."

"I've told Matt Prior a hundred times to tell his bosses at Greetwell Housing Trust to sort this matter out."

"Your friend Matt?"

"He's also a maintenance inspector at Greetwell Housing Trust."

"Oh, my God, that means he's a colleague of Mum's!"

"It's a small world."

"You could've asked Mum."

"As if *she's* going to lift a finger to help *me* …"

Kendal closed the laptop with uncharacteristic deftness and sat back in my chair with characteristic smugness.

"That reminds me," she said, a picture of executive self-assuredness. "He's coming here at six."

"Who is?"

"Matt," she said impatiently. "He called earlier."

The clock on the wall told us that Matt's arrival was at most ten minutes away. He would arrive at six on the dot, if he didn't arrive sooner.

"What does he want?" I wondered aloud.

"He's coming to look at that crack in the wall," Kendal replied with a nod at the blemish in question.

"Well, while he's here, he can tell us why he hasn't sorted out the problem with the telephones."

Kendal gave me one of her little-girl-lost looks. It was the look that she gave me when she needed to soften me up in advance of some cunning scheme of hers, so my suspicion was aroused immediately.

"Remind me," she said, "what *is* the problem with the telephone numbers?"

"As I've explained several times before, Greetwell Housing Trust sent their annual Christmas newsletter to all their tenants." My tone was watchfully reproachful, watchful because Kendal was given to hitting back with a waspish insolence. "The newsletter contained the usual information about the housing association's maintenance department, the number that tenants should call when they need something fixing, but, instead of giving out *their* number, they gave out the number of a North Oxford private detective, namely *myself.*"

"Why did they do that?"

"It was a mistake, Kendal." Sometimes, I wondered if she listened to a word I said. I'd furnished her with the very same explanation a few days before.

"Yes, I remember now."

My exasperation was expressed with a sigh.

"The two numbers are exactly the same," I continued, "except for the third and fourth digits' being transposed."

"And, in the newsletter, the number was given with the third and fourth digits wrongly placed, therefore giving *our* number?"

Kendal had a cheek in saying "*our* number". Anyway, I let it go.

"What a balls up!" she exclaimed with her customary elegance.

"Exactly!"

When Kendal changed the subject, suddenly, I knew that whatever cunning plan she'd hatched was about to break noisily out of its shell.

"The one genuine call that we did receive this afternoon, apart from Matt's … well, the woman's name sounded familiar."

"What was her name?"

"Belinda Waugh …"

"She's the woman I've been tailing for the past month!"

"I thought so."

"And I shall be tailing her tonight."

"She's not supposed to know that you're tailing her."

"I assume that she *doesn't* know."

"So why's she calling you?"

"God knows."

"Can I come with you tonight?"

"I knew you were plotting something."

"What do you mean?"

"You were giving me your butter-wouldn't-melt look just now, which told me that you were plotting something."

"You've such a suspicious mind, Daniel."

"I was a detective in the Metropolitan Police. Now I'm a private detective. Being suspicious is a way of life for me."

Kendal shot me with a conciliatory look. It was about as genuine as a fur coat at Peckham Market.

"I just want to watch a master at work, Daniel, that's all."

"Flattery will get you nowhere."

I uttered the words with a grudging admiration for the girl's powers of persuasion. She had both me and her mother dancing to her tune, whilst she played nonchalantly in our midst, now and then clicking her fingers so that we stopped dancing and started wrestling, or even boxing. One way or another, we always fell into line. We knew that we were being played. Rosie and I were jointly committing an act of semi-conscious submission to a peerless chancer and charmer. Kendal was the master, not I. If she were to attempt a coup—to usurp me, putting her name on the office door, and making me her would-be sidekick—I would likely yield to her machinations. She really was *that* beguiling.

"I need to concentrate when I'm on surveillance," I added. "I can't have you distracting me."

"How will I distract you?"

"Just by being there."

"I might be able to help you."

"Yes, all right," I said with a sigh, "but you mustn't interfere."

"Interfere with what exactly?" Kendal asked mockingly. "You'll just be sitting in the car, outside a house or a pub, listening to one of your CDs, waiting for something never to happen."

"That is what I'll *appear* to be doing."

"Well, I want to see you in action." Kendal peered down at the notebook on the desk. "And, while I remember, Belinda Waugh wants to meet you, at midday tomorrow, outside the main gates of the University Parks."

"Are you pulling my chain?"

"Look!" That single word contained Kendal's entire capacity for mockery and mischief. "It says so right here!"

"Why the University Parks of all places?"

"Perhaps she wants to feed the ducks with you."

At that moment, Matt bypassed the door that, in my desperation to reach the lavatory, I'd left wide open. He was my age, and he dressed much like I dressed, though usually with a tad more colour. He even looked a bit like me, the main difference between us being that his hair was receding, slowly but surely, whereas my widow's peak was stubbornly resisting the onslaught of time. He was clutching a large black briefcase, inside which rattled an empty lunchbox. He placed the briefcase on the desk and was momentarily transfixed by Kendal's fetching décolletage, which, as usual, she was making little effort to conceal.

"Why, hello," he said, sounding like a cross between Danny La Rue and Casanova.

Had Kendal been able to cover her exposed cleavage, she would have done so, but there was no material with which to do it.

"I'm Matt," he said, ignoring me completely.

"I'm Kendal," the girl snapped back at my salivating friend. "We've met."

"I think I would have remembered."

"You two *have* met," I put in, just to let Matt know that I was there.

"Have we?" Matt replied, as if I wasn't there.

"In the Dew Drop, just before Christmas," I told the still oblivious Matt. "Kendal was sitting in the corner, being chatted up by Gabriel Tolpuddle. We were propping up the lounge bar. She looked over at us and waved. We waved back."

Eventually, Matt gave me some attention.

"Yes, I remember now," he said. "I didn't see her clearly. She was sitting in a very dark corner."

"Dark corners are the kind of places where Kendal lurks," I quipped.

Kendal can always be relied upon to fight fire with fire. "That's where I met Daniel," she returned, "in a dark corner."

"You two bicker like a married couple," Matt said. He'd snapped out of his trance and was now giving me something approaching his undivided attention. His hands were in the pockets of his trousers. "I came up through the art gallery."

"Only *I'm* allowed to come up through the art gallery."

"It was open," Matt protested, "and the iron stairs outside are very steep, and I've had a hard day."

"My heart bleeds," I said.

"You're lucky having your office above that art gallery." Matt was in full oratorical flow now. He could be some performer when he got going. "I met the two women who run it, Natasha and Natalie. What a pair of honeys they are. Are they single?"

"I don't know," I said, "and, even if they were, they're not my type."

"I meant for *me!*"

"Either of those two would eat you alive, Matt. You should beware of girls with names like Natasha and Natalie. They're often cruel."

"Any chance of getting that coffee, Daniel?" Kendal enquired sarcastically.

Though I'd made two cups of coffee, they remained on top of the fridge and were getting cold. I gave Kendal her cup, took a sip from mine, and offered to make Matt a cup, an offer that he politely declined.

"Cruel?" Matt said with a laugh. "You don't half talk some nonsense, Winter."

"You should try living with him," Kendal said in a voice so low that it was probably not meant to be heard.

"You don't have to live with me." My rejoinder was fired only half in jest. "There's plenty of room back at Waterhouse Towers."

"Waterhouse Towers isn't big enough for your ego and your mum's." Matt was indulging himself with rumours and hearsay. "That's what I've heard."

"You've heard right," Kendal said. Then she took it upon herself to broach the subject of the muddle with the telephone numbers.

"Don't think that I've not had the right words in the right ears on the matter."

I'd heard some unconvincing responses in my time, but that one bore all the conviction of a politician purporting to tell the truth. My response was not uncharacteristically sardonic.

"As if we ever doubted you, Matt…"

"I'm afraid that you're going to have to put up with receiving Greetwell Housing Trust's maintenance calls for a while longer."

"Why doesn't that surprise me?"

"An extra newsletter is going out in February. That will show the *correct* number."

"Next month!" I exclaimed angrily. "I'll be going to your offices first thing tomorrow morning to demand an explanation. Who's your chief executive?"

"Her name's Ida McSweeney, but you've got no chance of getting an audience with *her*."

"Why's that?"

"She's never there." Matt walked over to the large bookshelf which covered the main wall. "We're not sure she even exists."

"So, your organisation's run by a phantom, is it?"

"So it would seem." Matt studied the books on the shelves with his eyes narrowed in disbelief. "Have you transferred all the books in your flat into your office?"

"It's called duplication, my friend."

"What do you mean?"

"They're copies of the same books."

"Are you telling me that you've gone out and bought copies of the same books, so that now you own every book of yours twice?"

"I had to fill the shelves with something."

"You must have more money than sense."

"It has been said."

"You can see why he's so hard to live with, can't you, Matt?"

"Yes, Kendal, I certainly can."

"The other day, we had to arrange all of Daniel's DVDs into alphabetical order, according to the directors' names."

"That's because all of my favourite films were made by *auteurs*."

Matt and Kendal regarded each other quizzically.

"Then we had to arrange his CDs alphabetically, according to the names of the singers and bands," Kendal rumbled on. "He agonised over whether to file Joy Division and New Order separately or together."

"And Warsaw," I added. "The band was called Warsaw before it became Joy Division."

"Now *that* I *can* relate to," Matt conceded.

"Yes, musically, we're cut from the same cloth," I declared. "That's how we met."

"Daniel *has* told me the story of how you two met," Kendal said, "but I wasn't listening at the time."

"We met in December, nineteen-eighty-two, in Brighton, at The Jam's last-ever gig," Matt began nostalgically. He'd finished perusing the display of books—he'd even subjected the crack in the wall to a cursory examination—and was now sitting on the desk, with Kendal looking up at him, daring herself to be intimidated by his size. "During the interval, we bumped into each other in the toilets. I was coming out. He was going in. I was wearing a brand-new pair of basket-weave Gibson's, which this little hooligan promptly trod on and split."

"It was an accident, of course," I said to Kendal, by way of appeal, as if she were the judge presiding over us. Then I turned back to Matt. "Anyway, I did you a favour. They were bloody awful shoes."

"They cost me a small fortune!"

"So, you two kept in touch, did you?"

Matt nearly fell off the table with laughter. For once, Kendal wasn't being sarcastic. She meant the question perfectly innocently. That's what made it so funny. I nearly laughed myself. I nearly fell on top of the fridge.

"Did we heck as like!"

Matt has a deep, booming voice, so the fridge was bound to shake, rattle and almost roll in protest.

"I nearly decked the little blighter!"

Matt was calm enough not to endanger the fridge further, though it did register a nervous reaction of some kind.

"The only reason why I didn't was that I wanted to get back into the front row, ready for the restart. Oh, and because, well, there was a sense of fraternity that night, we were a band of brothers, grief-stricken by the break-up of The Jam."

Kendal shook her head in bewilderment.

"Have you got over it?" Matt asked me.

"Not entirely," I replied, "but I'm getting there."

"Yes, one day at a time, eh?"

"Oh, my God, you two are so sad!"

"You wouldn't understand, Kendal," I said.

"Yes," Matt agreed, "your generation lacks the soul to produce anything like the Mod Revival."

"You're both as bad as Mum when she reminisces about the Seventies … and Steely Dan, and 10CC, and The Sweet."

This time, Matt did fall off the table, like a jockey thrown off his horse, but, once laughter had subsided, he saddled up and remounted.

"The Sweet!" he guffawed through suppressed laughter.

"You can see why Rosie and I never quite made it, can't you?" I returned in like manner, trying not to knock the bowl of sugar off the fridge.

Kendal's bewilderment had metamorphosed into outright despair.

"Anyway, to complete the story," Matt resumed, "one day, about five years ago, I walked into the Lamb and Flag, needing a drink, after an especially punishing morning working as a maintenance inspector for Greetwell Housing Trust, and I clocked this sad-looking weirdo brooding over a pint of Spitfire."

"That sounds like Daniel."

"So, I bought myself a pint of the same stuff, and we got talking, and we discovered that we had the same taste in music, and that we'd both attended The Jam's last-ever gig. That's when the penny dropped. 'You're the bastard who trod on my basket-weave Gibson's!' I yelled at him. He apologised, he bought me several drinks, and we staggered out of the boozer several hours later, best of friends, and we've been mates ever since."

"Jack-a-bloody-nory!"

"Again, Kendal, you wouldn't understand."

Kendal was keen to change the subject, to steer two middle-aged men away from their tawdry trip down Memory Lane.

"So, Matt, what about the crack in the wall?"

Matt's reply was emphatic and reassuringly commanding. "It's only superficial, so don't worry, the building's not going to collapse any time soon. A bit of Pollyfilla and the job's a good'un."

"That's a job for Kendal then," I said with a playful smile in her direction.

"You can whistle for that, mate!"

"Talking about jobs," Matt said. "What have you got on at the moment?"

"I'm investigating a case of potential multiple infidelities by a copper's wife."

"What a grubby business …"

"Indeed …"

"Well, I've got the mother of all jobs for you."

"You?"

"This is the juiciest case you'll ever take on." Matt sounded afraid of his own enthusiasm as he expounded on the case in question. "This case would test the sleuthing prowess of Holmes, Poirot, Spade and Marlowe combined."

"What about Hazell and Shoestring?"

"Them too …" Knowing that he had something dramatic to reveal, Matt paused to heighten the suspense. "What is the question that all Oxford is asking right now?"

"Who killed Laura Hart?" I guessed.

Kendal had been silent for all of thirty seconds, so a contribution from her was long overdue.

"The housing officer at Greetwell Housing Trust?"

"The very same," Matt said. "She was a colleague of mine…and of your mum's, of course."

Kendal nodded in sympathy. It was a touching gesture.

"She was murdered on Christmas Eve," Matt intoned gravely. "It's now the ninth of January, the Christmas decorations have come down, the police are getting nowhere, and they will continue to get nowhere."

"Why's that?" I asked.

"Because the killer is someone within Greetwell Housing Trust. The people at my office might be at each other's throats the whole time, but they've closed ranks. Someone is being protected. Laura was a good friend of mine. I want her killer—or killers—brought to justice. You're the man to do it. I'll pay you good money."

"I don't want your money."

"I'll pay you."

"What makes you think I can catch the killer?"

"You're a fine detective—so you keep telling me—and you're an outsider, so nobody will suspect you."

"How am I supposed to get on the inside track?"

"You befriend someone."

"Who?"

"One Rachel Bannerman…" Matt beamed like the Cheshire Cat in *Alice In Wonderland*, and, like the Cheshire Cat's, his smile almost consumed him.

"Why her?"

"Because that woman is trouble with a capital T. She attracts trouble like Oxford attracts students. There's trouble at Greetwell Housing Trust, and she's right at the heart of it. Get her onside and you'll crack the case."

"You make it sound so easy."

"It'll be a challenge, even for you. You'll have to get inside Rachel's head, which is a horrible place to be, and you'll probably have to get inside her knickers too."

"That's not how I operate."

"You'll have to do whatever is necessary, my friend."

"And how exactly am I supposed to insinuate myself into this woman's life?"

"She works at the Round House, in Headington, behind the bar, two evenings a week. Go over there tonight and turn on your charm."

"What charm would that be?"

Matt looked down at Kendal's grin—she, too, was now little more than an insalubrious smirk—and told her that I had a way with the ladies, that I was not exactly Charlton Heston in the looks department, so what success I enjoyed could only be put down to an abundance of charm. He was wrong on at least two counts.

"I'm busy tonight."

"It will have to be tomorrow then," Matt countered. "She works at the Round House on Monday and Tuesday nights. She's a good old-fashioned barmaid. Big smile. Big everything. Likes a bit of banter with the punters."

"I get the picture."

"And, of course, you've an added incentive to find out who killed Laura Hart."

Matt sounded less like a friend now and more like the policeman he never was. I was starting to feel a little threatened, as if a noose were tightening around my neck. I can't deny that I was also feeling the faint stirrings of intrigue. I was even a little thrilled.

"Have I?"

"You know full well you have?"

"What's he talking about, Daniel?"

"I'm giving you, my friend, a chance to clear the name of the prime suspect for the murder of Laura Hart, the person you've been hiding since Christmas Eve: Dominic Kane. The police don't know you're hiding him, but I do, and I don't like keeping other people's secrets, especially from the police."

"You didn't tell me about Dominic Kane, Daniel."

"I don't tell you everything, Kendal."

"Where are you hiding him?" the girl asked, insistently, as if she had every right to know.

"The more people I tell, the less of a hiding place it becomes."

"Donna Tamsin suspects that I know something," Matt said. "She badgers me every day about it."

"Who's Donna Tamsin?"

Kendal's interrogation was proving to be irksome as a wasp in summer.

"She's the housing officer at Greetwell Housing Trust who made Dominic homeless," I replied. "Dominic is twenty years old and is struggling with drug-addiction. His room at Windsor Court was his chance to start rebuilding his life. But Donna Tamsin had other ideas."

"To be fair to her, she was only applying the rules."

"Somewhat overzealously, I would say."

"Why did Donna Tamsin make Dominic Kane homeless?"

Matt looked from me to the questioner, and then back to me, visibly curious to know what the answer would be.

"I'll explain that to you later, Kendal, when we're on surveillance."

Kendal seemed satisfied with my answer. I struggled to remember the last time that had been the case.

"I'll also explain why I'm convinced that Dominic is innocent of Laura Hart's murder."

"An old lady walking her dog saw him at the scene of the crime, Daniel: Laura Hart's kitchen. Laura was lying on her back, in a pool of blood, with a knife in her chest. Dominic was kneeling beside her, covered in Laura's blood. It could hardly be a case of mistaken identity. Dominic has a large purple birthmark on the right side of his face. He would stand out anywhere."

"As I've told you before, Matt, the door had not been forced open. Dominic found it open. He's homeless. He was hungry. He simply wanted something to eat."

"Or something to *steal*. He's a junkie, after all."

"He's *off* the drugs, no thanks to Donna Tamsin."

"His bloodstained fingerprints were found all over the handle of the knife."

There was no denying that. I sighed. Then I told Matt that Dominic had thought that, by removing the knife from Laura's chest, somehow, she could be brought back to life. He had been confused and distressed.

My friend's reaction to that was to grimace. He looked like a constipated toad. He remained unconvinced by my version of events. He was in urgent need of further enlightenment, and I was more than happy to provide it.

"If I hand Dominic over to the system, it will eat him alive. I was a copper, remember? I've seen it happen a thousand times. The system's hardly been kind to him so far, has it?"

"So, before I dropped this opportunity into your lap, what was your plan to prove Dominic's innocence?"

That, indeed, was a perfectly reasonable question, for which there was a perfectly spurious answer.

"I was going to play for time, wait for the police to make a breakthrough, and then use what influence I have with the Thames Valley Police to avert a charge of conspiring to pervert the course of justice."

What I meant was that I was going to exploit the goodwill that I'd accrued with one Detective Inspector Stephen Waugh, for whom I was then working. Don't ask me how a private detective found himself working for a policeman—the custom is for the police to regard private eyes as something akin to vermin—but that is where I found myself. Of course, my working for the said policeman had nothing to do with his work as a detective, but it was an irregular compact, nonetheless. Naturally, Matt had no need to know any of this.

"You'll be waiting a long time for a breakthrough," Matt said.

"Don't I know it?"

At that moment, the phone rang, ominously. I could always tell what kind of call it would be by the way the phone rang. The tone was vindictive, and I told Matt in like vein that it was bound to be one of his company's tenants calling.

Kendal put the phone on speaker before she answered. When she said, "Daniel Winter's office," she sounded alarmingly professional. I could almost have imagined her working the switchboard at the Randolph and beguiling prospective visitors with her mellifluous tones.

"Oi!" came the voice from the phone. It wasn't the politest voice I'd ever heard. "My boiler's busted!"

Matt got to his feet and started pacing around the room with his head in his hands.

"Your boiler's busted," Kendal repeated facetiously.

"Yeah! Read my lips! My boiler's busted!"

"I can hardly read your lips over the phone, can I?"

"Are you being funny with me? Because, if you are, I know where you work!"

"Good for you…"

"Listen to me!" the voice went on. "If you bunch of cowboys haven't fixed my boiler by nine o'clock tomorrow morning, I'm going to the *Oxford Mail*!"

"They all give us that line," Matt interjected. "They think it's a threat."

"Go boil your head, numbskull." With that, Kendal put the phone down.

I couldn't help but laugh. Matt was closer to crying. For Kendal, it was just another problem dealt with.

"You played a blinder there, sweetheart." I was giggling like a schoolboy.

"Oh, my God!" Matt exclaimed. "There'll be hell to pay now! That was Noddy bloody Sanderson!"

"Noddy?" Kendal was laughing in disbelief. "Is that his real name or his nickname?"

"He'll be like a dog with a bone over this," Matt said in despair. "You've no idea what you've just unleashed."

"Good," I said. "Perhaps your people will sort out the problem now."

Matt winced and advised Kendal never to get a job in customer service.

"That was Kendal at her politest." I wasn't exaggerating either.

Matt suggested that we discuss that and other important matters in the Dew Drop.

"What other important matters?" I asked.

"The kind of matters that can only be discussed over a beer..." Matt jerked his head to indicate my esteemed personal assistant. "It's men's talk."

"Don't mind me," Kendal said. "Listening to you two is like watching an episode of *Teletubbies*."

I dismissed the jibe and told Matt that the drink would have to be a quick one, since I had a job on at eight.

Kendal was bound to correct me. "*We've* got a job on!"

As I prepared to leave the office, I told Kendal that I would be back by seven and that we would then eat dinner before going out on surveillance, whereupon she reminded me that we had no food in the house. I threw a crumpled ten-pound note on the table and told her to get us some fish and chips.

"Again?" she protested.

"We'll need plenty of protein for this evening's assignment," I said, "and lots of carbohydrates."

Leaving Kendal hanging, with my cryptic comments ringing between her ears, was the only time when I felt as if I had the slightest degree of control over her and her anarchic temperament.

I went to the pub quietly pleased with my little victory. It really was something to savour.

FOUR

"Why was Matt so eager to get you down the pub?" Kendal had asked this question as we ate our fish and chips.

"He wanted to ask a favour of me."

"What favour?"

"He asked me to take someone under my wing for a couple of weeks."

"Who?"

"A seventeen-year-old lad named Karl..."

Kendal had felt threatened by this development and she told me that she wasn't prepared to share the office with anyone, except, of course, me.

I'd told her that she could be Karl's boss. I'd gone on to tell her that Karl was a student of Business at the College of Further Education, and had been embarked on a programme of work experience at Greetwell Housing Trust since before Christmas, but that he was routinely ignored by everyone at the company and so was receiving no benefit from the experience. Matt, then, had asked me if I wouldn't mind keeping Karl occupied until his spell at Greetwell Housing Trust was due to finish at the end of the following week. "Why not?" I'd replied after my considered objection had been met with some gentle persuasion from Matt. "Every other waif and stray seems to come my way, so I might as well take another one."

The beauty of the arrangement from Matt's point of view, as I'd told Kendal, was that, owing to the mix-up with the telephone numbers, Karl would do more work for Greetwell working for me than he would whilst working at the office of Greetwell itself, another benefit being that not a soul at Greetwell would notice that Karl wasn't there. Everyone was a winner.

Kendal had protested that she liked answering the phones and that she did not take kindly to being usurped.

She would share the office for the small matter of two weeks, I'd told her, mistakenly thinking that such words of reassurance would mollify her to the extent that she would at least stop complaining.

***

Kendal was no less inquisitive when we were tailing Belinda Waugh to wherever it was she was going. Her husband had told me that she was planning to go out that evening, and I knew from my previous observations of her movements that she never went out before eight, or after nine, so I was ready to intercept her in Wolvercote from the very moment when the chocolate mints were being handed around at dinner parties. At eight-fifteen, she and her Mini Cooper emerged and my Jensen Interceptor and I were hot on her trail.

Kendal's questions were always forensically specific. They were relentless in their probing exactitude and economy of words. Not a syllable was ever wasted. No criminal would have stood a chance against her in a police interview room, or standing in the dock being cross-examined by her under oath. They would be worn down by her questions' remorseless sense of purpose. I'd been reticent about the case of Belinda Waugh; all that Kendal knew about it was that, ludicrously, I'd been following the wife of a policeman; but, since it was bound to be a long evening sitting in the car with only each other for company, and since there was an outside chance that Kendal could have shed some light on the case, I considered it expedient to furnish the girl with some details.

"So far, I've followed Belinda Waugh three times," I began as we drove down Woodstock Road towards the city centre. "The first time was two weeks before Christmas. She went to the Phoenix Picture House to watch a film with a man, who, when I described him to my client, was identified as her cousin, an Oxford don, no less."

"What was the film?"

"*My Summer Of Love* ..."

"Did you watch the film?"

"Yes, and I claimed the cost of the ticket on expenses."

"Of course ..."

"In any case, I saw no evidence of physical intimacy between them, so my assumption had been that they were simply friends. Then, between Christmas and New Year, she went to dinner at Gino's with a girlfriend. Strangely, there was much touching and caressing between the two women across the table. When I described the woman to my client, he had no idea who she was. I sat at a table, alone, eating spaghetti carbonara, discreetly watching them and trying not to look conspicuous. After dinner, they went for a drink at Jude The Obscure. Then they kissed and went their separate ways."

"They sound like a pair of lesbians."

"That's what I told my client."

"What did he say to that?"

"He didn't seem bothered."

"Some women!"

"In fourteen months' time, you'll cross the bridge from girlhood to womanhood, and I wonder what hazards for the world that particular crossing will occasion."

"What's that supposed to mean?"

When I regarded her with affectionate ease, she smiled at me: she knew that whatever had been meant by the comment, it was made in jest, or largely so. She then reflected that it was odd that Belinda's husband had no idea who the other woman was.

"Stephen and Belinda Waugh, though husband and wife, live entirely separate lives," I said. "The only time their paths ever cross is when they wake up next to each other in bed."

"Why bother being married?"

"Like every other married couple, they have their reasons."

"It makes no sense to me."

"The bizarre thing about this case is that Stephen doesn't suspect that his wife is having an affair, nor does he care much whether she is or not. He simply wants to know what she does with her time, because they never talk to each other, they never tell each other what they're doing."

"What a pair of fruitcakes they must be."

"Stephen told me that it's because his work is his life, and that he never talks to his wife about his work, because, in his job, careless talk can cost lives, so she gets equal by telling him nothing about *her* life."

"Like I said, fruitcakes, the pair of them."

"It's how some people roll."

"So, what happened the third time you followed this Belinda Waugh?"

"That was last week. She attended a lecture at Keble College. The subject was the open society and its enemies. Naturally, Karl Popper got a mention. I managed to buy a ticket at the door—someone had cancelled—and I sat at the back of the auditorium with both ears on the lecture and with one eye on Belinda Waugh. There was a drinks reception afterwards. She and I even spoke to each other. I hadn't intended to speak with her. We just bumped into each other, literally. Anyway, I suppose that that allayed any suspicions that I was spying on her. We chatted, naturally and amiably. One has to be a consummate actor in this game, you know."

"It's a bit like being a prostitute."

"Except that I'm paid to be somebody's eyes and ears..."

"And now this woman is going to ask you to spy on her husband?"

"I'll find out tomorrow, won't I?"

"You can't work for both of them, surely?"

"I plan to wrap up this case this evening, and I will, unless Mrs Waugh gives me reason to suspect that she's up to no good. By midday tomorrow, I should be free to work for Mrs Waugh."

"It still sounds wrong...weird, somehow."

"It's the most absurd scenario since two private detectives were paid to follow each other."

"Has that ever happened?"

"Everything's happened somewhere, at some time, in this crazy world."

The Mini Cooper indicated right, which ruled out another evening of liberal philosophising at Keble College.

"Look out," I said. "She's turning down Halstead Road."

Not only did the lady turn down Halstead Road, she parked her car in Halstead Road and then knocked on the door of a house in Halstead Road. A silhouette opened the door and Belinda followed the shadow into the house. Unfortunately, there were no parking spaces left in Halstead Road. However, providentially, there was a space on the corner of Chalfont Road, a spot which enabled me not only to park comfortably, but also to sit and monitor the house across the road as if I were sitting at home watching television. I'd been blessed with good luck. Even private detectives need a break from time to time, whether they deserve one, or not, in the practice of their grubby trade.

Once we'd settled down to our vigil, Kendal asked me if we were going to listen to some music. She was given to protesting that my taste in music leaned towards the antediluvian, but that had never stopped her from listening to it, and, often as not, voluntarily. I told her that I wanted to assess the job in hand before giving it a soundtrack.

We'd been sitting in silence for twenty minutes before the next question came.

"How come Belinda Waugh saw you three times, on three separate occasions, but never suspected you were stalking her?"

"She *didn't* see me, though, did she?" I replied. "Except the time at Keble. But, to her mind, that was the *first* time."

"But you were there the two previous times."

"She didn't see me."

"How could she have missed you?"

"She might have *seen* me, but she didn't *notice* me," I went on. "My presence simply didn't register with her. Why would it?"

"So, you can make yourself invisible, can you?"

"The art of surveillance is to *be* there, but *not* to be there."

"So, what do we do now?"

"We sit and wait."

"For what?"

"For something to happen …"

"Nothing's going to happen."

"If nothing happens after an hour, I'll think of an excuse to knock on the door."

"What kind of excuse?"

"Oh, I don't know. How about I ask to borrow some sugar?"

"You'll have to do better than that, Daniel."

"Okay, how about I knock on the door and ask them to turn the music down, because I live across the road and my three-year-old daughter is trying to sleep?"

"What if they're not playing any music?"

"Whilst I'm apologising for being mistaken, I'll sneak a look inside to get an idea of what's going on."

"Any chance that your brain will engage first gear tonight?"

"Or I could resort to my tried-and-tested ploy."

"What's that?"

"I could pretend to be a copper. Then all I would have to do is think of a pretext for knocking on the door."

"Not your Detective Inspector Maximilian Doublesnake impression again, please!"

"Why not? It served me well during the Miranda Ward-Homer case. It got me past that bonehead bouncer outside The Aquarium."

"The name's ridiculous, Daniel."

"Are you knocking my stroke of genius?"

"Anyway, isn't impersonating a police officer against the law?"

"Not if you used to be one ..."

"You're a piece of work, Daniel."

There were no more questions until we were eleven tracks into a Lou Reed compilation album. I put the track on hold whilst Kendal spoke. Even the great Lou Reed had to be quiet when Kendal Waterhouse was speaking.

"What's the time?" she asked.

"It's midnight in Moscow." I was unable to shake off the impression that the question had deserved such a facetious response.

"Is it?"

"No ..."

"I know why you became a private detective," the girl said, suddenly, "apart from the fact that you're nosey."

"Enlighten me."

"Because you get paid for sitting in your car listening to music ..."

"You know me too well."

"Why did you leave the police force?"

"I've told you a hundred times, sweetheart."

"Mum says it's because you refused to become a Freemason, which meant that you couldn't get higher than detective-inspector."

My eyebrows leapt at Kendal's words. Had I really told Rosie so much?

"I don't remember telling your mum that," I said, "but if that's what she wants to think…"

"So, it's not true?"

"There were other reasons, as you know."

"Somebody's going into the house!"

Kendal's announcement made me jump, not so much that my head hit the roof, but enough for me in one swift movement to reach into the glove compartment and pull out my binoculars. They were small but powerful: a pocket rocket of an ocular device. I put them to my eyes. A tall man of about fifty was standing outside the house waiting for the door to open. He was little more than a silhouette, an amorphous shadow in the gloom, but something about his body shape suggested his age, and his posture, too, gave me a sense of someone established in life, distinguished in some way, with a touch of arrogance. A man of similar age, eventually, opened the door.

"Bloody hell!" I said, my excitement barely suppressed. "The bloke opening the door! He's practically naked!" I could make out a mass of uncovered flesh by virtue of the light shining from behind him. He had a towel around his waist.

Kendal was never going to listen to such wanton titillation without getting a view herself, so I was hardly surprised when she snatched the binoculars from my grasp with all the haste of a Seventies' kid diving into a Jamboree Bag.

"What a gruesome sight." As she spoke, her face was screwed up in disgust. "That'll be you in ten years' time, Daniel."

"I doubt it."

"It will be if you keep knocking back the beer like there's no tomorrow."

"Shut up about the beer, will you?"

"They're going inside."

"There's always one who's fashionably late to the party."

"Now what do we do?"

"We let them settle down … and then I'll go in."

"*You'll* go in?"

"It won't need both of us."

"We'll see about that."

Ten minutes later, I broke the silence.

"When Belinda turned into Halstead Road, I was worried."

"Worried?"

"I thought we were heading for another night at the Phoenix Picture House."

"Would that have been so bad?"

"Yes, because there's a terrible film showing there tonight."

"You're a snob, Daniel."

"If you're accusing me of being a cinematic snob then I must plead guilty."

"When can I meet Dominic?"

Kendal was highly adept at changing the subject in the blink of an eye. It was her way: to catch people off-guard whilst in full conversational flow, before their brains had a chance to register the sudden change of direction.

I was in no mood for an argument, least of all with Kendal, so I promised that I would take her to meet the young man as soon as the evening's assignment was completed. Once she had recovered from my uncharacteristic largesse, she sat back in her seat, satisfied, a curious young woman eager to explore more of the curiosities of life. I could almost hear the cogs of her mind whirring inside her head as she plotted the next chapter of her life's story. I suppressed a grin. She was in for a shock when she found out where I'd been hiding Dominic Kane. She would surely rebuke me for my recklessness, and not for the first time. Then it occurred to me that I still hadn't told her about my prospective liaison with Helena Johnson-Roffey. I felt like an adolescent boy worried about telling his mother that he had a date with an older woman. I could almost feel my face itching with acne.

"Are you all right, Daniel?"

"Yes, I've just got an itchy face."

"I've got itchy *feet*, so I'm going in soon."

"Don't be silly."

"I've got a plan."

The girl's brain went back into plotting mode. That was always enough to make me tremble with a sense of gathering foreboding.

***

Another ten minutes later and my companion's plan was ready to be put into action. I was astonished to learn that mine had been downgraded to a watching brief, that I, the one ostensibly in charge, had been reduced to a mere spectator whilst the junior sleuth asserted ownership of the streets of affluent North Oxford. So, it was with curiosity that bordered on studied fascination that I acquiesced in what, on the face of it, was a plan so doomed to fail that it was like entering a donkey for the Grand National.

Kendal rubbed her hands together gleefully. "This is so exciting, Daniel!" she trilled.

"The Charge of the Light Brigade was exciting," I replied, "but it wasn't very effective, was it?"

"Your problem, Daniel, is that you lack imagination."

"And yours is the recklessness of youth."

"Fortune favours the brave, Daniel."

"I can't believe I'm letting you do this."

"Watch and learn, my friend. You've seen the rest. Now see the best."

Kendal's confidence was overflowing. I had to open the window to let some of it out of the car, so as not to be consumed by it.

"Go on then," I said. "Off you go. Don't expect me to be here when you're being chased off the premises."

"It won't come to that."

"We'll see."

It was entirely appropriate that the next track on the album, as Kendal trotted across the road, was *A Walk On The Wild Side*. I was barely able to look as she made her way to the back of the house. There was no gate, only an iron archway. I was again the Seventies' child, this time watching an episode of *Doctor Who* from behind the sofa. The basic plot of Kendal's plan was sound as a pound. It was the details that filled me with dread.

As Lou Reed burst into *What Goes On?*, I was mired in apprehension. The lack of movement from the house was ominous. All kinds of thoughts as to what might have been going on entered my head, most of which I managed to expel forthwith the better to protect my sanity.

Then my phone rang. It was Kendal calling. A voice in my head urged me not to answer the call, but, alas, ignoring it was not an option.

"Daniel!"

"What's going on?"

"You need to see this!" Kendal sounded as if she had just caught her worst enemy in the most compromising of situations, there was that much vindictive joy in her voice. "You *really* need to see this!"

She was right; whatever was going on in that house, I needed to see it; though I was far from sure that I *wanted* to see it. I was across the road, and round the back of the house, before Kendal had registered my silence. I found her crouching down at the intersection of two large French windows, across which curtains were partially drawn. We could see the spacious living-room and what was unfolding within its four elaborately decorated walls. What we saw was a festival of the bizarre. It was like seeing Her Majesty the Queen and the Duke of Edinburgh at Balmoral wearing shell suits.

"Bloody hell! Is this the latest suburban craze?"

"It's the Naked Book Club," Kendal laughed in reply.

"I thought I'd seen it all."

Sitting in a circle were fifteen middle-aged bookworms, all of them naked as the day they were born.

"What book are they reading?" Kendal wondered.

I peered through the glass and identified the book as *The Lie*, by Helen Dunmore.

Kendal put a hand on my arm and urged me not to move a muscle: she thought we'd been spotted.

"They won't be able to see us," I said. "From inside, all they can see is their own reflections. It must be part of the turn-on."

"Your Belinda Waugh keeps looking this way. We've been rumbled."

"Okay, stay still."

"Let's keep talking," Kendal said. "It will relax us."

The girl's logic was highly dubious, but I went along with it.

"Are you a virgin, Daniel?"

"Not yet, but I'm working on it."

"So, you and Mum never—"

"Never!"

"When did you lose your cherry?"

"When I was eighteen …"

"What was her name?"

"Lindy …"

"Lindy? What was she? A doll?"

"It was the sexual equivalent of the evacuation of Dunkirk."

"I can imagine."

"She made me wear two condoms. I'm not sure that it even counted."

"You're having me on!"

"Did you think I was going to dignify such ridiculous questions with the truth?"

"Hold on," Kendal said. "Your Belinda is reading aloud now. We're in the clear."

"I have to meet her tomorrow," I remembered. "I won't be able to look her in the eye."

"Being a peeper, Daniel, seeing people in their birthday suits is an occupational hazard, surely?"

"And what on earth am I going to tell her husband?"

"Don't tell him anything," Kendal replied as she snatched her phone from her jacket pocket. "Just show him this."

In taking the photo, Kendal lost her balance and fell on top of a terracotta plant pot to her right; the pot went to ground with her and broke into pieces with a smash. We were across the road, and back in the car, before any of the readers had reached for their trousers.

"Keep your head down," I said as I peered over the top of the dashboard and across the road.

"Is someone there?"

"Yes, a bloke in a dressing-gown," I replied. "He's looking around. He looks puzzled. It was a cat or a fox. That's what he's thinking. Now he's gone back inside."

We both sat up and agreed that we would now draw a line under the case of Belinda Waugh and the affair that she never had.

Kendal had more case notes to record.

FIVE

Before taking Kendal to see Dominic, I took her into Jude The Obscure for a much-needed libation. I had a whisky. She had a lemonade. It was time that I told her Dominic's story. It was a thoroughly depressing story, but, like all such stories, it contained the seeds of redemption. It was a story that she needed and deserved to hear.

In short, Dominic was a young man of twenty too traumatised by a single event ever to be able to live anything like a normal life. When he was fifteen, his family home had caught fire one night. He had escaped. His parents and his little sister had perished. He had opened his bedroom window and leapt onto a branch of the willow tree outside, the tree that his father had been due to cut down the following day because its roots had wrapped themselves around the pipes under the house. The guilt had started right then, before the fire had finished its work. What could I have done to save them? Why did I survive? Am I more worthy than they? Is my survival yet some sort of punishment? These are the questions that he never stops asking himself. He hears the cries of his father and mother and sister. He sees his exit blocked by the fire raging down the landing. He sees the smoke filtering through the gap under his bedroom door. He feels the room warming as the fire nears. He sees himself making his escape. The flashbacks and the nightmares and the recurring sensation of heat on naked skin make him wonder if death would not have been an escape more forgiving than the one with which he'd been afflicted.

Since that infernal night, life for Dominic had been nothing but a wish to escape. Wherever he found himself, he wished to be somewhere else. He spent two years at Field Place, the type of place that used to be called an orphanage. It was not too bad a place, it was hardly Dickensian, but all the same he had escaped. He took to the road. He kept bad company. He got himself a drug habit. Eventually, somehow, he found himself in Oxford, some sixty miles north of his Southampton home.

For a while, Oxford was good to him. Courtesy of Greetwell Housing Trust, it gave him a home: a room at Windsor Court, a home for reforming addicts of one substance or another. Alas, there, Oxford's hospitality died a sudden death. Three fellow residents made his life a misery. They tormented him, preying on his vulnerability. The last straw was their sabotaging the lock on his door: they poured glue in it, which hardened, thus trapping him inside, an experience that brought terrible memories flooding back. So, he fled. He took to the streets again. Three weeks later—a grimy, emaciated mess—he went back to Windsor Court and found that his room had been given to someone else. He went to the offices of Greetwell Housing Trust and asked his housing officer, Donna Tamsin, why his room had been taken from him. She told him that it was because he'd gone away without telling Greetwell, so Greetwell presumed that he'd absconded, something which tenants are all too inclined to do. Rules were rules, Donna Tamsin said. He was told that he'd made himself homeless again. He told her why he'd taken flight without informing Greetwell, but his protestations fell on deaf ears. He was told that he would have to go back on the waiting list; that he would be notified in due course of the next stage of his rehabilitation; and that he should report back to the office in seven days' time to learn of his fate.

Having wandered the city for two days—scavenging, rather than begging—he found refuge in a disused boathouse by the River Cherwell, in the Summertown district of Oxford. One day, whilst out looking for food, he ran into me. He told me his story. I offered to put him up until I'd helped find him somewhere else to live, but he refused my hospitality, saying that he didn't want to be a burden. Of course, I got in touch with Greetwell Housing Trust, but they simply told me what they'd told Dominic. They were nothing more than a bureaucratic brick wall.

So, every day for several weeks, I took food and drink to Dominic at the boathouse. In the meantime, Sylvia Blackman had contacted me and asked me if I wouldn't mind looking after Philip's old house—now *her* house, of course—whilst she worked out what to do with it. I'd met her in London, one day during the first week of December, to pick up the keys. That had been a strange—and, indeed, a strained—meeting, but that is a story for another day. I offered Dominic temporary accommodation in the house—Sylvia would have understood—but, again, he said no…until Christmas Eve last, when he was caught red-handed at the scene of a murder.

When I went to the boathouse, late on Christmas Eve, to invite him to spend Christmas Day with me and Kendal, he told me what had happened at the home of Laura Hart earlier that evening. That's when I smuggled him into my old friend's old house, now the house of the woman he'd loved but who'd spurned him and inadvertently caused his death thereby. It was a horribly tangled web.

"So, Daniel, let me get this straight," Kendal began as we drank, "you're hiding someone wanted by the police for murder?"

"That's right."

"And you're hiding him in a house in the same street as Mum's house?"

"Right again…" If Kendal had thought that I wouldn't have noticed her saying "Mum's", instead of "our", she would have been hugely mistaken.

"And, in hiding Dominic, what crime would you be committing?"

"Possibly, conspiring to pervert the course of justice…"

"Which is a serious crime, right?"

"Almost as serious as crimes come…"

"Daniel, what are you playing at, man?"

"He didn't do it!" Kendal had barked the question at me with righteous anger, and far too loudly for my liking, and I'd responded in kind. "The police won't care that he didn't do it." I was calmer now. "I used to be a policeman, in case you've forgotten. If they're offered a result on a plate, they'll take it. A result is a result. The truth is just a bonus. That's how they operate. That's one reason why I left the force."

"So, you're never going to hand him over to the police?"

"No, I'm not."

"The police might find him."

"They might."

"Then you'll be in trouble."

"I will."

"Then you need to prove his innocence, Daniel, and fast."

"Now that I know that the killer works at Greetwell Housing Trust—I trust Matt's judgement on that count—and that the police will get no joy from that quarter, it is imperative that I act quickly."

"What will you do?"

"Matt's pointed me in the right direction, hasn't he?"

"You mean that hussy, Rachel?"

"You've such a charming turn of phrase."

"How long do you think it'll take to get to the truth?"

"Matt told me that I should aim to identify the killer—or killers—by Friday evening."

"Why Friday evening?"

"Because that's when the Goodbye Golden Age Dinner and Dance is taking place, at the Wolvercote Hotel…"

"Yes, of course, Mum will be going…"

"Matt has invited me to gatecrash the event."

"Will you go?"

"I'll turn up for the after-dinner drinks and take a turn on the dancefloor with Donna Tamsin. She'll be dancing the Dance of the Seven Veils, I'm sure, Salome-figure that she is."

"I've often wondered…"

"What have you often wondered?"

"Why the office of Greetwell Housing Trust is called The Golden Age…"

"I'll add that to my list of things to find out, shall I?"

"I mean, it's just an old house converted into an old office."

"Have you asked your mum?"

"Yes, and even *she* doesn't know. Nobody at Greetwell knows."

"But somebody at Greetwell knows who killed Laura Hart, and I'm going to find out who."

"Does Matt know where you're hiding Dominic?"

"He's never asked me, so I've never told him."

"But he knows *that* you're hiding him?"

"You know he does."

"How does he know?"

"He knows about Dominic and how I found him. He knows that he was living at the boathouse, but that he's not there now, so he's worked out that I must be hiding him, or at least that I know his whereabouts, though he hasn't put that question to me. He doesn't want to know, because he doesn't want to be complicit in my subterfuge."

"And now *I'm* complicit. Thanks a lot, Daniel."

"Don't give me that, Kendal," I said. "You wouldn't have it any other way."

SIX

We found Dominic much as I'd expected to find him: a mess of a young man, sitting in the middle of a mess of spent plastic bottles and cartons and tin cans. The mess in the living-room would take five minutes to clear up; Dominic's personal and sartorial mess a little longer; and the mess that was his mind might never be tidied sufficiently to give him a chance to get a foothold on life. The mess into which, somehow, I'd contrived to get myself would depend on much good luck—some degree of divine intervention, perhaps—for its satisfactory resolution. My fingers were as firmly crossed as metaphorically my legs had been during my full-bladdered walk home earlier that evening.

The weirdness that I felt at being present at the home of my old friend had long since dissipated, aided by Philip's parents, who'd emptied the house of his personal effects. The house had become a kind of shell, with only the unadorned furniture suggesting that the place had ever been occupied and animated by a human spirit. Dominic's presence reflected his state of mind. He was there in body, but not in spirit, and not even his body betrayed much in the way of fellowship with its surroundings.

The last time I'd taken provisions to Dominic at the boat-house was on a freezing-cold morning just before Christmas. My feet had crunched on the frosty ground. The meadow had been draped in a white blanket and sheets of ice had floated down the River Cherwell. Crows had squawked and screeched around me, mockingly, as if to signal the futility of my efforts to heal a broken man. I'd been weighed down by a bag of shopping. When I'd entered the boathouse, the door had nearly fallen off its hinges. I'd found Dominic asleep on the floor, wrapped in a sleeping-bag.

I found him much the same now, except that he was spread out on a sofa. He was wearing a red sweatshirt with the hood up. Black hair was escaping from under the hood. His large purple birthmark was just about visible in the shadow of the hood and under the greasy, streaky hair. He groaned and made an effort to sit up.

"Oh, it's you," he said.

"Who else would it be?"

Furtively, almost guiltily, he glanced at Kendal. "Is she your girlfriend?"

Kendal looked at me and laughed.

"If she'd ever been my girlfriend, I'd have dumped her long ago," I replied.

Kendal looked at me again, this time without the laughter.

"This is my assistant," I said. "Her name's Kendal."

"Hello, Dominic," she said. "I'm sorry."

"Sorry for what?"

"That Daniel's got you involved in his little scheme..."

"I don't know what you mean," Dominic moaned as he straightened himself and sat up.

"I'm not sure that Kendal knows what she means either," I said.

"I'll clear up," Kendal announced, and she started to busy herself around the room.

"Where are the blankets I gave you?" I asked, sternly, my head dancing with the myriad possible grotesque replies.

"Someone nicked them."

"Who?"

"That filthy Irishman..."

"He came here?"

Dominic shook his head. "I went out. He took them off my back."

"You're supposed to be lying low, Dominic, yet you go wandering about."

"I can't stay here all day, every day."

"Just keep your head down for a few more days."

"Until what?"

"Until I've proved your innocence..."

"Good luck with that."

"Do you want the heating on?"

"No point, I've got the sleeping-bag...and the telly keeps me warm."

"Well, don't put it on too loud, will you? We don't want to alert the neighbours."

"Some old dear lives next door. I reckon she's as deaf as a post."

"Why do you reckon that?"

"She has her telly on full-blast. I could be letting off fireworks in here and she wouldn't hear a thing."

"Just be careful, will you? It's my head that's on the block, as well as yours."

As if I were a schoolteacher scolding him, Dominic sighed. Then he told me that, whilst wandering around Jericho, he'd seen the three "bastards" who'd terrorised him at Windsor Court. That was music to my ears, but emphatically the wrong sort of music. It was like turning up at the Royal Albert Hall to hear some Beethoven, only to find that I'd accidentally gatecrashed a Def Leppard concert. And that wasn't the last of the young man's stomach-churning revelations.

"Right!" I exclaimed. "Anything else you want to tell me?"

"Yeah," he said sullenly.

"What?"

"I saw the old cow who grassed me up."

"Where?"

"Don't worry, she didn't see me. I looked out of the window and there she was, walking that scraggly dog of hers."

"What's she doing walking her dog in Jericho? She lives in Summertown."

"Jericho's a short walk from Summertown, Daniel."

"When did you last walk from Summertown to Jericho, Kendal?"

"If I see that old woman again, I'll give it to her ... and the dog."

"Don't talk daft, Dominic."

"And Ginger, Nobby and Silkman, from Windsor Court: they're going to get it too."

I sighed and then asked Kendal to make us all some coffee.

"What did your last maidservant die of?"

"Inactivity!" I told Kendal. "I would hate the same to happen to you."

Dominic hadn't finished articulating his plans for personal vengeance.

"And Donna Tamsin: I'll save the last bullet for her."

"You don't need to worry about Donna Tamsin," I said. "*I'll* deal with her."

"She'll get what's coming to her!"

Dominic's sudden obsession with the settling of personal scores was a worrying turn of events, not that I suspected for one second that he would resort to violence, or even advocate a more vigorous prosecution of his grievances. It was just that he hadn't spoken in such terms before, he was so meek and broken. It was like watching Saint Francis of Assisi suddenly turn into Atilla the Hun. His new demeanour reinforced the urgency of my mission to find out who killed Laura Hart. I backed myself to do it. I had my methods, and they worked, though now I was under pressure to apply those methods within a compressed timeframe. I preferred to explore at leisure, to get to know the protagonists and their respective hinterlands. That's another reason why I'm no longer a policeman: results always came first, quick results, with the truth an optional extra. The police in Oxford would see Dominic not as a human being, but as a result, somebody so much in the frame as to be practically a portrait hanging on the Chief Constable's office wall. Hence my implacable belief that I was doing the right thing in shielding him from the long arm of the law.

Matt had done me a favour in giving me the opportunity to find out who killed Laura Hart and so to prove Dominic's innocence. I hadn't seen that at first, but I saw it now, or at any rate I'd been made to see the urgency of the task in hand. Now that I knew that Greetwell Housing Trust harboured

Laura Hart's killer—or killers—and that the people there had closed ranks to thwart the police and their investigation, waiting for a breakthrough was no longer an option, if it had ever been one in the first place.

I thought about Greetwell Housing Trust and how the place seemed to be assuming the role of stalker in my life in Oxford. It was stalking me for sure. Wherever I looked, it was there. It was getting closer all the time. I knew it was there, that I was in its shadow, but I couldn't quite shake it off. There was Matt, maintenance inspector at Greetwell, whom I'd encountered at a rock concert in Brighton, when I was seventeen, and again in Oxford some twenty years later. There was Rosie, administrator at Greetwell's Mother and Baby Unit, and mother of Kendal, my daughter-figure and unwanted sidekick. There was Detective Inspector Stephen Waugh, chief investigating officer in the case of Laura Hart's murder, for whom I was working, spying on his wife. Then there was that very same wife: now, it appeared, she, too, was on my case. Then there were the mixed-up telephone lines—my business line with Greetwell's—and the imminent arrival at my office of a young man by the name of Karl, whom Matt had thrust upon me. Then, of course, there was Dominic Kane. These were the players on the stage. Rachel Bannerman and Donna Tamsin were waiting in the wings.

"Within the next few days, Donna Tamsin will get her comeuppance," I continued to reassure Dominic. "I will expose her as someone not only prepared to harbour a killer, but also as someone prepared to let an innocent person take the rap for the killing."

"I'll leave you to it then."

Dominic's nonchalance was almost touching. Seeing him looking so lost and vulnerable increased my determination to set him free.

Kendal came out of the kitchen and into the living-room. She asked Dominic whether he took milk and sugar in his coffee. It was a commonplace question, one heard in every house up and down and across the land; but, coming from Kendal, a teenager with attitude, it sounded positively surreal. It was like hearing the words of Florence Nightingale coming from the mouth of Lady Macbeth.

Dominic looked at me and Kendal, his eyes flickering nervously in some act of minor derangement. For a moment, he was speechless, his words dammed behind thick walls. It seemed to me that he might never speak again.

"Milk and sugar?" he said at last, his voice tremulous and soft as a baby's. "I really…can't remember."

For every moment of lucidity that Dominic enjoyed, he suffered three moments of abject brokenness. The question about how he took his coffee had been beyond banal; and the answer should have been automatic, unthinking; instead, the response was telling, all too telling; indeed, it was nothing less than a cry for help.

SEVEN

After a fractious breakfast, over which Kendal and I had argued over who would have cereal and who would have toast, since there was not enough milk for us both to have cereal, Kendal had opened the office in readiness for the new day. When I arrived, some twenty minutes later, I found a tall, bulky, mixed-race youth pacing up and down the room whilst Kendal busied herself at the laptop.

"The cavalry's arrived, I see," I declared, not expecting either of my assistants to have the first idea what I was talking about.

"This is Karl," Kendal said without enthusiasm. "I've already told him that, if we're going to work together, he will have to learn to stop staring at me."

The boy stopped pacing around, though, in hopping on the spot, he still gave the impression that he had a box of frogs concealed in his trousers, and his head was not entirely steady upon his shoulders, as if there were frogs between his ears too. I put his demeanour down to first-day nerves. After all, who wouldn't be nervous upon seeing Kendal for the first time?

"She's cute," the boy said.

"About as cute as a Rottweiler," I replied. "She's your new boss. Just do whatever she tells you to do. I find that makes life a lot easier."

"My name's Karl with a K," the boy added. "I've got German blood." He laughed.

"Hello, Karl with a K," I returned. "Welcome to the team."

The boy grinned inanely as he continued to hop from foot to foot. I reflected that if he put as much effort into any work that Kendal might give him, he was bound to be a useful addition to the team, albeit a temporary one.

"Are you a student, Karl?"

Karl laughed again. "Sometimes," he said.

"Well, for the short time that you're going to be with us, you'll be a student of human nature," I said, "and, if you can work Kendal out, you're a better man than I."

Karl showed his teeth and sniggered.

"Has the phone rung yet, Kendal?" I enquired, not believing that the tenants of Greetwell Housing Trust had yet got into their Tuesday morning stride.

"You bet it has!"

"You're kidding me!"

"It hasn't stopped ringing!" Kendal looked down at her notebook. "Selena Wilcox phoned to ask why neither Rosie Waterhouse"—she glanced at Karl—"she's my mum, nor Grace Helm was at the Mother and Baby Unit. Then an old woman called Anne-Marie Denham-Staples-Jones rang to say that her toilet was blocked because she'd just emptied four days' accumulation into the pan."

"But she's constipated," Karl protested knowingly.

"She's not constipated today," Kendal said. "Then a guy named Roly Cheeseman phoned to report that his boiler was broken."

"At Greetwell, they call him Cheese Rolyman," Karl put in, his teeth again on display.

"Then this old bird called Scarlet Creamer started bending my ear."

"This just gets worse," I moaned.

"She's an old boiler." Karl tittered at his own comment. He, at least, was finding the catalogue of woe entertaining.

"What did this Scarlet Creamer have to say for herself?"

"She told me that she'd called the fire brigade."

"Do I need to know why?"

"Because she and her poodle were being driven mad by the squealing of her next-door neighbour, Bertha Garlick, and her wretched cat Horlicks…"

"What's up with them?"

"They're stuck up Bertha Garlick's walnut tree."

"Scarlet Creamer's just stuck-up."

"How come you know so much about the tenants, Karl?"

"They wouldn't let me answer the phones at Greetwell," Karl said, "but I was listening all the time."

"So, you saw and heard a lot at Greetwell, did you?"

"I saw and heard everything."

"Did you meet Rachel Bannerman at Greetwell?"

"Yeah…"

"What did you make of her?"

"She's got a nice arse. She's fit, man. She must be forty-something, but *I* would."

I tried to remember if I'd spoken like that when I was seventeen. I was trying to find some kinship with Karl, some point of contact, but it was like trying to engage with a creature from another planet. He made Kendal look almost human.

I sighed. "I'll make us all a coffee, shall I? Karl, sit next to Kendal, would you? Watch and learn."

Whilst I made the coffee, Karl manoeuvred himself gingerly so that he sat in the chair beside Kendal. It was a rickety old thing that nobody had sat on for years, so I was curious to see whether it would take Karl's weight without collapsing. I said a silent prayer and hoped for the best.

Karl was looking at Kendal in a most disconcerting fashion, as if she were an exotic animal at the zoo and he the fascinated onlooker, peering through the cage. Kendal looked poised to remind Karl not to stare at her, with the reminder coming from the back of her hand, rather than from her mouth.

"What are you doing?" she asked Karl, recoiling slightly.

"I'm watching you."

"I'm not doing anything."

"When you do something, I'll be watching."

The phone rang. How did I know that the call would not be for me and my little team?

"Answer that, would you, Karl?" Kendal said, her tone as commanding as a newly promoted sergeant in the Metropolitan Police barking orders at a hapless constable.

Karl picked up the phone as if it were a hand-grenade likely to blow up in his face. "Hello," he mumbled. He spoke cautiously, and with a hint of mockery, as if the entire charade were beneath his dignity. A voice boomed from the earpiece. He handed the receiver to Kendal. "It's for you," he said.

Visibly irritated to the point of anger, Kendal snatched the phone from the boy's tenuous grasp. She put the phone on speaker mode again.

"Hello, it's Lionel Watson here, of Flat Six Martyrs' Crescent! I've locked myself out! My neighbour's got the spare key, but he's on holiday, see! My methadone's inside! I can see it through the window! It's on the kitchen table! I need the methadone! It's my medication, see!"

Kendal made notes as Lionel Watson spoke: though vexed by the latest intrusion occasioned by Greetwell Housing Trust's error, she and I recognised the urgency of the calls and so were responsible enough to take down the details and to pass them on to the housing association.

"Somebody will be with you shortly," Kendal growled down the phone. She slammed the instrument down like an alcoholic slamming down an empty glass on the bar to indicate that he expects another whisky.

Karl was shaking his head as if he were trying to dislodge something stuck in his hair.

"What did you make of that, then, Karl?" I asked.

"I'm surprised that Lionel Watson is still in town," he replied. "He was last seen pushing his wife across Port Meadow in a supermarket trolley, heading for Southampton."

The entanglement with Greetwell Housing Trust was becoming weirder by the moment, by the hour, by the day, and the termination of my little enterprise's relationship with them could not have come soon enough. I thought about changing my number, the number of the office, but decided against it on the grounds of propriety. The problem was of Greetwell's making, and it was their job to find a solution. In any case, I was consoled by the thought that we might just receive a call that would shed some light on the mystery that was Laura Hart's murder.

"I bet school was never as much fun as this, was it, Karl?" Kendal said.

Karl simply bared his teeth in reply, a gesture that was as much lascivious grin as it was schoolboy smirk. I wondered for how long Kendal would put up with the boy's spaced-out inanities. By my reckoning, no more than two days. The boy had only just arrived, and already he was on borrowed time.

"Come on, Karl," I said, "we're going out."

"Where are you going?" Kendal's hackles were raised again.

"I'm taking Karl to the Bakehouse for a coffee."

"What about *my* coffee?"

"The kettle's boiled."

As we left the room, Karl winked at Kendal, an act so provocatively cheeky that I was forced to revise my estimate of the length of Karl's stay with us from two days to one day, and that was being wildly optimistic.

EIGHT

Karl's temperament was entirely in keeping with the madness that seemed to pervade the phenomenon that was Greetwell Housing Trust. Matt had often told me about the surreal capers at his workplace, and I was now seeing that he'd never once exaggerated for the sake of an entertaining story. Karl was merely one aspect of the madness, a case of like having attracted like, and I wondered if I, too, had not a touch of madness about me, since Rosie worked at Greetwell and Kendal was her daughter. If only there were a scientific instrument capable of measuring the extent of one's contamination by madness, as a Geiger counter measures radiation, I would have paid a lot of my hard-earned money for it. The hour or so that I spent with Karl on that Tuesday morning—an hour during which I'd intended to give him the benefit of my acquired wisdom about life: man talking to boy, maturity to youth, experience to innocence, prudence to untamed instinct—had gone horribly awry before we'd even reached the Bakehouse. The madness began even before we'd turned right out of South Parade and onto the Banbury Road. Scores of vehicles of all shapes and sizes zoomed and swished and screeched and groaned, up and down and right and left. People came and went. It wasn't exactly Piccadilly Circus, but it was noisy enough, but not so noisy that I was unable to hear Karl's madcap utterances with disturbing clarity.

"My dad keeps banging on about the future of this country," he began.

"Does he?" I returned.

"But he never says what the future is."

"Perhaps he doesn't know what the future is."

"So why does he keep banging on about it?"

"I don't know, Karl."

"Could *you* tell me?"

"Tell you what?"

"What the future of this country is …"

"How should I know what it is?"

"Just tell me *something*."

"Why?"

"So I can tell my dad."

"Why?"

"So he can shut the fuck up!"

As we passed Safeway, a woman in a burka walked by like a black cloud of smoke drifting aimlessly towards an unknown destination. A pair of eyes, snow-white in the slit amid the hooded darkness, darted from side to side. The eyes seemed to be guarding against intrusion; though they suggested fear and suspicion, I was conscious that I might have misread them, for might not a smile have lurked behind the veil, a smile that betokened benignant eyes? As I watched the woman pass, a breeze came from nowhere. It brushed against the black cloth, causing it to ripple around the hips and the back, and the hem to flap like the wings of the raven.

"Some people say that the answer is flapping in the wind, Karl."

"Eh?" Karl said with a bemused stare and a boyish grin.

"I was just being flippant, comparing hawks and doves, and wondering which was which."

"My dad says that Muslims—"

"We'll talk about your dad another time, Karl."

A few yards further up the street, we encountered Jeffrey, the *Big Issue* vendor on the Woodstock Road side of the Banbury Road through the Summertown shops. Sellers of the *Big Issue* were famous for their inventive and witty lines in sales patter. The best I'd heard was the oft-used line spouted by the young man selling the magazine outside Blackwell's Art & Poster Shop, in Broad Street: "The name's Bond, Basildon Bond, double-O-seven and licenced to sell." His badge number really was 007, but I doubted that his name was Basildon Bond, after the stationery company. Anyway, there was Jeffrey, who was reticent at the best of times, but who, today, was positively mute. Moreover, he was swaying from side to side, staring into the distance, his eyes glazed with a sheen of moisture. If it were possible to be comatose whilst standing upright, or just about, then Jeffrey was giving a demonstration of just such a state and just such a stance. Somehow, he was managing to cling onto a clutch of magazines, and there were more of them in the bag behind him, leaning against the wall.

Karl regarded Jeffrey as if he were a clown escaped from the circus.

"Are you all right, Jeffrey?" I asked, knowing full well that he wasn't.

Jeffrey departed from his customary wordlessness by launching himself into an incoherent monologue, which appeared to be a story of how Napoleon left his home in Ancient Greece, became a general commanding the British Army in the Crimea, returned home, victorious, and married the Queen of Sheba.

Karl's look was one of one freak looking dumbfoundedly at another.

"I haven't taken my medication," was the only coherent thing that Jeffrey said, to which I replied that he ought to take it before he started talking nonsense.

We had just crossed the road when Karl asked me what I thought the big issue was: was it homelessness?

"The environment is the big issue, Karl," I replied, "because, when it has been ruined, we will all of us be homeless."

The Bakehouse was busy with people enjoying mid-morning snacks and cups of tea and coffee; and the young waitress, Judy, was rushed off her feet trying to service the rush of customers. Eventually, she reached our table and I ordered two cups of cappuccino, both with a sprinkling of chocolate. Over our coffees, I tried to conduct an intelligent conversation with Karl, but it was like trying to discuss Wittgenstein with a blancmange. I'd seen enough of Karl to suspect that between his comically large ears was a brain capable of original thought and conducive to a devil-may-care independence of mind; however, his moroseness that Tuesday morning had nothing to do with a lack of brainpower; it seemed to derive from his preoccupation with his mobile phone, which he kept gazing at longingly and caressing with his thumb.

"Did you have a good weekend, Karl?"

"Yeah, not bad…"

"What did you do?"

"Not much…"

"Did you go out on Saturday night?"

"Yeah…"

"Did you drink much?"

"Yeah, ten pints of Stella and half a bottle of vodka…"

"That's a lot of drink."

"I woke up on Sunday morning on the bonnet of someone's car."

"You slept well then?"

"Yeah…"

"Why do you keep staring at your phone, Karl?"

The boy looked eaten up with regret, tenderness and remorse.

"Man, I want to phone her," he said.

"Who do you want to phone?"

"Maria…"

"Your girlfriend?"

"My *ex*-girlfriend…"

"I see."

"I haven't seen her for three weeks and, man, I miss her."

"Has she gone away somewhere?"

"She dumped me."

"I see."

Karl looked at me with desperation in his eyes. "Shall I call her?"

"Why not? She might want you back. Don't push it, though. Play it cool."

"But I've done some bad things, man."

"What exactly have you done?"

"I smashed her brother's car up and beat up her dad."

Mirth and a profound sense of alarm jostled in my breast for supremacy; neither won, but each was happy to call the contest a draw.

"I'd leave it if I were you," I said.

It was an opportune moment to change the subject.

"What's your surname, Karl?"

"Jaspers …"

"Is it really?"

"Why would I make up such a thing?"

"Karl Jaspers was a famous existential philosopher."

"A what?"

"Or should I say a philosopher of existentialism?"

"You've lost me, man."

It was time to change the subject again.

"What can you tell me about Rachel Bannerman, Karl?"

"Like I said, she's got a nice arse." Karl laughed as if he had just told a joke but nobody but he had found it funny. "When I first started working at Greetwell, they stuck me at the back of the office of the maintenance department," he went on. "Every time Rachel went to the filing-cabinet, I got an eyeful of her arse. She was doing it on purpose. She knew I was watching. She's got the hots for me."

"It sounds like *you've* got the hots for *her*."

His laughter signified his assent.

"She's in her mid-forties. She's a bit washed-up. She's just your type, Karl."

"She's hot, man."

"She's old enough to be your mother, Karl, and some!"

"You're old enough to be Kendal's father."

"Except that I don't want to sleep with Kendal…"

"*I* do."

"Don't even think about it, Karl."

"Anyway, listen to this, man."

Karl sounded earnest, as if he were on the verge of saying something sensible. Stranger things had happened. I held my breath in anticipation, though still more in hope than expectation. He leaned towards me confidentially.

"The people at Greetwell… well, they ignore me, especially that stupid cow, Harry Fenwick, the manager of the maintenance department. I walk around the building and hear all sorts. It's like I'm invisible. And Rachel… she makes personal phone calls, all the time, whenever I'm the only other person in the room. It's like I'm not there."

"Why are you telling me this, Karl?"

Karl leaned forward again and, to ensure that nobody could overhear, looked over both his shoulders. "Because I know you're on the Laura Hart case," he said.

"How do you know that?"

"Matt told me."

"Oh, did he now?"

"Anyway, Rachel, she makes these calls, see, and I've worked something out."

"I'm all ears."

"Well, Rachel Bannerman, Donna Tamsin—she's a housing officer at Greetwell…"

"I know who she is."

"Okay, those two, Sheryl Henry—she's another housing officer at Greetwell—Laura Hart and Caitlin Mallett, they're all part of a lesbian sex group."

"This sounds like an adolescent fantasy, Karl."

"I've worked it out, man."

"Who's Caitlin Mallett?"

"She, Donna and Rachel were all at school together, so they all go back years. Sheryl and Laura, I'm not sure what their stories are, but they're both on the scene now…or Laura *was*. And they all know who killed Laura Hart, and they're telling the police nothing, to protect whoever killed Laura."

What Karl was telling me now was beyond sensible. It was dynamite. I felt as if some beautiful act of providence had sent Karl my way. After an inauspicious start, he was proving his worth more than I could ever have dared imagine.

"There's more."

I was hyperventilating by this point.

"Caitlin is the wife of Rick Mallett…"

"I've heard of Rick Mallett," I confessed. "He was best friends with Matt at school. Matt talks to me about him."

"Well, word is that Rick's the father of Selena Wilcox's kid. She lives at Greetwell's Mother and Baby Unit. She was sixteen when she had the kid, but she was only fifteen when she was knocked up."

Karl's latest nugget of information, on the face of it, was not strictly relevant to the Laura Hart case, but I was mindful that it might yet prove to be useful.

"Whose word would that be, then, Karl?"

"Harry Fenwick sent me over to the Mother and Baby Unit to change a lightbulb." Karl had leaned back in his chair by now and was expounding like an Oxford don at a tutorial. "Just before I knocked on the door, I heard Rosie Waterhouse and Grace Helm talking about it."

"You do know that Rosie is Kendal's mother, don't you?"

"Yeah, Kendal said so, back at the office."

"Anything else you want to tell me, Karl?"

"Yeah …"

"I'm listening."

"Did you hear that Selena Wilcox was busted by the cops for having weed growing in her flat?"

"I read something in the newspaper about it."

"Okay, well, it turned out that she was just looking after the pots of weed for her boyfriend, so she got off and he was nicked instead."

I waited for the punchline with bated breath. I knew there was more.

"One day, last week, after work, I was leaving the building by the back door, and I saw, standing in the carpark, talking, Selena Wilcox and the copper investigating Laura Hart's murder."

"Detective Inspector Stephen Waugh?"

"That's the one."

"What were they talking about?"

"I don't know, but they looked very cosy. There's definitely something going on there."

"You think they're having an affair?"

Karl shook his head in disgust, as if the very idea of an affair between the two was too gruesome to contemplate.

"No, but there's something going down between them, and it might be relevant to you, you know, in the Laura Hart case."

"Indeed, it might, Karl."

We had both neglected our coffees, so we drank them in a hurry, before they became undrinkable. I could tell that drinking coffee was rather alien to the boy. Strong beer and vodka were much more up his street.

"Thank you, Karl, you've been most helpful. I have to be somewhere now. I want you to go back to the office and help Kendal do whatever it is she does. But don't tell her a word of what you've just told me. She'll quiz you about all sorts of things, including—especially—the Laura Hart case, but just pretend to be as stupid as she thinks you are. Mum's the word, right?"

"Right…"

"I'm seriously thinking about telling that Harry Fenwick what a huge mistake she's made in neglecting you."

"You tell the stupid cow."

"And forget about Maria, Karl."

"No, no, I want you to help me get her back."

"I've got enough on my plate, Karl."

"All I want you to do is tell me something that I can tell her, something romantic. You're good with words."

I reached into my jacket pocket for my little notebook and pen. Then I wrote down a sentence that was so ludicrously over the top that the girl would hear it and never talk to the boy again. I was doing him a favour. I passed the slip of paper across the table.

Karl's eyes lit up as if I had just conjured the most magnificent bouquet of flowers and invited him to give them to Maria, the girl of his dreams. When he read the words, they sounded yet more absurd coming from his lips than they'd looked written down on the slip of paper.

"May I congratulate God on creating such a radiant flower as yourself?"

The man sitting at the table next to ours choked on his coffee.

"Wow, man!" Karl said. "She'll melt when she hears me say that!"

"All you have to do is get an audience with her," I replied. "You'll have to sort that out yourself."

"I'll go back to the office now and practice saying it."

"You do that," I said. "I'll be back this afternoon to test you."

NINE

The Covered Market is one of Oxford's many gems. If not the jewel in the crown exactly then it is without doubt one of the precious stones encrusting the regal headpiece. It is to a provincial shopping centre what a bottle of vintage Château Lafite is to an off-the-shelf flagon of Blue Nun. Every shop adorning its precincts is superior almost to the point of being supercilious, containing its grandiosity just within the bounds of decency. The shops are small but reassuringly expensive, a guarantee of quality in a world festooned with a glib superabundance of quantity. Whatever you buy in Oxford's Covered Market, it will cost you four times as much as it would cost you elsewhere in the city, but only because it will be three times better.

My only problem with the Covered Market is that, whenever I go in, I can never find my way out, even when I'm simply using it as a shortcut from Market Street to the High, or from Cornmarket to the Broad. If I enter looking for the barber's, I go round in circles and keep returning to Brown's, the greasy spoon, yet, whenever I fancy eating at Brown's, I make myself dizzy and return again and again to the shoe-repair shop, the café forever eluding me. Once, for some reason that escapes me completely, I had cause to visit the florist's, but the only shop that seemed to want my business that day was the butcher's. It was a case of taking a butcher's at the butcher's, walking around the block looking for the florist's, and coming back to the butcher's, before giving up and buying the flowers at Interflora in the High, once I'd found my way out.

To help me navigate my way around and through the place, I always try to picture in my mind the Covered Market as two figures-eight, situated side by side; the reality, however, is that it's more like two entangled snakes enjoying each other's company.

If it is not quite unfathomable, I have no hesitation in calling it all but unnavigable.

***

Before my rendezvous with Belinda Waugh, I hurried to Brown's in the Covered Market to avail myself of brunch in the form of ham, egg and chips. There might have been a sausage thrown in for good measure, and a few baked beans. It was all helped down the hatch by a mug of tea the size of a beer keg. There—having found the place somewhat fortuitously as I searched—I met three of the sort of people who, in my days as a policeman, would surely have been among my small army of snouts, people who blew down my ear once in a while, letting me know who was up to no good and where they were up to it. They were three very different characters with one thing in common: they loved Brown's, one of two restaurants of that name in Oxford, the one at the cheap end of the market, and, with a bizarre irony, the one in the Covered Market, the exception, if you like, that proved the rule. Perhaps they had two things in common, for none of them seemed to work.

Pig greeted me upon my arrival by holding out the spare seat at their table and beckoning me to sit beside him. He was on the point of finishing a full English breakfast, mopping up as he was the sauce of his baked beans with a slice of pasty buttered bread. He was called Pig because he was Polish and he played in goal for his pub football team, that pub being, coincidentally, the Round House; nobody could pronounce either his first name or his surname, so he was known as "Pole In Goal", or Pig for short.

"Morning, Daniel!"

Pig's words came out with an orange spray, most of which fell short of the plate of Osney Mick, a burly middle-aged chap who lived on Osney Island, in the west of the city, on the way to Botley.

"How are you, Pig?"

"I tell you something," he replied. "You English could never produce something as totally delicious as bigos, but your fry-ups aren't bad."

"The people who run this place are Italian," I said, and I braced myself for another shower of tomato sauce, this time directed at me.

"Your usual, Daniel?"

I looked over my shoulder at the counter and said "Yes, please" to Sonia.

Mercifully, the hailstorm of half-swallowed tomato sauce was over: Pig had finished his breakfast. It can't be said that he didn't do his nickname some justice whilst eating.

"I'm depressed, Daniel!"

"When aren't you depressed, Lorry?"

He was called Lorry because he used to drive one. Nowadays, the only thing he drove was staff at Brown's up the wall with his endless demands for extra slices of bread, which he always expected to be given free of any extra charge.

"Another slice of bread over here, Sonia, please!"

Thankfully, Lorry always managed to keep what he was chewing within the confines of his mouth, though his habit of talking with his full mouth open often had me recoiling in disgust. His tendency to gulp his tea and then belch loudly hardly endeared me to him either.

"Why are you depressed, then, Lorry?"

"My lot, we've signed another sicknote, haven't we?"

"That's one more player than my lot will be signing in the January transfer window," I said.

"Yes, but we've signed someone from AEK Athens, a bloke called Diogenes."

"He's a good player."

"Yes, but Diogenes is Greek for 'dodgy knees'," Lorry returned ridiculously. "We've spent millions on another bloody crock-merchant."

"Lorry, the club you support is so rich, it'll just buy the bloke a new pair of knees."

"You reckon?"

"It's a certainty," I said. "Now, will somebody please tell me something sensible."

Pig rejoined the conversational fray, though whether any of what he said was sensible would depend upon one's definition of sensible.

"Guess who we're playing on Saturday," he challenged me.

"Real Madrid?"

"The Dog and Trumpet…and you know what happened last time we played them."

"Remind me."

"Four players were sent off and the referee was attacked by a guy with a chain and by another guy with a meat-cleaver."

"That's right, the game was abandoned by riot police," Osney Mick put in.

"Weren't you one of the players sent off?" I asked Pig.

Pig ran his fingers through his greasy hair. "I was provoked," he said. "Their big centre-half kept calling me Blondie and blowing me kisses, like I'm a bloody girl, and then he called me the son of a German whore. I was furious. Nobody calls a Pole a bloody German."

Sonia placed a plate of food before me; it was accompanied by a mug of tea so strong that, when I added sugar, it resisted my attempt to stir it. I thanked her and smiled my winning smile, the smile that often got me into trouble. Her husband Mattia looked over at me, just to check that I wasn't flirting with her, as if it were possible for me to find a beautiful and endlessly charming woman with gorgeous Mediterranean features in any way attractive.

Pig asked me if I fancied going to the game on Saturday.

My answer came after my first mouthful of chips.

"Do I look like I have a death wish?"

Osney Mick had devoured a mountain of food and was in the mood for spreading a bit of gossip, something which, as a former policeman, and as a working private detective, was never to be sniffed at.

"Hey, Daniel!" Osney Mick addressed me as if I were at the other end of the city, in a soundproof room in Risinghurst, instead of on the other side of the table. "There were two birds in here the other day talking about you!"

"Really? Who were they? And keep your voice down, will you?"

"One of them had shoulder-length shaggy hair, was about forty, bit of a hippy, and the other looked like a malnourished stick-insect, about the same age, and had rings and studs all over her face, and she was wearing a white T-shirt with an arrow pointing downwards, and below the arrow the words 'This Way'."

Providence had done me another good turn when it pointed me in the direction of these three reprobates, who did nothing but drift around Oxford, seeing and hearing things that I'm not able to see and hear because I cannot be everywhere at once. Oxford is a small place, and I moved among its spires and domes looking for clues to solve my cases, so having three extra pairs of eyes and ears was a valuable resource, not to mention a source of comradeship that was rewarding for its own sake. Osney Mick had done me proud. His unerring eye for the nefarious activities of the city's lowlife had allowed him to describe Donna Tamsin with such penetrating accuracy that I could almost have reached out and touched her, there and then, and I was left hoping that his ears had been attuned with like precision.

Osney Mick had more to say about Donna Tamsin's metallic proclivities.

"I nearly warned her never to go in a magnet factory!" he roared. "When she gets old, she won't go grey, she'll go rusty!"

Laughing uproariously at his own jokes was one of Osney Mick's more endearing traits. I confessed that I knew exactly who he was talking about. I asked him what he'd managed to overhear.

"Oh, well, the hippy bird was telling the skinny bird—the one who looked like Metal Mickey—that she'd seen you with someone…someone she reckoned you shouldn't have been seen with."

"Who?" I asked.

"I didn't catch the name."

"It was Dominic Kane," Lorry interposed. "The hippy bird said she'd seen you with the lad who killed Laura Hart."

I looked around the café to see if anyone had heard Lorry's broadcast to the nation. Lorry took the hint.

"Don't worry, Daniel," Pig interjected. "She said she'd seen you two together weeks before Laura Hart was killed."

"The timing's not so important," I said. "I was seen with Dominic Kane, who's now wanted for murder, there's no trace of him, so therefore I must be hiding him. Donna Tamsin knows that I've been looking out for Dominic. She and I have had a run-in."

"*Are* you hiding Dominic Kane?"

Instead of answering Osney Mick's question, I filled my mouth with ham dipped in egg. Better egg in my mouth than on my face. My comrades seemed to understand my reluctance either to tell the truth or to lie. They all looked at me solemnly, which I took to be a gesture of collective solidarity. I've long been of the view that for detectives, of whatever ilk, having friends in low places is better than having friends in high. After all, was a crime ever solved by the detective's knowing personally the Commissioner of the Metropolitan Police? Snouts are like gold dust for detectives, especially when they don't even know that they're snouts, because then they don't need paying.

Inbetween mouthfuls, I told my three friends that they reminded me of the three old boys who drifted around Holmfirth in the television comedy series *Last Of The Summer Wine*; that I had no idea what they did all day, apart from eating Brown's out of eggs and bacon, and that I had no wish to know. Brown's, then, clearly, was to Lorry, Pig and Osney Mick what Sid's Café was to Compo, Clegg and Foggy. I wondered which one of my friends was Compo and who was his Nora Batty.

I found myself proposing a toast to eyes and ears. It was a bizarre proposal, but I had my reasons. Four sturdy mugs were raised and clinked together without a drop of tea being spilt. I then proposed another toast: to success. The ritual was repeated.

That left me only to invite the three men for drinks at the Dew Drop on the following Saturday night, an invitation that was accepted with alacrity all round, and not just because I was paying.

"And what do we owe this unexpected pleasure, then, Daniel?" Lorry asked.

"We shall be celebrating my latest success," I replied with all the confidence of Casanova in a harem, "and the part that you three played in it."

The three men regarded each other with satisfaction, though they had no idea what they were supposed to be satisfied about.

"We shall also be celebrating Brighton and Hove Albion's victory over Leeds United," I said.

"Always pleased to celebrate a victory over dirty Leeds," Osney Mick declared.

"Not forgetting the Round House's victory over the Dog and Trumpet," Pig said.

"Let's hope you live to tell the tale," I replied.

The mug-touching ritual was repeated.

By that time, we had an audience of a scattering of lonely-looking individuals all wishing they'd been invited to the party. If only they'd all known just how welcome they would have been to join us.

TEN

Fortified by brunch and a cup of tea strong enough to keep me awake for a week, I waited for Belinda Waugh to arrive for our rendezvous with the ducks at the University Parks' famous Pond, for that's where strolls amid that green expanse of Oxford invariably ended. The time was three minutes past midday. I was late. But then so was Belinda Waugh. My phone rang. I saw that it was Matt calling. I wondered if I had time to chat with him.

"It's not a good time, Matt," I said.

"What are you doing this afternoon?"

"I've a meeting now."

"After that?"

"I thought I'd do some thinking."

"Where? In the King's Arms?"

"I thought I'd try the Turf Tavern."

"Forget the booze, Daniel, you're coming with me."

"Where are we going?"

I looked down Parks Road, and up Keble Road, past the red-brick colossus that was Keble College Chapel, but there was no sign of my prospective new client.

"We're going up to the Littleworth Housing Estate," Matt continued, though I could barely hear him above the noise of the passing traffic. "There's someone I'd like you to meet."

"Who?"

"An old friend of mine called Rick Mallett..."

"You've talked about him...and Karl mentioned him."

"Rick and I go way back. We went to school together. He's married to Caitlin Mallett—O'Donovan, as was—who went to school with Donna Tamsin and Rachel Bannerman. We're all the same age, but we went to two different schools. Rick and I went to Frideswide Upper, in Cowley, and the girls went to Saint Thomas More, in Headington. Today's a difficult day for Rick. He's a troubled man and today will bring him further troubles that he really doesn't need. I'll explain later."

"What does Rick have to do with me?"

"Again, I'll explain later."

"Why have you kept so much from me, Matt?"

"What do you mean?"

"I've gleaned from Karl this morning a lot of details that I should have got from you."

"That boy was a fly on the wall at Greetwell, he saw and heard things, he's a mine of information, which is why I sent him to you. I knew he'd open up."

"It seems that, as well as being highly perceptive, Karl also has a violent streak."

"I know nothing about that."

"Really?"

"The boy can be your minder."

"I can look after myself, thanks."

"That's just as well, given what's happening today."

"What do you mean?"

"I'll tell you later."

"Stop keeping me in the dark, Matt."

"I don't want to overload you with too much information, too soon, Daniel. Don't worry, one way or another, you'll be told everything you need to know, as and when."

Mainly because I didn't have time to argue with him, I shook my head and sighed. Matt was keeping much else from me. I could tell. I didn't like it, not least because it made no sense, since he'd asked me to do a job, and he was paying me to do it, and it wasn't as if I had unlimited time in which to get it done. There was also the small matter of justice and the fate of a young man accused of a crime that he hadn't committed.

"I don't want to be making fruit salad without any fruit, Matt."

"What? You don't even like fruit."

I sighed again.

"This morning, I learnt from my three amigos at Brown's that Donna Tamsin knows for certain that I've been hiding Dominic Kane. They overheard her being told by another woman that she'd seen me and Dominic together. Evidently, Donna Tamsin has drawn her own conclusions, but we knew that already."

"How did they know it was Donna?"

"They didn't. But they described her. Built like a stick of spaghetti and with enough metal on her face to hang keys on. Who else could it be?"

"Who was the other woman?"

"She was described as a hippy."

"That sounds like Sheryl Henry."

"Karl mentioned her too."

"And when did Sheryl say she'd seen you with Dominic?"

"It was before Laura Hart was killed, but that's not important."

"Perhaps not, but it's odd that she took so long to mention it."

"Perhaps she'd only just remembered. Perhaps something jogged her memory. You know how these things are."

"This is all good news," Matt enthused. "The more cages that are rattled the better."

"Donna Tamsin wants to nail me."

"But *you're* going to nail *her*."

I still couldn't rid myself of the suspicion that Matt knew much more than he was telling me. I was even toying with the idea that he knew who killed Laura Hart, that he was making sport of me, albeit at his own expense. I couldn't help thinking that he was exploiting my enthusiasm for solving puzzles, which (he knew) overruled my sense of danger, and that he now had me beyond the point of no return on a path littered with hazards. These hazards I would be allowed to discover for myself, if he didn't condescend to warn me first.

"Matt, my client's coming. I have to go."

"Okay, I'll pick you up at one-thirty."

"Where?"

"Outside the Randolph…"

"Okay…"

Belinda Waugh approached me and actually said, "Daniel Winter, I presume."

"Well, I'm certainly not Doctor Livingstone," I replied, if only to communicate to her that I'd understood her allusion to the famous words of American reporter Henry Morton Stanley upon his uncovering the Scottish physician and explorer, assumed lost or dead, on the shores of Lake Tanganyika.

We shook hands. Belinda was wearing a black raincoat and a red silk scarf was tied loosely around her head to protect her mane of hair from the drizzle that was continuing to sweep across the park; as she stepped ahead of me, as if to indicate the way, gravel crunched under the weight of her leather boots. Hers was quite an intimidating presence. She was about the same age as Helena, though not quite as elegant, and nowhere near as pretty. Somehow, now that she was a client of mine, she seemed different, a different person almost. All in all, she was making quite an impression on me, again.

"We've met," she said as I scurried to catch her up.

"Have we?"

"Don't bother with the flannel, Daniel. I know my husband paid you to follow me. I knew the first time I saw you."

"Where was that?"

"At Gino's," she replied. "You stood out like a spare one at a wedding."

It seemed that I'd overestimated my ability to conduct a successful undercover surveillance operation, but there was no need for Kendal to know that.

"So, you didn't see me at the Phoenix Picture House, on the tenth of December, when you went to watch the film, *My Summer Of Love*, with your cousin, one Professor Maurice Cobbold, teacher of History at Saint John's College?"

Graciously, she conceded defeat on that score. "You had the advantage of darkness on that occasion," she said.

"If only I could operate under cover of darkness every time," I said. "I'd be a much more effective private detective."

"You were operating under cover of darkness last night, Daniel, but I still saw you."

It was my kind of winter's day: wet, murky and bleak. I looked around at the trees that clawed at the grey sky with their multitudinous scrawny fingers, mindful that, in eight or nine weeks' time, they would be starting to show signs of life as spring approached, slowly but inexorably, a season that would be as wet as the season preceding it and as wet as the season coming after it. I was hoping that my sudden immersion in the nature surrounding us would serve to deflect a substantive reply to Belinda's last comment; alas, my embarrassment notwithstanding, it had to be addressed.

"I'm sorry about that." My words were as feeble as a schoolboy's excuse for not doing his homework.

"I hope that what you saw didn't shock you."

"I didn't see much." That was a lie. "But I saw enough to enable me to tell your husband that you'd simply enjoyed an evening with fellow bibliophiles at a book club."

Belinda looked at me as if she knew that I'd seen quite enough and more.

"It was a good choice of book, by the way," I went on, emboldened by the conversation's turn and feeling more relaxed in Belinda's company. "I like Helen Dunmore."

The University Parks were deserted. There weren't even any students throwing frisbees at each other, or any lovers holding hands and stealing kisses under the trees. It was just us two and nature, not forgetting the birds, of course—crows, mainly—that added a wintry soundtrack to our verbal meanderings and tentative entreaties. If we'd had the first idea where we were going, we wouldn't have been able to see it, such was the murkiness given by the fog and the rain. We were walking along the path by the cricket pavilion, a famous old building that, like every other structure of its type, brooded restlessly during the winter, willing spring to come. The students were playing Sussex in April. I looked forward to that.

"I'll get to the point, shall I, Daniel?"

Not before time, I thought.

"I want to turn the tables on my husband, Daniel." She managed to say that without sounding pompous. "He's paid you to spy on me, and now I'm going to pay you to spy on him. I trust that meets with your approval."

As it happened, I was able to think of at least ten good reasons why my spying on Detective Inspector Stephen Waugh, for his good wife, most certainly did not meet with my approval; however, I was paralysed by curiosity even as I was being drawn irresistibly into the murky lives of people whose fates appeared to be hopelessly intertwined. Little did I know—though I should have guessed—that those lives and fates would become more elaborately intertwined yet.

"We peepers have no scruples," I said. "We'll work for whoever's paying us." I hoped that she'd know that I'd spoken in jest, though what was that saying about many a true word being spoken in jest? "What exactly should I be looking for?"

"Does the name Selena Wilcox mean anything to you?"

"It does."

"So, I needn't tell you about her recent difficulties with a former boyfriend and drugs?"

"I know all about that."

"My husband was involved in that case, and I have it on good authority that he spent a lot of time with Selena not just during the investigation but after it, too, and that they appeared to be intimate."

"Oxford seems to have eyes and ears everywhere," I said. "You can't sneeze in this city without everyone knowing about it."

"Doesn't that make your job easier?"

"It makes it rather too easy sometimes."

"I'm not bound to assume that Stephen and this Selena girl are having an affair, but I would like confirmation—reassurance, if you like—that he hasn't stooped to something so grubby as to take advantage of a vulnerable girl whom he'd been investigating. Our marriage is not blessed—if that is the word—with much in the way of passion, never mind love, but it does depend on a measure of mutual respect. I hope that you'll tell me what I want to hear, Daniel."

"I'll do my best."

We had walked through the middle of the park, eschewing the delights of Mesopotamia Walk and Parson's Pleasure, and arrived at the Pond, an insulting misnomer if ever there was one, for to my eyes the secluded stretch of water was very much a lake. To our left ran the footpath to Wolfson College and Old Marston; to our right loomed the High Bridge over the River Cherwell which joined with another footpath, this one going to Marston, the newer one; and everywhere there were ducks, quacking hungrily in the rain. I looked at my jacket and was surprised to see that the drizzle had left only faint little spots on the black polyester surface.

The ducks were in a state of apoplexy courtesy of a young couple: a man in a tasteless blue cagoule and a woman wrapped in a hideous plastic poncho. The young have an excuse for being fashionable, yet all too often they choose to dress as if fashion has gone out of fashion. Everyone around me looked cold and wet, but I was neither. Even the ducks looked like they would rather have been on a beach in the Bahamas. The lovers were throwing bread into the water and the ducks were scrambling for every crumb.

"Are you married, Daniel?"

"Yes, but only vicariously."

Belinda looked at me as if I were an enigmatic portrait hanging in a gallery: she knew that I'd meant something profound, but to preserve the mystery she wished not to probe me. She was an immeasurably deeper person than her husband, deeper, perhaps, than she gave herself credit for being.

"I work at Oxford University Press," she said. "We've just published a book about policing in the Thames Valley. My husband features in the book. It's funny: in helping to put together the book, I learnt more about him than I have in twenty years of marriage."

"If you don't mind my saying so, Belinda, your marriage does seem a trifle unorthodox."

"That's how we are. Even on our honeymoon, we barely spoke. Two weeks of near-silence in Corfu. But we were blissfully happy in our own way. We still are."

"He's a good man, your husband."

"But am I a good woman?"

"He thinks so."

"Does he?"

"He has the highest regard for you."

Belinda gave a satisfied nod at the ducks, as if they themselves had reassured her in some way. I was struck by the idea that the utter futility of the ducks' existence was making her feel better about being human, as if the lesser futility of our own collective existence was cause for muted celebration. "I'm not a duck," she seemed to be thinking, "and there's value in that."

As for myself, I saw the attractions of being a duck.

"Never marry for love, Daniel," she said after a while, "unless, of course, you find that rarest of things, true love, a thing so rare that I'm not sure that it exists."

"My father once gave me the same advice," I said, "and circumstances proved his advice to be sound."

"True love is like the poem, Daniel: it is 'somewhere behind'. We merely discover it. If we're lucky, that is."

"Some people just trip over it."

"Are you familiar with the works of Jan Skácel, Daniel?"

"No, but I've read some Milan Kundera." It seemed like a sensible response at the time.

"I had no idea that a man in a Harrington jacket, and a former policeman to boot, could be so erudite."

"I'm full of surprises," I said. "Next, I'll be telling you that I used to be a trapeze-artist."

She smiled at the ducks again.

"Ducks are lucky," she mused. "They don't have the responsibility of loving. They don't have the burden of *being* loved."

Belinda Waugh was proving to be a curious creature. It would be unfair—and grossly inaccurate—to say that my earliest impression of her was that she displayed all the emotional depth of a kitchen table, but there had been something discernibly cold about her, something frigid, something detached. Now, she was invoking giants of Czech literature and philosophising about the unbearable heaviness of being loved. She was even investing ducks with noble bearing. All of which suggested only that she had some sense of being, a sense that most people singularly lacked. Akin to that sense of being was the sense of realism about who she was, about marriage, and about the type of man with whom she might share a marriage. She had picked the right man in Stephen Waugh, and he had picked the right woman in her. Those two were made for each other.

Love between the Waughs was impossible—I felt entitled to surmise that much—but the mutual respect which glued them together was something worth cherishing, and certainly worth preserving, and it was for that that I felt I owed them both another thorough investigation. It might be that I was kidding myself, that I was investing my profession with a nobility that it did not warrant, or even want. Did I embark upon my every investigation without a trace of voyeurism? Did I never want to catch the subject in the act? Did I always wish my clients' suspicions to be allayed? Any private detective answering yes to all three questions is at best deluded and at worst a liar.

Karl had introduced me to the idea of a relationship of some kind between Detective Inspector Stephen Waugh and young Selena Wilcox. He'd also furnished me with the idea that Rick Mallett, long-standing friend of my friend Matt Prior, was the father of Selena's child. Belinda Waugh knew about the former, she knew nothing about the latter, yet it was entirely possible that a thread now joined Belinda Waugh, through her husband and a teenaged single mother, to Rick Mallett, a man she'd never met and was never likely to meet.

The plot was thickening.

Surely, nothing else would be added to the mix?

ELEVEN

When Matt's car pulled up outside the Randolph Hotel, a man dressed as a Coldstream Guard leapt from the steps of the luxury establishment and opened the passenger door. Nobody got out. But I got in. It was nice to have somebody opening doors for me. It made a pleasant change from having doors slammed in my face.

"The old boy thought somebody was getting out," Matt said as he drove down Beaumont Street in the direction of Worcester College.

I voiced my gratitude about doors being opened for me, instead of being slammed in my face, and we were sliding down the High Street before I'd worked out how to broach the subject that was foremost in my mind. As I was about to open my mouth, as we were passing The Queen's College, Matt forestalled my opening gambit by speaking first.

"So, how did your meeting go?"

I decided to tell Matt as little as possible.

"We got wet."

"Anything else to report?"

I reminded myself that, though Matt knew about Detective Inspector Stephen Waugh—obviously, since he was the chief investigating officer in the Laura Hart murder case—and about the irregular confidence that the policeman shared with Selena Wilcox, he had no idea that I'd been paid by the detective to follow his wife, or that I'd just been engaged by the same wife to keep tabs on the very same detective. I was tying myself in knots trying to remember who knew what and who *should* know what. Indeed, I was struggling to keep up with all that was happening, so fast were events unfolding and so intricately intertwined were the various strands of the story. If I'd been at home, watching the story as a film, I would have been constantly rewinding the DVD to refresh my memory or to remind myself who said what to whom.

"Have you not heard about client confidentiality?" I ventured to reply.

"Don't give me that!"

"My new punter has nothing to do with Greetwell Housing Trust," I said, knowing that my reply was at the same time both the truth and a lie. That was another problem I was having: separating truth from lies and reality from fiction. Still, it was all good fun.

"I've got some good news for you, my friend."

"There's a first time for everything."

"Our esteemed chief executive has agreed to compensate you—and handsomely—for your troubles with the mixed-up telephone numbers."

"Not before time…"

"She wants to see you tomorrow, at two o'clock, in her office."

"At The Golden Age?"

"Where else?"

"But that means—"

"It means that you'll have to enter the lions' den," Matt said. "That shouldn't be a problem. You are called Daniel, after all."

"Ingenious…"

"And you can do some snooping around while you're there. It's a golden opportunity. If anyone challenges you—even if it's Donna Tamsin herself—you'll have the perfect excuse for being there. You might get lost, of course. As I've told you, the place is like a rabbit warren. And you might fall through the floorboards. The building's falling down. It was condemned months ago. The other day, I put my foot through one of the stairs. The wood's as rotten as North Korean justice. And there are cracks in all the walls, *real* cracks, *gaping* cracks. By nine o'clock on Friday evening, the whole place will be boarded up. Still, you'll have fun tomorrow observing the local wildlife."

"I can't wait."

We had come to a halt just outside the main entrance to Magdalen College. Matt was impatiently trying to see what had happened ahead to bring the traffic to a standstill. The fog had become so thick that it was impossible to see more than thirty yards ahead, so we were stuck and we had no idea why.

"I knew I should have taken the ring road," Matt grumbled.

"That, too, is just a carpark," I remarked. "It's like the M25 in miniature."

"This whole city is grinding to a halt," Matt complained. "Even the pavements are clogged up."

Looking across the road at the arched entrance to another of Oxford's major attractions, for tourists and residents alike,

I asked my friend if he'd ever graced the Botanic Garden with his presence.

"Once," he said. "I bunked off school with Penny Jones and we took a tumble amongst the hydrangeas."

"How romantic!" I laughed.

"You ever had a look round the Botanic Garden?"

"No, but I've a feeling that one day a prospective client will meet me there. It's the kind of place where people meet for confidential conversations that only orchids might overhear."

"Or hydrangeas!"

"There's nothing much there to take a tumble in this time of year," I said.

"Listen, I'm sorry that I was less forthcoming than I might have been, you know, about the details of the case, but I know what Karl knows, we talked, and I knew that he would tell you all that he knew. I didn't have to put him up to it. There was no need for you to hear it all from both of us, and I wanted Karl to be useful."

"You did me a favour in sending Karl to me," I conceded. "He's a bright lad."

"He's a bright lad in a dozy kind of way."

"He gives the impression of being half-asleep sometimes," I agreed, "but he doesn't miss a trick, that boy."

"I'm working on the assumption that what he told me is exactly what he told you," Matt said.

"Let's assume that to be the case," I replied.

"It's mind-blowing, some of it."

"So, what about your friend Rick?"

Matt looked troubled. He frowned and pursed his lips. He looked like he'd just been intercepted by a rattlesnake and didn't know which way to turn.

"Poor Rick," he resumed with a sigh. "He must be in turmoil. A year ago today, his nine-year-old daughter, Melissa, died of meningitis; he's devoted to his wife, Caitlin, but word is that he got a fifteen-year-old girl up the duff; today, his old mucker, Greg Tinnion, comes out of the nick after serving three years for GBH; and, on top of that little lot, this morning his boiler broke down."

"So, we're going to counsel him, are we?"

"I just thought he could do with some company."

"His wife works?"

Matt nodded. He then told me that Caitlin worked at Tesco by the ring road and that Rick hadn't worked for years.

"Why don't you ask him about Selena? You're his best friend. He'd tell you, surely?"

"I can't bring myself to ask him. I'm not sure that he knows about the rumours about him and Selena."

"So who does know?"

"Only people within the four walls of Greetwell Housing Trust…"

"The walls that are tumbling down, you mean?"

Matt nodded his appreciation of my reference to The Style Council, the band that Paul Weller set up (with Mick Talbot) after he disbanded The Jam.

"His wife?" I added.

Matt shook his head. "If Caitlin knew, there would be ructions, and I would know about them."

"Do you believe the rumours?"

"Yes, but only because Rick is given to doing the daftest of things. At school, when we were about thirteen, he slapped our French teacher, Miss McBlaine, on the arse. She'd bent down to pick up an exercise book that she'd dropped on the floor. He was suspended for a month. The old girl probably enjoyed being slapped on the arse. It must have been her first erotic experience for years."

"What's Rick's connection with the girl? How does he know her?"

"Rick used to do voluntary work, during the school summer holidays, at the Littleworth Youth Centre. Selena had been going there every summer for years. She used to flaunt herself in front of Rick. At fourteen, she had the body of a twenty-year-old. However, I struggle to believe that he would be so stupid—or so depraved—as to give in to her wily attempts at seduction."

"When was the baby born?"

"Last May, a month after Selena turned sixteen, which means that the wicked deed was done round about August time, right in the middle of the school holiday."

"There is circumstantial evidence to implicate Rick then…"

"It doesn't bear thinking about, Daniel."

"Just ask him."

"He might open up to me if you're there with me."

"Why would my presence make a difference?"

"Male solidarity," Matt said. "You know, boys together and safety in numbers."

"Okay, we'll see."

"Isn't it funny how all the people we've been talking about are connected in some way?"

Matt seemed to have forgotten that we were parked on the cusp of Magdalen Bridge and hadn't moved for ten minutes. We might have been propping up the bar in the Dew Drop for all he knew.

"I mean, the copper Waugh, Selena, Rick, Caitlin, Donna, Rachel, Sheryl, Rosie, Kendal, Dominic, you, me, and anybody else I might have missed out: it's like we've all been made into a soup, put in a big pot, and are being stirred by a chef with a warped sense of humour."

"And it's a pretty thick soup at that," I said.

"When you go to the Greetwell office tomorrow, to see Ida McSweeney, go and see Rosie at the Mother and Baby Unit and try to find out what she knows about Rick and Selena."

"That's not one of your better ideas, Matt."

"I'm serious."

"What does the Rick-and-Selena business have to do with the murder of Laura Hart?"

"You never know…"

"You've already told me that Rachel Bannerman is the key person in all of this."

"Absolutely, she is." Matt was exercised by apparent movement up ahead and he prepared to put the car back into motion. "Do you know what else I think about Rachel?"

"Enlighten me."

"She's part of a group of people centred on Greetwell that knows who killed Laura Hart. I believe that Rachel doesn't want an innocent young man—namely, Dominic Kane—to take the rap for Laura's murder. She's gagging to tell the truth, or at least to help somebody discover the truth. That's where *you* come in, my friend. You won't have to work too hard to get the truth out of her. She'll talk soon enough, in her own way. Pillow talk, probably."

"I'm glad that you're prepared to entertain the idea that Dominic might just be innocent."

"Look, for what it's worth, I don't think he killed Laura, but you should let him be questioned, to let justice run its course."

"We've been through this."

"Now, thanks to me, you have Rachel Bannerman to help you prove Dominic's innocence. That's what friends are for, eh?"

"I guess so."

"On our way back from Littleworth, once we've seen Rick, I'll tell you more than you'll ever need to know about Rachel Bannerman."

"If you think that's necessary..."

We were moving again. We soon learnt that there'd been an accident at the Plain—the roundabout connecting the High Street with Saint Clement's and the Cowley and Iffley Roads—involving a bus and a cyclist. Matt said that he'd suspected another suicide attempt by a student on Magdalen Bridge. Just before Christmas, a student with girl troubles had decided to end it all by leaping into the Cherwell, but he'd succeeded only in breaking his leg when he landed on a submerged supermarket trolley. What lay beneath the murky waters of the Cherwell boggled the mind.

We'd left behind the Oxford of God and the Mind, heralded as they were by Magdalen College Bell Tower, and were finally on our way to Littleworth, via the multicultural thoroughfare that is the Cowley Road.

"Talk of the she-devils," Matt announced as we drove past the Bullingdon Arms and saw three women stepping out onto the street. "There they go: Donna, Rachel and Sheryl. The middle one's Rachel. Now that you've clocked her, I bet you've changed your mind about the pillow talk."

I couldn't deny that she had an alluring deportment, though she was more Raquel Welch than Julie Christie.

"She dresses like that for the office. You wait till you see her tonight behind the bar. If I were you, I'd take something to prop up your eyes."

"My eyes are quite capable of defying gravity without artificial props, thanks all the same."

"Can you imagine those three in bed together, with Caitlin and Laura thrown in?"

I took that to mean that he knew what I knew, and we said not a word more on that sordid subject until the case was closed.

TWELVE

I had seen people who were clean yet fundamentally dirty, people who were neat and tidy, smooth around the edges, too, but whose underlying griminess was given away by signs here and there: an unpleasant smell, dirty fingernails and mouths the inside of which resembled old graveyards. As soon as he opened his front door, Rick Mallett struck me as being the opposite: dirty yet fundamentally clean. Though his hair was tousled and greasy, and he was decidedly rough around the edges, there was something wholesome about him, as if a lack of soap and water could never sully his basic decency of body and mind. I sensed an immediate affinity with him and the feeling, I felt sure, was mutual. His eyes passed quickly from Matt and lingered on me, for so long that I was almost troubled. There was an audible stroking of his stubbly cheeks and chin, a scratching and shuffling sound, like a thousand termites chewing on bark. He looked like he'd just got out of bed and hadn't quite got to grips with the day.

"Oh, it's you, Matt," he groaned.

He was wearing a black T-shirt across which, in red letters, was written: "Just Do Nothing."

"Were you expecting someone else?" Matt replied.

"Yeah, your Rapid Reaction Team, to fix my bloody boiler…"

"Ivor Bagshot, Hugh Windlesham and Ronald Blythe wouldn't react rapidly to rockets up their arses," Matt said, "and, anyway, they don't fix boilers, so why are you waiting for them?"

"I asked them to come." Rick adjusted his jeans, not that they needed adjusting: he was simply fidgeting nervously, as if we were policemen. "One of your blokes, a Scouser, said he'd send them."

"Lester Bloodworm," Matt said thoughtfully. "He should know better. The Rapid Reaction Team only attend to little jobs, quick jobs, like blocked toilets and broken taps."

"Well, the Scouse bloke told me he'd send the Rapid Reaction Team."

"They won't be coming, Rick. You'll have to wait until the contractor, Bullard's, arrives, which might not be until tomorrow morning."

"Can *you* have a look at it?"

"If I ever get across the bloody threshold…"

Rick turned on his heels and walked away from us; as he went, a streamer fell from the ceiling and did its best to wrap itself around him. We followed him into the house.

"It's time you took the Christmas decorations down, my friend," Matt laughed. "It's nearly Easter."

"You sound like my wife!"

"And I thought you'd given up smoking."

"I have!" Rick yelled from the kitchen.

"There's cigarette ash all over the carpet, man!"

"The vacuum-cleaner broke down two months ago and we can't afford a new one!"

"I tell you what. I've got a spare one at home. You can borrow it. You can *have* it."

Matt, too, was now in the kitchen. Somewhat bewildered, I was standing beside him.

"Bloody hell!" he exclaimed. "It's colder in here than it is outside!"

"That's because there's no heating."

"Haven't you got any electric heaters?"

"What do *you* think?"

"I'll give you one of mine." Matt tilted his head towards me. "This is my friend Daniel Winter."

Rick fixed me with another hard stare. I tried to read his eyes, but they betrayed only a sense of loss, and for that he could not have been appealing to me, a stranger.

"I think we've met," Rick said.

"I'm not sure that we have," I returned.

"You've heard about Daniel, I'm sure, and not just from me," Matt said. "He's a famous private detective. He can't do proper surveillance because everyone in Oxford knows him. He always goes on surveillance in disguise. Last night, he tailed someone dressed as Guy Fawkes. People just thought he was going to a fancy-dress party."

Rick shook his head and I was his mirror image.

"What can I get you gentlemen?"

The man of the house was endeavouring to be a good host.

Matt said that a cup of tea would be nice, and I agreed wholeheartedly.

"Sit down while I make it."

"We're men, Rick," Matt replied. "We stand."

"Suit yourself."

"We stick together and we stand united," Matt declared with unnecessary and unbecoming fervour.

When the drinks were made, we three stood around the table, as if we were standing guard over something, with cups of tea in our hands, eyeing each other awkwardly, wondering what to say. The thing that seemed to be stymying conversation was resting in the middle of the kitchen table. Matt eyed it as if it were a hand grenade just about to go off. To me, it was just a piece of paper. Its significance would soon be made apparent to me.

"You're not still poring over that bloody letter, are you, Rick?" Matt said at last.

"Today's the first anniversary of Melissa's death," our host said in reply. "Surely, today of all days, I'm entitled to mourn my little girl."

Matt nodded his sympathy. "Of course you are," he said. "That's why we've come today."

"My condolences, Rick," I put in. "I'm so sorry about what happened to your daughter."

"Thank you," he replied earnestly. "That means a lot to me."

As Rick had been making the tea, I'd watched him like a hawk. He'd seemed lost, dazed, as he staggered around the kitchen as if he had no idea where he was or where anything was kept; it had actually been painful to watch a man look so disorientated under his own roof, a man so ill at ease with his surroundings that he might have just been lifted out of the sixteenth century and dropped in the twenty-first. It was a wonder that the tea had been made at all. Now, Rick watched me as I tried not to watch him watching me. I distracted him by mentioning the piece of paper on the table, whereupon he snatched it up and offered it to me. It was double-folded. I didn't open it. Instead, I stood there clutching it, as bemused as he'd been five minutes before.

"It's a letter from the health authority informing the parents of Melissa's schoolfriends about Melissa's meningitis," Rick announced sadly. "It's dated Friday the seventh of January, of last year. The parents received it the following day. Two days after that, Melissa was dead."

"I can't even imagine how you must be feeling," I said.

"Keep it," Rick said. "Don't destroy it. Just put it somewhere out of my way."

I looked at Matt, who nodded vaguely, which I took to mean that I should do as I had been asked.

"I keep looking at it, see," Rick added. "It's kept in the top drawer of the sideboard. Caitlin keeps telling me to stop looking at it, but it's like an itch that I can't help scratching. The only reason why she doesn't destroy it is because she knows that I would go straight down to the health authority to ask for a copy."

"You might do that if I take this away," I said.

Rick shook his head. "Not if I know that it still exists somewhere beyond my reach," he said. "I know that I can trust you. You look trustworthy."

"I'll put it in the safe in my office," I said. He didn't need to know that Kendal had changed the combination, and then promptly forgotten what she'd changed it to, so that I would have to employ a safe-cracker—somebody from the criminal fraternity—to get inside my own safe.

I slipped the letter into the inside top pocket of my jacket and prepared myself to guard it with my life; in spite of what people were saying about Rick, about what he might have done, he seemed like a man whose interests were worth defending, and even fighting for. I resolved to find out the truth about him and Selena Wilcox, though there was little doubt in my mind that he was innocent.

"You know, whenever I read that letter, I hear Mel's music." Rick was still looking at me, as if Matt had vanished, as if he'd not been there at all.

"She was a musician, was she?" I asked.

"She played the violin," Rick answered. "Her school said she was precocious. I didn't know what the word meant. I had to look it up. She was eleven years old and she played like a maestro. She even brought a long-forgotten composer back from the dead."

Matt and I looked at each other like two men trying to find their way out of a fiendishly elaborate maze.

Rick shot Matt with imploring eyes. "You know? Kopetsky?"

The penny dropped finally. "Yes, yes, of course, that obscure Austrian composer whose works Melissa revived," Matt said, as much to explain the matter to me as to signal belated recognition to Rick.

"That's my girl," Rick said, his voice crackling with emotion. "She was special."

Matt went up to Rick and gave him one of those manly hugs that ends with a couple of slaps on the back. He did not look comfortable doing it. He looked like he would rather have been up close and personal with a crocodile. Rick bore the gesture with commendable fortitude.

"I'll take a look at your boiler," Matt told his friend. "It might be something I can fix."

The two men parted and Matt urged Rick to take down the Christmas decorations while he attended to the boiler, to which Rick replied that he would give me a guided tour of the house. To my eyes, it was an unremarkable dwelling on a nondescript housing estate, but if my host felt that there was something in the house worth showing me then I was more than happy to indulge him.

The tour began with the living-room. Rick showed me where the letter had been housed for the past twelve months, and indicated that the drawer had been endowed with a forbidding mystique, and that it had been a constant challenge to the strength of his will to resist opening it. I told him that I had the same experience with the drinks cabinet in *my* living-room. He told me that Caitlin called him twice a day, when she was at work, to make sure that he hadn't been reading the letter. He never lied to her. He always told her that he'd read it. She always threatened to burn it, though she preserved it for his sake. He told me that, each time he read the letter, he saw something different; that, each time, his daughter's music was unlocked; and that the melancholy strains of Kopetsky would fill the house. He said that, thanks to the letter, he knew that there was only one T in "vomiting". Not a lot of people know that, he said, especially on the Littleworth Housing Estate. He asked me why there was only one T in "vomiting" when there were two Ts in "committing". I said that one could say the same about the Ms. There was a little display of books in the cabinet adjacent to the sideboard. Two of the books caught my attention: Sylvia Plath's *The Bell Jar* and Zelda Fitzgerald's *Save Me The Waltz*. Rick told me that they were his wife's two favourite books. I told him that I had both books at home and that I had read them. He urged me to read the letter that he'd vouchsafed to me. I said that I would.

The next port of call was Melissa's bedroom. I knew the Master of Saint Benet's Hall, one of Oxford University's permanent private halls and, as such, one of its teaching institutions; he was a Catholic priest by the name of Father Felix Stephens and he often invited me to dine at Saint Benet's as his guest; most of the time, lunch was taken in the magisterial dining hall, but sometimes we ate in the cosy little enclave of alternative colour known as the Yellow Room. Melissa's domain put me in mind of the Yellow Room. The room could not have been more unlike that of an eleven-year-old girl's, for accoutrements of girlhood were conspicuous by their absence. The ambience was spartan. The walls and the carpet and the bedclothes were all plain yellow. The winter sunlight streaming through the yellow curtains illuminated the pervasive colour further so that it glowed like burning gold. In one corner stood a chest of drawers upon which were stacked, in several columns of CDs, the works of all the great European composers. In another corner stood the violin, his daughter's mouthpiece, the instrument by which she had brought from obscurity the Austrian, Franz Kopetsky, a man whose story (I had a vague recollection of it) was no less tragic than was her own. Somehow, the sparseness of the room made it seem large, an altogether more capacious vessel for the girl's prodigious spirit.

"We haven't touched the room since she died," Rick said with a note of anguish in his voice, "except to clean it."

It's the proverbial shrine to a deceased loved-one, I thought, with everything within having been left exactly as it was at the time of death, as if to preserve the memory of the deceased in a fixed moment of time, not as if they had died, but as if they had simply stopped continuing to live. I reflected at that moment that there was no such shrine for Albert, my father, except for the headstone in Saint James the Less Church, in North Lancing, a grave to which I could never quite bring myself to go.

"Do you know Kopetsky's music?" Rick asked.

"No," I replied, "but I've heard of the man."

Rick led me out of the room and closed the door behind him.

"I suppose I have to be grateful to Franz Kopetsky," he said. "Without him, I would not have had a prodigy for a daughter. Without him, she would not be alive to haunt me now."

Rick went down the landing and took me to another room, one that was unmistakably a teenaged boy's.

"This is the room of Jordan, my son," he said. "He's thirteen. Melissa was precocious. Jordan is just plain weird. I haven't a clue what he's talking about half the time."

"I know someone like that."

Rick looked at me as if he were about to ask me who that person was; instead of asking me the question, he allowed me to look around the room and make my own judgement about the occupier. The room was in a mess. The contents of the wardrobe had been emptied onto the floor. I could think of no reason why anyone, even a teenaged boy, would do such a thing, other than to look for something in a desperate hurry. The duvet was in a heap on the bed. Underpants and socks were liberally scattered across the floor and over items of furniture. The walls were covered with the strangest posters. Above the headboard was a poster that read: "F*** Censorship!" The irony was not entirely lost on me. A cage, inside which a rat slept, stood upon a desk by the window.

"This room is alien territory for me," Rick sighed. "What makes it worse is that he charges me and his mum a quid to enter, when he's here, that is. I ask him if we ever charge *him* money to enter *our* room. He says that he didn't ask to be born. That's his answer for everything."

"Teenagers are a law unto themselves," I said.

"Do you have children, Daniel?"

"Not exactly…"

Again, I'd left Rick momentarily speechless. He remained silent until he nodded at the poster of Nok Nee and informed me that the drum-and-bass outfit was his son's favourite band, and that they had lyrics such as "I'm gonna take you up the back way, baby", which was enough to make any sensible person's knees knock. He despaired of a world in which thirteen-year-olds could listen to such depravity.

Then came the sound of scratching from the cage of the rat. Rick went to it and I followed him.

"It's neat, isn't it, the cage?"

"Yes," I replied, "unlike the room."

"Jordan spends hours cleaning this cage, but not so much as a second cleaning or even tidying his room. He talks to the rat as well, which is more than he does to me and his mum. It's called Churchill. I've no idea why he called a bloody rat Churchill."

"I think I know why."

"Really?"

"It's because Winston Churchill ratted in leaving the Conservatives to join the Liberals, and then re-ratted when he left the Liberals to rejoin the Conservatives."

"Would Jordan know that?"

"Well, if he doesn't, it's a remarkable coincidence."

The rat pushed its twitching nose out of the cage and into the stale air. Rick leaned over the cage and opened the curtains. The surge of daylight had the rat scrambling for the cover of its cardboard hut.

The room looked even more of a tip in the cold light of day than it had in the half-light allowed by the closed curtains; and the sweat glistening on Rick's face and forehead was even more noticeable. In spite of the bristles' suggesting masculinity, there was something inescapably effeminate about Rick Mallett, a quality which I gleaned from the way he spoke (softly, kindly, almost maternally), by the way he moved (economically, but artfully and gracefully), and by the way in which he indulged me, a fellow man and a stranger to boot, so earnestly and (it seemed) so needfully.

"Jordan's fallen in love," Rick said as he surveyed the wreckage around him. "Caitlin's worried that it will make him like every other teenaged boy, whereas I'm happy about it because it will make a more normal boy of him."

"Do you know the girl?" I enquired.

Rick nodded. "Sally Whitehead," he said. "She lives around the corner. She's a nice girl."

On the way to the bathroom—God only knew why Rick wanted me to see that—I caught a glimpse of the matrimonial bedroom; in that split second, and with the door pushed-to, all I could make out was a riot of crimson; indeed, it was arrayed beyond the door in such abundance that it was almost overflowing, clamouring to escape, like water trying to burst a dam.

All that Rick wanted to tell me about the bathroom was that the day before it had been the scene of a personal triumph; and before I'd begun to wonder what that might have meant, he informed me that he and Jordan had, for the first time, accomplished something together, and something that was greatly appreciated by his wife and Jordan's mother: they had evicted a monstrous spider from the bath. It had taken them some fifteen minutes to accomplish the deed, so large had been the creature and so tenacious had it been in standing its ground. Caitlin, an arachnophobe of the first order, I was told, had been moved not only by the collaboration of father and son, but also by their sacrifice, for neither was a lover of spiders.

Then came a strange confession and one that heightened (and it was high enough already) my suspicion that Matt was leading me a merry dance in my pursuit of the killer—or killers—of Laura Hart.

"If I seem a little on edge, it's because I'm expecting a visit from an old friend of mine. He was released from prison this morning."

"Greg Tinnion, you mean?" I said.

"Do you know him?"

"Matt told me about him earlier."

"Did he also tell you that he'd done three years for GBH?"

"He didn't go into details."

"You might know the victim."

"Might I?"

"Yes, Greg's old flame, Rachel Bannerman…"

So, that's what Matt had hinted at when we were stuck in traffic by Magdalen College. His economy with the facts had at first rendered me curious, but now I was furious. I could not abandon my search now, even in the knowledge that another troubled and troublesome character had entered the fray, a character with whom there was every chance I would clash in the coming days.

"There's an injunction forbidding Greg from going any-where near Rachel," Rick went on, "but that won't stop him."

"Does Rachel know that Greg comes out of prison today?"

Rick nodded. "She knew the day would come...and she knows what's coming."

"He knows that he'll go back inside if he goes anywhere near her."

"He's not a rational man, Daniel. Heaven help any man that she's been with these past three years. He'll find out who they are, if he doesn't know already. She's had a few, I can tell you."

"Is she with anyone now?"

"Nobody who will still be with her tomorrow..."

"I would worry about yourself, Rick, before you start worrying about Rachel."

"I'm not worried about myself so much. I'm worried about Caitlin worrying about me. She knows that Greg is a bad influence on me, and always has been, and she's worried that he'll lead me astray again."

"Will he?"

"He's got a hold on me. I've never quite been able to shake him off." The softly-spoken Rick, in voicing his terrible sense of foreboding, had just spoken so softly that his words had reached me as a whisper.

"It's time you did."

"Easier said than done…"

"Now's the time, Rick…"

"The trouble is that he's unstable with me *in* his life, but he would be ten times more unstable *without* me. God knows what he would do if he came round here, shouting the odds, and I told him to sling his hook."

"What time are you expecting him?"

"He could be here any second now."

At that moment, there was a knock on the front door and Rick looked like a man condemned to his fate.

"I'll get it!" Matt called from the foot of the stairs.

To Rick's relief, not to mention mine, it was not Greg Tinnion calling but two members of Greetwell Housing Trust's three-man Rapid Reaction Team. Rick and I had joined Matt in the doorway.

"Ivor Bagshot," one of the men announced.

"Hugh Windlesham," proclaimed the other.

We three regarded the two men who stood before us wearing overalls that were too big for them and who clutched toolboxes that threatened to sink them into the ground.

"You must be the Rapid Reaction Team," Rick said, his voice betraying a note of sarcasm.

"That's us," the two men replied in unison.

We three took a step back.

"Come in," Rick said.

The two men entered. They were not young.

"Is this the door?" Hugh asked, nodding at the front door as Rick closed it.

"What do you mean?" Rick asked.

"The lock that needs changing?"

Rick shook his head. "I've a *boiler* that needs *fixing*."

"No lock that needs changing?" Ivor asked.

"No lock that needs changing," Rick repeated.

"Then we've been misinformed," Hugh said.

"There does appear to have been a mix-up," Rick returned.

"Greetwell Housing Trust wouldn't be Greetwell Housing Trust without a mix-up," Ivor said.

"Life wouldn't be life without a mix-up," Rick replied.

"We'll call the maintenance department," Ivor said. "They'll call Bullard's, who will call you."

"Hasn't that been done already?" Rick asked.

"Well, yes, it has," Hugh replied, "but there's been a mix-up, so we'll have to start again."

Rick sighed. "I'll call Bullard's myself."

"Oh, no, you can't do that," Ivor said.

"Why can't I?"

"The job has to be booked through Greetwell," Ivor replied.

Rick was getting angry now. "The job's been booked already."

"Let's hope so, Mr Mallett," Ivor said vaguely, somewhat cryptically, and incongruously from a man who seemed so harmless, with a hint of menace.

"*I'll* call Greetwell," Rick said. "Can I do *that*?"

"If you wish, Mr Mallett," replied Hugh.

"As I did, what"—Rick looked at his watch—"six hours ago." He opened the door and waited for the two men to take their leave. "Goodbye, gentlemen."

The two men shuffled onto the garden path.

"I hope that your boiler gets fixed sooner rather than later, Mr Mallett," Ivor said in a jocular tone that annoyed Rick.

"With you lot on the case, that is some bloody hope!" Rick barked back.

He slammed the door shut.

"Sorry about that," he said.

Matt was falling about laughing.

"Even allowing for the fact that this is Greetwell Housing Trust, that was surreal," he garbled through his mirth. "I opened the bloody door to them. I've been a colleague of theirs for donkey's years, but there was not so much as a pang of recognition from either of them. I was just waiting to see how long it took before one of them recognised me."

"Perhaps you're not as well-known as you thought you were, Matt," I suggested.

"No, those two old grippers are blind as well as stupid," Matt replied.

"So, what about my boiler then?" Rick demanded.

"I've fixed it," Matt declared.

"What was wrong with it?"

"Nothing much. I'll call Bullard's to cancel the job."

"I'm grateful."

"What are friends for?"

"Well might you ask." My words were a challenge to Matt, who must have known to what I was alluding. Words would pass between us, most of them mine.

The next knock on the front door was aggressive, as if the person knocking was being pursued and was desperate to get inside. I looked at Rick. What I saw wasn't fear, it was sadness, sadness at an opportunity lost, sadness, perhaps, about a situation that had become hopeless. He radiated vulnerability too; here was a man who had lost his little girl and, one way or another, might lose his wife too. The last thing he needed was Greg Tinnion coming back into his life to imperil the good that remained to him. That I hardly knew Rick Mallett was not going to stop me from fighting his corner should he be threatened by the newly liberated jailbird.

"Is that him?" Matt's was possibly the most superfluous question asked anywhere in the world that day. It was like asking Her Majesty the Queen if she wanted the Corgis feeding.

The knocking continued. There was a bell on the door, as well as a knocker, but the caller evidently preferred to hammer on the door itself, as if determined to beat it into a pulp. Whoever was calling, it wasn't the Dalai Lama.

Resigned to his fate as he was, Rick came over all philosophical.

"It was inevitable that he would come," he began. "My life is hopeless, so it might as well get worse. I can't blame anyone but myself for having this man in my life. I've had countless chances to tell him to get lost. I visited him only once in prison, and that was eighteen months ago, yet here he is, calling on his only friend in the whole world, good old Rick Mallett, his poodle. I'm stuck with him now."

"No, you're not, Rick," Matt said. "Take this opportunity to kick him into touch. We're here to back you up."

"I can't walk away from him when he's just stepped out of the slammer and he's drunk on freedom. If I do that, he will tip over the edge again."

"He'll do that, anyway, without any help from you."

The knocking on the door had reached fever pitch.

A voice boomed through the letterbox: "Open up, Rick! I know you're in there!"

"You know, this morning, I thought to myself that I might do one great deed in my life, just one, that would redeem me, that would make sense of my life. Perhaps reforming Greg—or at least *trying* to reform him—could be that one great deed."

"Greg Tinnion is irredeemable, Rick," Matt said helpfully.

The integrity of the door was in danger now. Rick placed a cigarette in his mouth with the nonchalance of a Hollywood star in a movie; if his intention had been to exude a calm, detached indifference then lighting the thing might have helped. He went to the door with the unlit cigarette in his mouth, and it was missing from his mouth completely by the time he returned to the kitchen.

"Jesus, man, it's brass monkeys out there!"

"It's called winter, Greg."

Greg rubbed his hands together. "And it's even colder in here!"

"That's because the boiler's broken."

"There's a bloody great Rottweiler loose across the road!"

"That would be Gwendoline Caspar's," Rick replied, deadpan as a stupefied zombie. "She's been told a million times not to let it loose."

"Do you want it taken out? It would be practice, like, you know, for my new career."

"If you're going to talk like that, you're not staying."

"I see the operation was a complete success."

"What operation?"

"The sense-of-humour bypass…"

Rick sighed heavily. "Did you have to come here today?"

"I've been telling you for months, in my letters—which you never returned—that today's the day."

"Did you have to come here at all?"

"Oh, that's nice, isn't it? And what's this? A reception committee?"

"Matt, I think, you know. And this is Daniel Winter."

"Who's he? Your boyfriend?"

"You haven't changed, have you, Greg?" Matt put in bravely. "Ever the wind-up merchant, eh?"

For one horrible moment, which seemed like an hour, Greg thought about punching Matt's lights out, but, mercifully, he thought better of it. Then he seemed to have been overtaken by geniality, but even his geniality was like a flick-knife being thrust before one's face. Then he clapped his hands together and asked Rick if there was any chance of a cup of tea. Rick said that he was just making one. Matt and I did not stay for a second cup of tea.

"It's time you took the Christmas decorations down, man." Even in trying to sound charming and jocular, Greg failed to disabuse me of the notion that somewhere on his person were a knuckle-duster and a Stanley knife.

"I left them up just for you."

"I'm touched, man."

"But only because we didn't have a hundred yellow ribbons to tie around the old oak tree."

***

Matt and I stepped onto the garden path and walked to the end of it. Before I got into the car, I looked around me. Cross Crescent looked grimmer than a disused textile mill in Blackburn. Weak sunlight bathed the houses grudgingly. A car with no wheels was parked on the drive next door. Filled with bits of broken furniture, foam, rotten cloth, rusty iron, sand, gravel, cardboard, plywood and an old mirror, a skip was rooted at one end of the street like a burnt-out tank in the aftermath of battle. An emaciated whippet approached the house next door and sniffed at the decomposing flotsam that had burst from one of the bin sacks that were piled up in the front garden. Though there was no breeze to speak of, a tin can twirled and bounced across the road.

"Greg Tinnion and Rachel Bannerman," I said to Matt across the roof of the car. "That's another little secret you kept from me. Well might you look sheepish."

Not one to labour a point that is perfectly capable of labouring for itself, I got into the car with Matt and left the matter of Greg Tinnion and Rachel Bannerman at that.

Matt produced a ham roll from the glove compartment. It looked at least three days old. He grimaced, before lowering the window and throwing the roll onto the street. The whippet pounced. Then Matt looked across the road and told me that he had been scheduled to visit Gwendoline Caspar that afternoon but had called in a favour and asked Doug Loft, the other maintenance inspector at Greetwell, to go in his place.

"What's Gwendoline Caspar's problem then?" I asked.

"She took it upon herself to hang some wallpaper in her living-room, and then she wondered why, when she got up the following morning, it was all over the floor. She wants us to inspect the walls for rising damp."

"Is rising damp not a possibility?"

"It's more likely that she used something other than paste to hang up the wallpaper."

"Such as?"

"Rottweiler snot, I shouldn't wonder."

I couldn't help but laugh at that.

"Poor old Doug," Matt reflected. "He's in there right now, having his ears bent by Gwendoline Caspar and his leg chewed by a rabid Rottweiler. He'll be cursing me right now. That'll teach him to owe me a favour."

No sooner had the words left Matt's mouth than a rotund middle-aged bald man bolted from the house in question and made a dash for his car. The man was wearing a white tank-top that was much too tight for him and sky-blue chinos that stopped halfway down his calves. Anyone would have thought that he'd put on his clothes first thing that morning and grown six inches by lunchtime. I was surprised that he could move in that clobber, never mind run. He was being pursued by a snarling Rottweiler and a woman with an Afro the size of a small hedge sitting on her head. All that was missing was the Benny Hill music. The man very nearly beat the dog to the car. The woman beat the dog off the man, which gave him time to scramble to safety. The woman waved the dog into the house, before following it inside without so much as a word of apology to the man.

"He'll be more than cursing you," I said.

Matt was in hysterics. "Doug must have been in and out of that drum like a fiddler's elbow," he chuckled.

"Shouldn't we be helping him?"

"What could we do for him now that a surgeon and a shrink couldn't do?" His eyes were watering with mirth, as if he'd been peeling a bucketload of onions.

"What about Rick?"

"What about him?"

"He's in there with that madman."

"Greg is Rick's friend. Rick will have to deal with him. I've told him that we're here for him, should he need us."

"We? Us?"

"Yes, why not? You two seemed to be getting on famously. It was very sweet, almost homoerotic, if you ask me."

"Leave it out, will you?"

THIRTEEN

On the way back to my office, Matt told me what he knew about Rachel Bannerman and her life, which was quite a lot. He could have penned a biography about the woman that would have taken up no little space on a Blackwell's book-shelf. I looked forward to matching biography and subject when I met her that evening. I looked forward even more to my first engagement that evening, dinner with Helena Johnson-Roffey, which promised to be altogether more plea-surable than the morass of secrecy, death, double-crossing and squalor that had claimed me during the last twenty-four hours. It seemed like twenty-four days, so much had hap-pened since I last saw Helena.

My trip back to the office was curtailed somewhat, since I asked Matt to drop me off outside the Hobgoblin, the pub where (Matt had told me in the car after we left Cross Crescent) Rachel liked to drink and to pick up men. I knew Simon Fairweather, the manager of the bar. I could have done with a drink and Simon was potentially a rich source of information. I only hoped that he would be working. Matt understood that I needed to poke around the Hobgoblin without him and, anyway, much to my surprise, he said he had work to do. I had one foot inside the pub when my phone rang.

"Kendal?"

"What are you doing, Daniel?" Her tone was somewhere short of conciliatory, though not quite belligerent.

"I'm on the case."

"A case of what? Beer?"

"Both!"

"When are you coming back?"

"In about an hour…"

"Can't you get back sooner?"

"No," I said firmly. "How's Karl doing?"

"At the moment, he's not here."

"Where is he then?"

"He went out for a walk…an hour ago."

"He's a turbo-charged executive. He needs to clear his head."

"He's been driving me mad."

"What's he been doing?"

"He's filled my notebook with sketches and doodles, and he keeps repeating this ridiculous sentence."

"What ridiculous sentence would that be?"

"He keeps saying: 'May I commiserate with God for creating such a redundant flower as yourself?'"

That was easily the funniest thing I'd ever heard.

"I'm glad you find it funny, Daniel."

"I'll explain later."

"You bet you will." Kendal added: "And he told me that you'd called him an exquisite pie-thrower."

That was the second-funniest thing I'd ever heard.

"Why did you call him that?"

"I called him an existentialist philosopher."

"What the hell for?"

"Because his name is Karl Jaspers."

"So?"

"Again, I'll explain later."

"You've got a lot of explaining to do."

"So I have."

"See you in an hour and no later."

"Count on it."

Luckily for me, Simon was behind the bar busy drying glasses with a soaking-wet tea-towel. He had some customers, but not enough to keep him on his toes. Mind you, it was three-thirty on a Tuesday afternoon. Most *towns* are not open on a Tuesday afternoon, never mind public houses.

"A pint of your usual?" Simon said.

"Yes, please, Simon, and a whisky chaser ..."

"Coming up!"

"I need a drink, I can tell you."

"How are tricks?"

"Never a dull moment in my racket," I replied.

"I still can't see you as a copper."

"I'm *not* a copper."

"But you *were* one."

"I'm still a copper really," I admitted. "I'm just not working for the police."

Simon placed my drinks on the bar and I paid him. He waited for me to explain why I'd come to his pub at such an hour, other than my needing a drink, of course.

"I was hoping you could help me with something," I said.

"As long as it doesn't get me into trouble ..."

"Trouble is *my* business, as a private detective more famous than I once said."

"Oh, yes, but Philip Marlowe wasn't real."

"Sacrilege!" I joked.

"Tell me your worst, then, Daniel."

"I understand that you know Rachel Bannerman."

"I'm surprised that *you* don't know her, Daniel. She comes in here often enough, and so do you."

"I guess our paths just haven't crossed."

"Avoid her. She's trouble."

"For the moment, avoiding her is not an option."

"Don't get involved with her."

"I'm involved already. What can you tell me about her?"

"Well, let's just say that there aren't many blokes who frequent this boozer who haven't spent some quality time between her ample thighs."

I choked on some whisky.

"Next you'll be telling me that she's bound to be buried in a Y-shaped coffin."

"Since when have I been that predictable, Daniel?"

"You've given me a double whisky and charged me for a single. Who could have predicted that?"

"I guess I was just pleased to see you. Don't tell the boss, will you?"

"I thought *you* were the boss."

"Often, Rachel doesn't stay long enough to have a second drink before she ensnares a man and lures him back to her boudoir, or wherever it is she takes them."

"She's quite an operator then."

"You're telling me. On Saturday, I'm not sure that she'd even *ordered* a drink before she left with no fewer than *three* blokes in tow."

"Does she wear some kind of love potion that makes her irresistible to men?"

"I don't know, but guess who the three men were?"

"I haven't got time to guess."

"One of them was Dane Goldman."

"Bloody hell! The Great Dane himself!" The whisky disappeared down my throat quicker than a rabbit down a hole in the ground.

"The other two were his Diddy Men, Tweedledum and Tweedledee."

"All of a sudden, I feel sick."

"It was a sickening sight, I can tell you." Simon returned to his glass-wiping. "You've had a run-in with Dane Goldman, haven't you?"

"Indeed, I have," I replied, shuddering at the recollection. "At the fag-end of last summer. Now I'm a marked man."

"Trouble really *is* your business."

"One makes enemies in this game."

"What else do you want to know about Rachel?"

"For the moment, I think I know as much about her as I need to know. What do you know about Greg Tinnion?"

"Enough to advise you to steer well clear of him ..."

"I've already had the pleasure ..."

"When?"

"Just now ..."

"What did you do? Meet him at the prison gates?"

"I was visiting somebody, and he just turned up, bold as brass."

"He'll turn up here soon enough." Simon had finished drying the glasses and now took to stacking the lower shelves with bottles of fruit juice. He seemed more than happy in his work, though I had often been of the view that he was wasted in such a menial job and that he was capable of doing so much better for himself. "He knows he'll find Rachel in here."

"He also knows that, if he goes anywhere near Rachel, he'll go straight back inside."

"He'll take his chances."

"He's a bit of a nutcase, right?"

"Too right!" Simon returned to the bar to indulge me, as if what he had to say next was of the utmost importance. "He used to be in the army, in the Paras. He did a tour of duty in Northern Ireland. Word is he had links with Loyalist paramilitary groups."

"I've met a few of that type before."

"If I were you, I wouldn't even make eye contact with him."

"Like I said, it's a bit late for that."

"And don't, whatever you do, be seen with Rachel, not with Greg Tinnion sniffing around."

"It might be too late for that too."

"On her own, Rachel Bannerman is trouble enough," Simon warned, sounding like an Old Testament prophet who'd just been troubled with an especially harrowing vision of fire and brimstone, "but add Greg Tinnion to the mix and it's a case of double trouble."

"Thanks for the warning…"

"You'd be well advised to heed it," Simon said. "Now I need to pop down to the cellar to change a barrel. Mind the bar for me, will you?"

"I'll help myself, shall I?"

"Be my guest!" he called back on his way down.

My phone rang. It was Kendal again.

"Daniel! The Greetwell Housing Trust tenants are on top form today! They're driving me up the wall and round the bend!"

"No change there then …"

"I'm beating these morons off with a stick while you sit around drinking!"

"I'm working, sweetheart."

"It's funny how your work always involves a pub!"

"All of humanity is in a pub."

"I can't take much more of these idiots phoning me!"

"I have news on that front."

"It had better be good news!"

"When have I ever given you bad news?"

"When will you be back?"

"I'm on my way."

FOURTEEN

Walking the short distance to the home of Helena Johnson-Roffey afforded me the most uplifting five minutes of my life. I felt liberated. For two hours, I would be in another world, a better world—a *perfect* world, I dared to believe—a world in which not only did nothing bad ever happen but also one in which nothing bad *could* ever happen. I decided to harness some of Helena's wholesomeness, some of her goodness, some of her sheer beauty of body and soul to help me get through the case of Laura Hart's murder and to solve it in my own way, if not exactly in my own time. Spending two hours with Helena would be like emerging from a cramped and dark underground cavern onto a beach of golden sand and blue sea overlooked by a yet bluer sky and burnished by a yet more golden sun.

Some three hours earlier, I'd arrived back at my office to the news that Karl's stint as an assistant in the office of a prestigious Oxford private detective had been cruelly curtailed after he'd fallen partway down a manhole and broken his left leg. How he'd managed to do that I looked forward to finding out. He now had his feet up—or one of them at least—in a bed at the John Radcliffe Hospital. When Kendal had first broken the news, I thought she was winding me up again, having a laugh, indulging herself in a bout of wishful thinking; only when I'd seen just how pleased she was by the turn of events had I realised that she was telling the truth, the awful truth, and that fate had played another rotten trick on me, not to mention poor Karl.

I'd added visiting Karl in hospital to my to-do list. I'd made a list in my head: visit Dominic, check out Caitlin Mallett at her workplace, look up Franz Kopetsky, read Rick's letter, and visit Karl in hospital.

Of course, I'd also to dine with Helena, visit Rachel at the Round House, and keep my appointment with Ida McSweeney at Greetwell Housing Trust the following day, but none of those engagements needed to be added to a list of things to do, not even in my head.

In the office, Kendal had asked me how productive my morning and afternoon had been, so I'd furnished her with the edited highlights and informed her that Greetwell Housing Trust was a classic case of an organisation—if one could call it that—the right hand of which had no idea what the left hand was doing.

Kendal had then regaled me with the highlights of her day, but they were scarcely edited, more a barely sanitised blow-by-blow account. She'd handed me her notebook.

"Three more broken boilers," I'd read. "Bullard's will earn their money this week." I'd read the rest of Kendal's scrawl. "Charlene Titterbridge, of number ten Jackson Court, thinks that she's swallowed a bird and that insects are eating her from the inside; Morrison Tonypandy, of number thirteen Lucas

Terrace, woke up thinking that his dog had chewed off its leg; and Sigmund Bonk, of number twenty-three Lucas Terrace, phoned to say that his boy, Billy, had been taking things from bins, kissing other children at school, including boys, and pulling down the pants of his classmates, including the boys'." I'd taken a deep breath. "God preserve us!" I'd sighed in disbelief. "Is all this for real? Are these *names* for real?"

"You couldn't make up any of that," Kendal had replied.

Then I'd continued reading.

"Rocky Midgett complained about dodgy electrics, Bartlemas Trouncer wants new window frames, and Ernest Waldock wants a burglar alarm fitted in his flat." I'd sighed again. "Well, at least these last three scenarios are believable," I'd said.

Then the phone had rung and Kendal had put it on speaker, and I'd been treated to another surreal exchange, this time with Kendal acting as if her blood were boiling and she didn't care who knew about it.

"Hello?"

"Yeah?"

"It's Pedro Ponce here!"

"Pedro who?"

"Ponce!"

"Is that your real name or your nickname?"

"What?"

"What do you want?"

"I want someone to come and fix my boiler, that's what I want!"

"What's wrong with your boiler?"

"It's broken!"

"That's a shame."

"It's an old boiler, a bit like my missus, but it's given me no trouble up till now!"

"I'll take a message."

"I don't want you to take a message, I want—"

Kendal had put the phone down with a clinical brutality, with a fearful combination of the teenager's disdain for the adult world and the adult's knowing cynicism.

The next phone call had come before we'd got our breath back. Kendal had moved to intercept the call like a semi-comatose gazelle.

"Hello?"

"What?"

"Hello?" Kendal had repeated.

"Is that all you can say?"

"What do you want me to say?"

"You could be anyone."

"So could you."

"I'm Amy Clutterbuck."

"Yeah, I recognise your voice. You called earlier."

"No, I didn't."

"Well, you're calling now. What do you want?"

"My house has rising damp."

"Well, that's better than *falling* damp. At least you won't need an umbrella."

"I want a maintenance inspector round here right away, and not that Matt Prior either."

"He's the best we've got."

"He's the *rudest* you've got, you mean, and the *sleaziest*. Last time he came round here, he eyed me up."

"Did he do the business?"

"I beg your pardon!"

"Did he fix your problem?"

"Well, as a matter of fact, he did, but that's not the—"

"I've taken a message," Kendal had said in a hard-hitting monotone. "Goodbye." She'd put the phone down.

"Heaven help the next person who calls!" I'd laughed. "You're like a bear with a sore head!"

The next call had not been long in coming.

"Hello?"

"It's Norman Ruby here."

"That's an expensive name."

"What?"

"Can I help you?"

"Yeah, you can tell me where that useless tosser Matt Prior's got to!"

"You want to speak to him?"

"Is he there?"

"No ..."

"Well, he's not there, and he's not here, where he should be, where he should have been an hour ago, so where the bloody hell is he?"

"I don't know."

"Do you know anything?"

"I know that you're a rude old git."

"Are you a kid?"

"No, because I'm not a goat."

"What?"

"I'll pass on your message."

"Tell Matt Prior to get his fat arse over here!"

"Whatever! Goodbye!"

Kendal had put the phone down, masterfully, and reclined in the chair, smug at having produced another satisfied customer. I couldn't help but feel that life as a fast-lane executive was much too easy for her. I'd wondered when the job would provide her with a challenge to which she couldn't rise.

Then I'd told her the good news regarding Greetwell Housing Trust and the substantial compensation that the chief executive Ida McSweeney had agreed to pay us—yes, *us*, me and her—and that I was going to see the woman the following day; and I'd promised Kendal that I would reward her with new clothes befitting her station in life as office manager and part-time private detective. That had mollified her somewhat, though her mood had darkened again when I told her how I was planning to spend the evening. With a stroppy sigh, she'd said that she'd go and see Dominic, and I'd agreed that that was the perfect thing to do all round.

Then the phone had rung again and Kendal had ordered me to be the receptionist because she couldn't face taking another call from yet another tenant of Greetwell Housing Trust. I'd been in no position to argue with her.

"Good afternoon to you." My enunciation had been crisp, theatrical, and as overblown as a Thespian's marriage proposal.

"Hello," had come the voice of a sweet old lady. "Can I help you?"

"No, can *I* help *you*?" I'd said.

"I'm sorry?"

"*You* rang *me*."

"I know I did."

"Then it is *I* who should be helping *you*."

"Yes, indeed, that's why I rang."

"So, how can I help you?"

"My name's April Fouracres," the old lady had continued, her words rhythmic, so that they'd seemed to be dancing before my eyes. "I'm one of your tenants."

Kendal laughed at my sigh of exasperation.

"And?"

"And I'm disabled."

"I'm sorry to hear that Miss Fouracres."

"It's *Mrs* Fouracres. I've never married."

Kendal had risen from the chair and was bouncing off the walls in laughter.

"Do you wish to report something, *Mrs* Fouracres?"

"Only that I'm disabled."

"How long have you been disabled?" I'd asked a stupid question, but better stupid than rude.

"Oh, more than eighty years now. I'm seventy-one."

I'd put my index finger to my temple to suggest that the old lady was barking mad, whilst Kendal signally omitted to record the incident in her beleaguered notebook; though the call hadn't been registered, Matt would be hearing about it, that much was certain.

"Well, I must be going," the old lady had trilled. "Bye for now."

The line had gone dead before I'd had a chance to bid her good day.

"I must have done something terrible in a previous life," I'd told Kendal. "I feel as if I'm being visited by a lot of bad karma."

Then I'd asked her why she was still cackling like a deranged fishwife.

"Because I've just realised that, somewhere out there in the big wide world, is a kid called Billy Bonk!"

I was halfway down Portland Road, in Summertown, outside Helena's palatial dwelling, when it hit me that I had another job on my hands: tailing, somehow, Detective Inspector Stephen Waugh. How on earth was I going to do that? As I knocked on the cherry-red portal, on the other side of which was a soothing place of beauty and warmth, I was hit by another thought: that I'd been charged with finding out what, if anything, was going on between Stephen Waugh and Selena Wilcox; and that the best way to find that out was through the girl rather than through the man.

***

The door opened and it was like being at the Pearly Gates. If this was heaven, I thought, then I absolutely must get serious about religion to ensure that I get there. But that thought made me think about Roseanne, about my tardiness in visiting her, and I wanted to put off the thought as much as I wanted to put off the deed.

The word that best describes Helena's home is not "opulent" but "elegant". That was quite in keeping with everything else about the lady, right down to her name. By elegant, I don't mean that her house was immaculate; it was more a case of its being refined without being pretentious; it wasn't flaunting itself; it wasn't saying, "Hey, look at me and how grand I am." It was an understated refinement that seemed embarrassed to be looked upon at all.

With an all-too-becoming finesse—and, I have to say, expertise—Helena removed my jacket and placed it on a hook on the inside of the door of the cupboard under the stairs. That darkened crevice, it seemed, served as the cloakroom, and even that, I had no doubt, was wholly consistent with the unselfconscious elegance that was the theme of the house.

I was standing on the doormat, wiping the rain off my feet, and the mat was laid upon a richly coloured and textured carpet that left exposed around its perimeter richly polished floorboards. To my right was hanging a painting that I recognised.

"I know a Matisse when I see one," I announced.

"It's a copy, of course," Helena answered.

"And I recognise the music of Bach when I hear it." That was coming from what I soon discovered was the sitting-room.

Helena led me into the room and I looked around. What elegance I beheld. Over a disused fireplace hung a gilt-edged mirror. Two large white sofas adorned the room, the one up against the window looking out onto the street and the other hugging the wall facing the fireplace and the mirror. A fluffy white rug was draped over the floorboards like a sleeping polar bear. Dry flowers towered from large ornate vases and silverware was arrayed like royal knick-knacks—there because it was expected to be there, splendidness in splendid surroundings—on a white antique cabinet facing the window. Before leaving the room, I almost missed the Art Deco lamp which shone from a tall stand in the corner by the window.

"My word!" I exclaimed. "There's more silverware in here than in Liverpool's trophy cabinet!"

"I know nothing about football, I'm sure," the lady replied with a beguiling innocence.

I gave her the bottle of rosé that I'd bought for the occasion. It was a compromise between red and white. It wasn't the most expensive wine displayed on the shelves of Safeway, but it was by no means the cheapest either. Helena thanked me and took the wine into the kitchen. She'd left the doors of the sitting-room and the kitchen open to allow Bach's mellow strains to reach us at just the right volume.

"The music will sound less intrusive coming from the sitting-room," my hostess declared. "We'll eat here in the kitchen."

I was bound to ask whether Bach could ever be considered intrusive.

"He can at the volume I play him," Helena responded. "I'm surprised the neighbours don't complain. They must like Bach."

"They'd complain about my music, that's for sure."

"What do you listen to?"

"I'm very much a rock-and-roll man, though I'm branching into jazz. I'm saving classical music for my retirement."

"Do you like opera?"

"You mean fat Italians in tights?"

Helena's smile was nothing short of an exhibition of perfect white teeth. "I'll take that as a no then," she said.

Having been dismissed as an outright philistine by my hostess, I was delighted to tell her that I'd seen three operas live (Puccini's *La Bohème*, at the Marlowe Theatre, in Canterbury; Offenbach's *The Tales Of Hoffman*, at the Düsseldorf Opera House; and Verdi's *The Masked Ball*, at the Royal Opera House, in Covent Garden) and that I adored Puccini's *Suor Angelica* because it condensed so much beauty and pathos into a single act.

Helena's estimation of me having been restored to its former place somewhere between the clouds and heaven, I accepted her invitation to take a seat at the large circular oak table in the corner of the kitchen, just inside the doorway; the table had been laid and the first course, avocado, was ready to be eaten.

"I hope you like avocado."

"Oh, yes, even when it has a big hole in the middle."

"You're in a jovial mood this evening, aren't you?"

"After the day I've had, there's no other mood to be in," I said.

"You'll need some wine then."

"Music to my ears…"

"We'll start with your rosé, shall we?"

"Why not?"

Conversation flowed as freely as the wine during the starter. I told Helena that my only previous encounter with avocado had been in a West End café, where I'd consumed it with crispy bacon in a sandwich whenever my work as a detective had taken me to that part of London.

Hitherto, Helena and I had done most of our talking in the courtyard of the Oxford Oratory, the Roman Catholic Church of Saint Aloysius Gonzaga, in Woodstock Rock, and we'd never discussed anything consequential, we'd simply passed the time of day and, anyway, there were usually other people around us, talking with us and across us. Helena knew that I wasn't a Roman, but she'd never deigned to ask why I spent so much time in the Oratory, attending Mass (and even Benediction of the Blessed Sacrament) without taking part in it and without approaching the altar for so much as a blessing. That evening, however, before I'd worked out whether I liked avocado in the raw, she ventured to ask me why I was drawn to the Oratory and its esoteric rituals. With relish—for I'd long wanted to tell her—I explained that my mother had disappeared from the scene when I was eight years old, and that, five months ago, I'd discovered that not only was she alive and well but that she'd become a nun and was based at the Carmelite of Our Lady, a convent in Upper Midmarsh, about seven miles north of Oxford.

Helena was so intrigued by my story that she poured us both some more rosé in an early stage of stupefaction. She looked charming and graceful as ever in cream-coloured slacks and a royal-blue blouse that accentuated the natural blondeness of her hair; that hair was frizzy that evening, when the day before it had been straight; and that was the pattern with her hair, frizzy one day and straight the next, so that I wondered which of the two styles was the affectation.

"But you've been going to the Oratory for about a year now," Helena said.

"Perhaps I had a premonition about Roseanne, my mother," I said. "I *am* psychic, you know." I winked at her. "For the moment, I'm happy to observe proceedings from the back of the church. I guess I'm just waiting to connect with it all. I'm just waiting for the penny to drop."

"Do you think you'll become one of us?"

"If the penny drops…"

"So, to paraphrase Saint Augustine, it's a case of 'Lord, make me a Catholic, but not yet'?"

"That sums it up nicely."

"Do you believe that the Catholic Church is the One True Fold?"

"Who was it that said that the Catholic Church must be divine because 'no merely human institution conducted with such knavish imbecility would have lasted a fortnight'?" The question had been posed with a nod at the knavish artfulness of the rhetorician.

"That was Hilaire Belloc..."

I nodded knowingly. "A fellow man of Sussex..."

The main course was not yet on the table and already we'd stumbled upon religion. Let's say that we'd invoked Faith, the first of the Theological Virtues. Faith, then, had corresponded with the first course. Would Hope similarly correspond with the second, and Charity the third?

***

The main course was a total surprise to me. I would not have been more surprised if Helena had lifted an octopus out of the oven. Not only was it a surprise, it was beautifully arranged on our plates, and the dish had a name, svíčková. It consisted of sirloin steak, cooked with vegetables, spiced with black pepper, bay leaf, allspice, juniper, and thyme, and boiled with sour double cream. It was a teeming metropolis of a dish. It was served with what I'd thought were slices of bread, but which were actually dumplings, known in Czech as houskové knedlíky.

It turned out that my hostess was half-Czech on her mother's side, having been born in Brno (the Czech Republic's second city) and come to England when she was thirteen years old. Her father had taught Slavonic and Eastern European Studies at both Brno and Oxford Universities, and she had followed in his illustrious academic footsteps by becoming a Professor of Philosophy and Theology at Oxford. Her father had not been a communist, nor had her mother; they had met in Brno two years after the Prague Spring and a year after her father had gone to teach in Brno, in what was then Czechoslovakia. The family had moved to Oxford when her father changed jobs. There were no politics involved when he'd moved to Brno, and likewise none when he and the family had moved to Oxford.

"He was able to go and work on the other side of the Iron Curtain?"

"Yes, and there was no suspicion of any communist sympathies when he returned to England, in nineteen-eighty-three. None that I'm aware of. My parents were pleased when the Velvet Revolution occurred, in eighty-nine, but they were left devastated by the Velvet Divorce."

"You mean the breakup of Czechoslovakia?"

"Yes, in ninety-three," Helena replied. "They saw it as an amputation of the country, as did most Czechs at the time."

"How did you feel about it?"

"I was only twenty-three at the time, and I'd been living in England for ten years, but I was quite upset about it. The Slovaks were most unpleasant about it all. It was they who wanted the divorce."

"You do realise, don't you, that I've now worked out your age?"

"And I know that you'll be forty-one next week."

"How do you know that?"

"A little bird told me."

"Who? Actually, don't tell me. I'd rather not know."

"How do you like the svíčková?"

"It's gorgeous," I replied, looking beyond Helena's eyes, into her soul, and noticing that the colour of her eyebrows matched the colour of her hair perfectly. The frizziness might not have been natural, but the colour was, and why wouldn't it have been when she was at the tender age of thirty-six? "Where do your parents live now?" I asked, hoping that she wouldn't tell me that they were dead.

"After Dad retired, they moved back to Brno. It was two days into the new millennium. They live in the family home in Líšeň, in the east of the city, next to the church. Grandad's dead, but Grandma's still alive. Mum will inherit the house when Grandma dies."

"How often do you visit Brno?"

"Three or four times a year…"

"Can you speak Czech?"

"Czech is my first language."

"Does your dad speak Czech?"

"Yes, he learnt Czech when he was in his teens. He was a precocious—rather freakish, if truth be told—Slavophile. He learnt Russian, which enabled him to learn Czech quite easily."

"Why Czech?"

"He just had an inexplicable affinity with Eastern Europe in general and Czechoslovakia in particular. Anyone would think that he was descended from Bohemian or Moravian royalty."

"Is he?"

"Not as far as I know…"

"You know what Neville Chamberlain said about Czechoslovakia during the Munich Crisis, don't you?"

"He described Czechoslovakia as 'a faraway country about which we know little'." There was a hint of resentment in Helena's voice when she spoke those words, and when she spoke the words that followed. "Nothing's changed in that respect, I can tell you. Even educated Oxford folk seem to revel in their ignorance about my homeland. I come back from Brno and people say to me: 'How was your trip to Slovakia?' 'Fine,' I say, 'except that I went to the Czech Republic.' 'Oh, it's all the same to me,' they say. So, I tell them that Slovakia is a separate country, that it seceded from Czechoslovakia in nineteen-ninety-three. Other people say to me: 'How was your trip to Czechoslovakia?' So, I tell them that the country ceased to exist in ninety-three. The best one is when people ask me about my trip to Czechoslovenia. I tell them that the country has never existed, and that Slovenia was part of Yugoslavia. It's all rather insulting, don't you think?"

"Yes, very much so," I replied.

"Have you been to the Czech Republic, Daniel?"

"I spent a lonely long weekend in Prague two years ago. I visited Franz Kafka's old house. Then I bought all his books. When I got back home, I read them all."

"In English, I trust?"

"Naturally…"

"I'm impressed."

"Wasn't Milan Kundera born in Brno?"

"He was, indeed, and he grew up in Královo Pole," Helena said. "Come to Brno with me sometime and I'll show you the house where he grew up."

"That would be fabulous."

"More wine?"

"Why not?"

Out of the blue, simply because she was there and I was curious, I asked Helena how, in a sentence, she could best inspire somebody to convert to her faith.

"I would invoke Saint Augustine."

"'Grant what you command, and command what you will.'"

Helena's raised eyebrows expressed not just surprise but approval too.

"You've read his *Confessions* then?"

"Oh, I'm steeped in it all," I quipped. "Was that the sentence you had in mind?"

"No, it was: 'Every saint has a past and every sinner has a future.' It shows the unconverted what lies ahead for them, if only they would choose the City of God, and it reminds them—and the converted, too, it must be said—that holy people were not always holy, that they, too, once chose the Earthly City before they saw the light."

"We must all choose between the City of God and the Earthly City, mustn't we?"

"Which one will you choose, Daniel?"

"Many are called, but few are chosen," I said. "Is that not so?"

Helena nodded, her eyes widened in wonder.

"If you were to pray for me, I might yet be chosen."

Faith and Hope had been covered. That left only Charity.

***

The pudding was a reassuringly bland apple pie with custard. My taste buds delighted in the soothing balm of the custard. I sensed that Helena had known that traditional fare would be the perfect end to the perfect evening, at least for me and my underdeveloped Anglo-Saxon palate. By this time, she'd opened another bottle of rosé and, without being incoherent, our conversation had become decidedly ragged.

"Taste buds are funny things," I was saying. "I dislike cherries, but love cherry-flavoured yoghurt. I detest rhubarb, but like rhubarb-flavoured sweets. And, though I could eat peanuts all day long, peanut butter tastes to me like half-set concrete."

Helena giggled suggestively. "Policemen who become private detectives are the funniest things of all," she said.

"Oxford philosophy professors are downright weird," I joked back.

"Shall we talk about our respective professions when we're less drunk than we are now?"

"Mine is not a profession, it is an occupation, in the sense that it keeps me occupied."

"It keeps you off the streets, you mean?"

"No, it keeps me *on* the streets."

"I want to know all about policing and private detecting and novel-writing."

"And I want to know all about professing and philosophising at Oxford University."

"There's not much to tell."

"I know Karl Jaspers."

"*The* Karl Jaspers?"

"The one that fell down a manhole and broke his leg..."

"You're drunk!"

"I am, but I know what I'm saying."

"Say 'Hot coffee from a proper copper coffee pot'."

"I could barely say that when sober."

"Who is your favourite fictional private detective?"

"Eddie Shoestring..."

"Who?"

"Or James Hazell..."

"Who?"

"Before your time, sweetheart..."

"Have you noticed that private detectives always find themselves chasing after lost and stolen statues?"

"Yes, and I dare say that my time will come to go after one. Knowing my luck, it will be worth millions, I will track it down, get my hands on it, and then drop it."

"Did you say that you have to be somewhere at nine?"

"I did."

"It's eight-thirty now."

"The work of a private detective is never done."

"What is the nature of tonight's assignment then?"

"A gentleman never tells."

"A spot of surveillance, no?"

"Rest assured, whatever the nature of my assignment, I would rather be here with you."

"Do you think that your work is compatible with being a Christian?"

"Who said I was a Christian?"

Helena met my cheeky smile with a smile of her own.

"Our Lord said that Faith, Hope and Charity—that is, Love—are the three greatest virtues, and that the greatest of these is Love. I imagine that much of what you do as a private detective involves suspending any impulse towards Charity. It is our compassion, as much as our reason, that makes us human."

"I *am* compassionate and I can prove it."

Her pudding consumed, Helena shot me with a wry grin and sat back and awaited my outpouring of eloquence, though I could see that she half-expected it to be flannel.

"I went to a comedy gig the other day," I began. "It was one of those events for up-and-coming young talent. Anyway, one of the acts was downright awful. He was about as funny as an all-night stake-out in Deptford in January. Nobody laughed. I felt sorry for him. So, I started laughing. I was pretending to laugh. But my pretend laugh sounded funny. So, people started laughing at my pretend laugh. Every time I laughed with my ridiculously overblown pretend laughter, the audience was in stitches. The comedian was happy because people were laughing. They weren't laughing at him, but he didn't care about that."

"I can see that you're a true man of God, Daniel."

"Rest assured, if and when I do become a Roman, I will quit being a private detective, such is the incompatibility."

"But you must become the *right sort* of Roman. You must be a Traditionalist: a Trad."

"You mean reject Vatican II?"

"Absolutely!"

"I've heard that most Trads are converts."

"That's true. I'm a Cradle Catholic. But I'm a Trad. That doesn't mean that I don't attend Novus Ordo Masses. As you know, I do. But it does mean that, given a choice, I will attend the Traditional Latin Mass. That's why you'll always see me at Mass at eight o'clock on Sunday mornings. We're lucky to have that choice at the Oratory. We owe it to Pope Benedict. He reinstated the Tridentine Mass. The current pope is a great man. The next pope will not be so great. In fact, he might not even be a Catholic."

"Are you serious?"

"You don't know much about me, Daniel, but I have three words for you: Bishop Richard Williamson. Read all that you can about him, and you will know all that you need to know about me."

"I will add that to my long list of things to do."

FIFTEEN

Many moons ago, when I was in my twenties, I found myself up north, in a small town. It was a stereotypically grim post-industrial landscape. I cannot remember where it was exactly, or what I was doing there. Needing a stiff drink, I'd chanced upon a rundown public house. It was (as James Hazell had once said of a similar establishment in the Smoke) the kind of place where the mice bring sandwiches and, if you get the right change, it's a mistake. Adjacent to that northern fleapit had stood—incongruously, in both time and place—a glitzy bar that resembled a hospital operating theatre with its antiseptic sheen. Neither place had appealed to me, so I'd gone thirsty. The Round House (in the Oxford suburb of Headington, though it was only a dropkick away from Risinghurst) was emphatically on the fleapit end of the spectrum.

There was a hole in the bar that shouldn't have been there, as if Jaws had taken a chunk out of it; the carpet was so threadbare that one could see through it; and the furniture was so shabby that it looked as if it had recently been lifted from a rubbish tip. If that doesn't quite set the scene then imagine that flies were buzzing around the sorry-looking collection of tarts and cakes housed in a see-through plastic container on the bar. That would be flies, and plenty of them, on the tenth of January! The cakes and tarts themselves looked like rock specimens in a geologist's laboratory waiting to be carbon-dated.

The place screamed at me, gloatingly, that my glorious interlude, my all-too-brief immersion in the chaste and virtuous world of Helena Johnson-Roffey was over. I'd taken a taxi to the Round House with my head spinning—and not just because of the wine—trying to work out how I would feel in the morning. "Beer before wine, you'll feel fine," I told myself. "Wine before beer, you'll feel queer." In that case, I'd reflected sourly, I'll have a rotten headache in the morning.

A woman who could not have been more different to Helena approached me at the bar and asked me what I'd like to drink. Politely, almost deferentially, I told Rachel Bannerman that I'd like a pint of best bitter. I paid her and wondered how I was going to prop up the bar without looking like I had an ulterior motive for being there. Rachel saved me the trouble by telling me that she'd never seen me in the Round House before. I lied by replying that I *had* been there before, to take part in a pub quiz, and that my team had suffered an ignominious whitewash at the hands of teams many times more knowledgeable than my own.

Rachel laughed. "I doubt that," she said, her voice surprisingly childlike for a woman of her age and worldly experience. "The combined IQ in this place wouldn't reach double figures, even on a quiz night."

"That just goes to show how ignominious my team's effort was then."

"If you can use the word 'ignominious', you wouldn't have any problems winning any pub quiz in this place," Rachel said, "so you must be telling me fibs."

I held up my hands in defeat. "Okay, I lied," I said. "I was trying to impress you."

"That's a funny way to impress a lady."

It was safe to say that I hadn't hit the top of my game since stepping nonchalantly into the Round House to general indifference, even if I was the only person in the place who could say 'ignominious', never mind spell it.

There was a scruffy old man beside me on a barstool. I hadn't noticed him until he piped up.

"Not seen you 'ere afore," he growled. "Oo be you then?"

"I'm your new best friend," I replied. "And who might you be?"

"The name's Poldark. A born-and-bred Cornishman, I be."

His accent was such that I had no reason to disbelieve him.

"His name's Norman Catchpole," the amused Rachel put in. "He's never been further south than Littlemore, or further west than Botley."

Another man who'd seen a bit of life came up to me, introduced himself as Trevor Peach, and then staggered towards the toilets.

"Are people in here always this friendly?" I asked Rachel.

"Some of them are … and some of them I'd advise you to cross the road to avoid."

Another man who'd long laboured under the cares of the world suddenly appeared beside me, as if he'd been beamed down from another planet. He scrutinised my every feature, as if they contained the answer to whichever question he'd been asking himself, before making his own unsteady way to the men's room.

"He must be Trevor Apricot."

"Believe it or not, his name is Trevor Cherry."

"Unlike some of us, I'm sure you don't tell fibs."

She smiled a smile that was alluring as it was innocent. I couldn't fathom how such a sensual woman could be so much like a little girl, and a little girl lost at that. Then all that Matt had told me about her was in that moment condensed into a synopsis of her life, a sad little tale of loneliness, betrayal and bitter cynicism. The potted biography came at me from her eyes in shafts of melancholy that struck at me with shapeless, formless blows, bypassing my five earthly senses but impregnating my other-worldly sixth sense with notions of a life lived at the very edge of existence.

My eyes, then, were drawn inexorably towards Rachel's. She was staring at me across the bar. I told myself that she'd attracted my gaze by an act of will, though she seemed to possess precious little of that, the path of least resistance seeming to be the one that she walked. My thoughts about Rachel became admixed with more thoughts about Helena, as if my mind, my unconscious mind, wished to remain in the realm of the good and not to shift to a darker realm, a place where good things never happened, but somehow I managed to focus my thoughts on Rachel and to put away thoughts of Helena, happy in the knowledge that they were a wondrous place to which I could always return.

Though Rachel looked as if she had tried too hard not to look cheap, her power was overtly sexual, making of her a dissolute woman whose dissolution was expressed in an addiction to sex as an act of conquest, a deed whereby men were told that they existed solely for her to play with. She exuded more sex appeal than she could manage. She was earthy. She was alive. She affirmed life and the force that drives it on. She was basic, primitive and raw. Her idea of violation was a man who declined to respond when she called. But I doubted that she had ever been so humbled.

She was an only child, estranged from her parents. Most only children are smothered by affection by their parents, but she hadn't been. She just hadn't been able to bond with them. It worked both ways, of course: she hadn't exactly been a loving child, and she wasn't exactly a loving adult either. All she had to offer was her body, and she offered that to men, to just about any man who wanted it, because she was lonely, because she hated herself, because having sex made her feel alive, it dulled the pain of nothingness, it showed both her and the world that she existed and that she must be taken notice of.

Greg had been just sex with regular beatings, and the beatings had made her feel more alive than sex alone would have. After all, if a man took the trouble to knock her into the middle of next week then she must be a player, someone to be reckoned with. Greg had been out of her life for three years now. Now that he was out of prison, he would expect to walk straight back into her life. He would want to enjoy her once more. Then he would want to beat her for what he assumed: that, in his absence, she'd had a succession of casual lovers. Indeed, she had had a succession of casual lovers, but Greg didn't need to know that. He wouldn't know because he couldn't know. Only, for Greg, what he couldn't know was worse than what he did know. His imagination would make him fear the worst. Little did he know, however, that the reality was worse than even his imagination could summon. She really had been *that* bad.

These were the people in her life: her mum and dad, the strangers who'd brought her into the world; Greg Tinnion, the monster who'd beaten her; and several hundred more strangers who'd known her in the biblical sense. The people she worked with didn't count. What a bunch of losers they were. Not one of them was worth a second of her time, even those whom she indulged, except Lester Bloodworm, whom she'd happily spend all day torturing before she put him away. As for the tenants, they weren't even human. She didn't want to think about them. They made her sick.

She was giving me the glad eye. In a manner of speaking, she was sizing me up. She had plans for me. She wanted to give me a taste of her charm and see where it took us. She had no doubt that it would take us to her bed. All the others had ended up in her bed, she was thinking, so why should this one be any different? True, he looked different from the others, but he was still a bloke, and no man could resist her charm when she turned it on.

Bloody men, she was thinking. She hated them. But she needed them.

My reverie was dispelled not by an irruption—a crash or a bang—but by the sudden hush that fell upon the Round House and its chattering and pool-playing punters. Greg Tinnion was not a tall man, he was not imposing, and nor was he beefy enough to inspire fear through his physical presence alone, but he did possess an aura, some malevolence of spirit that made one wish to look anywhere but straight into his eyes. The fear in the place was palpable. Everyone waited nervously for someone else to make the first move back to whatever they'd been doing sixty seconds before, or to speak the first word in resumption of a conversation truncated by the insidious invasion of evil.

Greg looked around the pub at the many worried faces that were looking back at him. He was daring people not to look scared. My excuse for neither feeling nor (I hoped) looking scared was the considerable amount of alcohol that I'd consumed that evening. I wasn't sure what Rachel's excuse was. But then she did have the full force of the law on her side.

"Well, well," he said as he approached me with the executioner's air of unalloyed sadism, "look who it isn't."

Three more mouthfuls of beer, quickly taken, further strengthened my bravado and weakened further my sense of self-preservation.

"Come to celebrate your freedom, have you, Greg?" I said, trying not to back away from him, even as he practically trod on my toes.

"I've been celebrating my freedom ever since they locked me out of the nick first thing this morning."

He wasn't exaggerating either. I could smell the booze on his breath, and I dare say he could smell mine.

"You wouldn't be sniffing around Rachel, would you?" His voice was hard as glass and sharp as a dagger's edge.

"I just came in for a quiet drink."

"How about you go and have a quiet drink somewhere else?"

"I think you'll find that *I'm* the one entitled to be here."

He fixed me with a stare that was harder and sharper than his words.

"You really think you're something, don't you?" he growled. "But you're such a sad little bastard."

"On the contrary," I returned, "being born within wedlock is one of my few accomplishments."

Greg's eyes darted left. He looked at Rachel as if she were a stray dog, *his* stray dog, that he'd come to collect and take home to her rightful place. He should have known that Rachel had long since ceased to be his obedient bitch.

"One word from me, Greg, and you're back inside," she said as confidently as if she had a company of Scots Guards standing right behind her.

"And I can blow down the ears of any number of coppers," I added, just to ram the point home. "But I'm a reasonable man, which is why I'm going to give you thirty seconds to make yourself scarcer than a condom in a convent."

"You'd better hope that our paths don't cross again."

"What do you do for an encore?" I asked. "Threaten women?"

"He doesn't threaten them," Rachel said. "He just goes ahead and hits them."

"So I've heard," I said, not taking my eyes off the chips of ice above Greg's nose.

"She'll come back to me. *I* know it. *She* knows it."

"Your time's up, Greg."

His time was up, and the game was up for him, at least for the time being. He was about to withdraw, but it was merely a tactical retreat. He would be back. Casually, he plucked his mobile from his jacket pocket, dialled a number, and waited for the reply. "Rick," he said with a sinister lack of intonation. "The Bullingdon Arms. Half an hour." He didn't wait for the reply. Then he was gone. Then there was a rush at the bar as punters sought to top up their Dutch courage. Better late than never, I supposed.

"Poor Rick," I said. "He doesn't deserve a friend like Greg Tinnion."

When the rush was over, Rachel omitted even to mention Greg; instead, she told me that she knew who I was and why I was there. Talk about having my cover blown. It turned out that I'd had no cover in the first place.

"Your name's Daniel Winter," she said, grateful to be able to converse again after the scramble for drinks. "You're a private detective. Matt Prior has put you up to poking your nose into the affairs of Greetwell Housing Trust."

"You mean the small matter of someone being murdered?" I replied. "And the equally unimportant matter of a group of people in the know conspiring to keep the police in the dark?"

"I'll tell you what you want to know, but you will have to give me something in return."

"A quid pro quo, I suppose?"

"That'll be three quid for that drink."

I paid her and wondered what it was that she wanted me to give her.

"How do you know that Matt Prior put me up to looking into the death of Laura Hart?"

"He knows that we're hiding something."

"We?"

"A few of us at Greetwell ..."

"I see."

"And we know that he's a friend of yours, and that you're a private detective, so we put two and two together."

"And why are you so happy to tell me what I need to know?"

"Because I believe that the truth must come out."

"So why don't you just go to the police?"

"It can't happen that way."

"Why not?"

Rachel was thoughtful for a moment. She was a thoughtful woman, an admirable woman in many ways. I'd taken an instant liking to her. Though she was no Helena Johnson-Roffey. But then Rachel was her own woman, and that was fine by me.

"I will give you the information that you need, soon, and it will be up to you what you do with it."

"How soon is soon?"

"Meet me after work tomorrow."

"At what time?"

"Six o'clock…"

"I've a meeting at your office tomorrow, at two o'clock, with Ida McSweeney."

"About the mix-up with the telephone numbers?"

"You know about that?"

Rachel nodded contritely. "Typical of Greetwell, that is."

"Engaging with your tenants has been fascinating, not to mention fun."

"You think the tenants are weird? Wait till you meet the staff."

"I can't wait."

"You can tell me all about your visit to The Golden Age when we're together tomorrow evening."

"I look forward to it."

"I bet you've never solved a case so easily, have you?"

"I haven't solved it yet."

"You will."

There was a touch of "You will, if…" in Rachel's voice, and I was still wondering what that "if" entailed. Her tone bespoke both a threat and a promise. All at once, she was the compassionate soul, bent on giving a man in need a helping hand, and the hard-nosed peddler of bargains with her foot on a man's throat and quite prepared to keep it there. I couldn't make up my mind whether she was saint or sinner.

I raised my glass to Rachel's health. I told myself that Helena brought out the best in me. I hoped that Rachel would not bring out the worst in me, and that I would not have the same effect on her. I wanted us both to emerge from this quagmire liking ourselves more than we had liked ourselves before it had sucked us in. I would no more have compromised Rachel to get the information I wanted than I would have profaned the name of the Blessed Virgin Mary. Though she was desirable, I did not desire her, and I wouldn't have desired her even if I hadn't had a job to do. She wanted to give me the key to the case inside which was the answer to the question that all Oxford was asking: who killed Laura Hart? To get that key, I would have to give her something in return. Whatever that something was, it had nothing to do with sex. Rachel was better than that.

I wanted so much to believe that.

SIXTEEN

I was contemplating ordering another pint when my phone rang. It was Kendal, of course. She summoned me to the house in Canal Reach, Philip's old house. Apparently, Dominic was on the rampage. By that, I mean that he was rampaging silently through his own head: outwardly, he was as still and as silent as the grave, stupefied, inert, unable to move so much as a muscle, except for the blinking of his eyes. The boy was simply sitting upright on the sofa, like a block of ice, staring straight ahead at the wall. I went to the house, straightaway, by taxi, and arrived to find the young man frozen in a bizarre posture, as if he were sitting to attention, like a Grenadier Guard whose legs had gone. I arrived also to find Kendal eyeing me accusingly, as she is wont to do, as if Dominic's state of torpor were my fault and mine alone. I was in no mood for one of her lectures. I had to keep reminding myself that I was the adult, and she the child; with each passing day, she was making me feel more like the roles had been reversed, such was the level of censure to which I was being subjected. I was almost permanently ensconced in the naughty corner. She was the perennially agitated scold.

"How long has he been like this?" I asked.

"I found him like this." Kendal's eyes were ablaze with indignation. "You smell like a brewery."

"Funny that, because I've drunk more wine than beer tonight."

"You need to lay of the booze, Daniel. You're setting me a bad example."

"I drink in the line of duty, as well you know."

"You keep telling yourself that."

I waved my hand, back and forth, across Dominic's face. There was no response. I clicked my fingers before his eyes. He didn't even blink. I was starting to think he was in a coma.

"Why don't you breathe on him?" Kendal's question came at me like a boxer's jab. "That'll bring him to."

That was not a bad idea, so I blew a gust of air at him. Again, there was no reaction, not even a blink.

Kendal laughed. "He must be in a coma if that failed to move him."

"I've never seen anything like this."

"We need to get him to hospital."

"No, we don't."

"Yes, Daniel, we do."

I'd been leaning over Dominic. I straightened myself and looked down at Kendal. She looked up at me with her wronged teenaged face, the look designed both to pull at my heartstrings and to shame me into backing down.

"You want to be a private detective one day, don't you, Kendal?"

"I guess so."

"You'll find that being a private detective means that often you have to make difficult decisions, that you have to think on your feet, that you often have to act tougher than you feel."

"Look at the state of him, Daniel. He's like a zombie."

"At least he's not going anywhere he shouldn't."

"He needs to eat and drink and go to the toilet."

"That's when he'll move, I'm sure."

"I'm not so sure."

"After tomorrow, he'll be able to go anywhere, vindicated, exonerated, a free man."

"You always back yourself, don't you?"

"I know how to grub around the cesspits of humanity for long enough to get the right answers."

Kendal sighed. For one crazy moment, I thought she was agreeing with me.

"Okay," she said, "but what do we do with Dominic until tomorrow?"

"We keep an eye on him."

"You mean *I* keep an eye on him?"

"Well, if you're offering to babysit…"

"You want me to spend the night here?"

"That would be asking a lot of you."

"But you're asking me, anyway?"

"I'm appealing to your sense of justice and to your compassion."

"You're a piece of work, Daniel."

"Whatever you say, sweetheart."

Kendal shook her head like a schoolmistress unable to fathom the recidivist tendencies of a recalcitrant pupil. "This is actually unbelievable. I'm having to spend the night with a zombie, somebody you're hiding from the law, and only thirty yards from Mum's house."

"There are a lot of walls between here and your mum's house."

"Nowhere near enough of them, believe me!"

"What is life without an adventure once in a while?"

"I suppose it's better than doing A Levels."

"That's the spirit."

"By the way, I meant to tell you …"

"That sounds ominous."

"I misinformed you earlier."

"Misinformed me? How?"

"About Karl …"

"What about him?"

"He didn't break his leg falling down a manhole."

"You know, I thought that was too ridiculous to be true."

"He broke his leg falling down a pothole."

I put my head in my hands and wondered if Karl's falling down a pothole were not even more ridiculous than his falling down a manhole. The upshot was that his leg was broken, regardless.

"Where in this fair city is there a pothole anywhere near big enough to fall down and break your leg?"

"Rawlinson Road …"

"I thought they'd filled that in."

"Obviously not …"

"Even if they haven't, you don't miss a hole that size and walk straight into it."

"You do if you're Karl …"

"Even Dominic in this comatose state would not miss a crater in the middle of the road."

"Dominic and Karl are a right pair, aren't they?"

"Yes, and I'm not sure quite which one of them is giving me more grief."

SEVENTEEN

Wednesday of that week began wet and stayed wet. The first thing I heard that morning was the sound of rain washing against my bedroom window. I went back to sleep content that the morning would not be cold and frosty, and that another winter day without sunshine and cold could be ticked off as spring waited patiently in the distance for its time to come. As I dozed in the moments before dragging myself out of bed, I managed to steel myself for the momentous day ahead, and I was mindful that if each stage of the day passed without mishap then I would finish the day not only knowing who killed Laura Hart but also with my bank account considerably swollen.

The second thing I heard that day was my phone ringing. I kept it on the kitchen table at night so that, if it rang in the morning, I would have to get out of bed—and quite swiftly—to answer it. It was my way of ensuring that if the call were related to my work then I would be standing upright when I took it, and so more likely to act upon whatever was demanded of me, and so less likely to go back to sleep. I threw on my dressing-gown and made a dash for the phone. The caller was Kendal. Still half asleep as I was, I had forgotten that she had spent the night babysitting Dominic and was wondering how she had managed to slip out of the flat without waking me up, which was her habit, for she crashed around in the mornings like a herd of elephants. Even when undertaking a simple task like making my morning cup of tea, she sounded like she was re-enacting the Battle of Waterloo in the kitchen. Also, she was given to leaving a mess for me to clear up, so I surveyed the spotlessness around me and wondered what on earth had happened to the old Kendal that I knew and loved so.

"Daniel?"

"Thank you, Kendal…"

"For what?"

"For not leaving the usual mess in the kitchen…"

"What are you talking about?"

"What?"

"I'm with Dominic, remember?"

"Oh, yes, of course. How is he?" I was expecting an answer that would get the day off to the worst possible start.

"He's fine."

"Really?" The shock was bringing me out of sleep as effectively as a bucket of cold water.

"I knew he was all right when he started yelling 'It wasn't me!' in the middle of the night."

"Where did you sleep?"

"On the floor. It was bloody uncomfortable."

"You could have slept upstairs."

"In your dead friend's bed? How creepy would that have been? It was bad enough being downstairs with Dominic."

"Well, you've played another blinder, sweetheart. I owe you."

"Damn right, you do!"

"Like I said, I will receive some compensation money from Greetwell Housing Trust today, and much of that money will be spent on you."

"When can we go shopping?"

"On Saturday…"

"I can't wait!"

"Has Dominic had something to eat and drink?"

"I made us some breakfast—bacon and eggs—and some tea. He was chatting away like an old biddy. For someone so young, he doesn't half chat like an old woman."

"It's good that he's talking at all, whatever he's talking about. Do you think he will be able to look after himself today?"

"I should think so."

"You'll go to the office now?"

"Yes, I'm just about to leave. What are you doing this morning?"

"I have some research to do."

"What research?"

"It's what teachers at my school called reading around one's subject."

"I wouldn't know about that."

"I have to read up on the composer Franz Kopetsky, and I want to read something that Rick Mallett gave me."

"Why?"

"Because Rick asked me to. He's a decent guy caught up in things he doesn't want to be caught up in. I feel sorry for him and I want to help him."

"You're all heart, Daniel."

"That's always been my trouble."

"Will you come to the office today?"

"I doubt it…and I won't be home until late either."

"I'll see you when I see you then."

***

The Internet and a couple of books of mine about classical music, between them, enabled me to construct a potted biography of the obscure nineteenth-century Austrian composer Franz Kopetsky, who died in his hometown, Linz, in eighteen-seventy-three, broken, penniless, and barely known. His story was a sad one and it put me in mind of Roseanne.

Isabel Kopetsky left her husband and only child when the boy was eleven. She eloped with as impecunious a painter as Franz would become a composer. On the day she left, Tomas Kopetsky's spirit went with her. From being a provincial city's most eminent lawyer, he became a broken shell of a man, going through the motions of the law and feeding his soul by giving his every penny to the poor. To his friends, he became a stranger. To his son, he became a ghost. Where once he had walked tall, held in awe by some and respected by all, from the day of Isabel's flight to Vienna, he was a shuffling, vacant, white-haired figure of pity. The loss of his childhood sweetheart left him stunned, all but speechless, unable to conjure a single thought as to why she had gone. Then a thought came to him. The Lord had taken his beloved from him in order to test him. His love for his wife was being used to test a yet greater love. He remembered Job, who, having lost all that he owned and all that he cherished, appealed to God as to why such a fate had befallen him. Tomas Kopetsky saw no reason to appeal. If God had deprived him of his earthly love, the love of body and soul that he and his wife shared, then he was damned if he would honour Him, never mind love Him. Having lost the love of his wife, then, he lost his love of God. He hoped that the love of his son, and the love for his son, would fill the void. They did not fill it. They did not begin to fill it. Tomas Kopetsky died whilst still alive.

Forced to bring himself up, and to grieve alone—for he would never see Isabel again—Franz found comfort in music. He found inspiration too. He learned to play the piano and the violin to reveal the music that played in his head, the music of a soul broken like his dreams of mother. Aged twenty-one, he went to university to study music, but he left after six months because university could teach him nothing.

In his forty-three years, he wrote ten pieces for the piano, six for the violin, and three for both. He earned little money for his troubles but spent much more. Harassed by creditors, he roamed from city to city, and from land to land, proclaiming, joyful in his melancholy, that a man without hunger can make no music.

With his body ailing under the curse of consumption, he left his austere lodgings in Paris and made for Linz, where he would die, under medical supervision, of a known disease and of a broken heart.

Some thirteen decades later, a girl in an English city brought Franz Kopetsky back to life. Her bow and strings stirred a soul. At last, Kopetsky heard his own music. The world rediscovered his every surge of exhilaration that was tempered by prolonged bouts of despair. The girl raised him so that he might serenade her to the grave. Then he might raise her from the dead.

***

With a cup of coffee in hand, I sat down to read the infamous letter. It was addressed to the parents of Littleworth Primary School. It was the saddest thing I'd ever read, even sadder than the first novel that I read, *Great Expectations*, by Charles Dickens, with its bittersweet denouement.

The parents were told that a child who attended Littleworth Primary School had been admitted to hospital the day before with suspected meningococcal infection; that, happily, the girl's condition was stable; and that no link to any other case in the area was known.

Meningococcal infection, it was stated, could take the form of meningitis or septicaemia (blood poisoning) and could be transmitted by close contact within households. The readers were told that, as this was not the sort of contact that would normally occur in school, children should attend the school as usual. The author declared that close family contacts of the child had been given an antibiotic in order to prevent spread. The advice given was that any other contacts should not seek antibiotics.

The letter informed parents that the infection was caused by bacteria carried in the nose and throat. Most people did not fall ill, the letter continued, but became immune without having symptoms. If a person was going to fall ill, it was usually two to four days after first meeting the bacteria. The importance of knowing the signs and symptoms of meningitis was emphasised. They were fever, headache, vomiting, an aversion to bright light, drowsiness, confusion, rash and neck stiffness.

More often than not, the letter went on, these symptoms will be due to a less severe illness, but, if anyone in the family had these symptoms, meningitis should be thought of and medical advice taken. Meningitis was commonest in young children, the author wrote, but could occur at any age. It was uncommon for there to be a second case amongst the close contacts of one case. All the same, it was felt that parents should be informed about the illness.

Parents were advised that, if their child was well, he or she should not be given antibiotics, as the problems with antibiotics would be greater than any slight benefit in these circumstances.

The letter gave the telephone numbers of Oxfordshire County Council's Public Health Department and the twenty-four-hour helpline of the National Meningitis Trust. It was signed by Doctor Kathleen Huntley, Consultant in Communicable Disease Control, and dated January the seventh of the previous year.

EIGHTEEN

Oxford's John Radcliffe Hospital is almost as big and as populous as Oxford itself. It is a sprawling monster of a building where one can get lost so many times as to forget why one went there in the first place. On my only previous visit, I'd gone to see a friend who'd just had a baby, but I'd given up trying to find the Maternity Ward after I'd spent an hour following all the signs, only to end up in the Blood Transfusion Centre. It had been like trying to find one's way into a city, by negotiating a complex of roundabouts, only to discover that the signposts for one's destination suddenly disappeared for no apparent reason. In that respect, Coventry was the worst place I'd been to. With all that in mind, I'd entered the behemoth that Wednesday lunchtime convinced that I would not be able to find my way to Karl's bedside. As for Karl himself, he was so spaced out that the only way that he would ever be able to reach his destination in so labyrinthine a place is if he were wheeled in on a trolley, which is precisely what he had been.

Eventually, I located Karl, but only after I'd been told that he'd been moved from the Accident and Emergency Ward to the Intensive Care Unit owing to a lack of beds in the former and a temporary surplus of beds in the latter.

I entered the hospital shortly before eleven o'clock. I was at Karl's bedside not much before midday. On the way there, I observed injuries and illnesses of all kinds but all of them horrific. Just before entering the ICU, a man passed me in the corridor wearing a tartan-patterned dressing-gown; he was confused and it was evident that he was lost; he asked me for directions to the toilets, but I had to tell him that I was lost myself. He then stood rooted to the spot and wet himself, so that a puddle formed at his feet, one that spread around him until a nurse came running to his aid. I didn't linger to witness the messy aftermath.

Karl was propped up in bed reading the *Beano*, his right leg in a sling. He lacked the air of someone suffering any sort of inconvenience. I fell into the armchair at the side of his bed and made myself comfortable, which wasn't easy given the amount of misery into the midst of which I'd been plunged.

"You've got some intellectual reading there, Karl, I see."

Karl averted his eyes towards me for long enough silently to acknowledge my presence. I wasn't expecting to be greeted with trumpets and a fanfare, but a word of acknowledgement would not have gone amiss.

"What's Dennis the Menace up to nowadays?" I asked. "Falling down potholes and breaking his leg, is he?"

Karl dignified me with a belated response. "Well, he isn't shagging Minnie the Minx, more's the pity." He laid the comic on his chest and then complained that the *Beano* was racist for not making Bananaman a black character.

"I think the *Beano* would have been accused of racism if Bananaman *were* a black character, Karl."

Karl looked me up and down with accusing eyes. "Did you bring me anything?" he asked.

"Only my sparkling personality…"

"I don't like grapes, but you could have brought me some."

"Aren't you going to tell me how you managed to fall down a pothole the size of a lunar crater?"

"I didn't see it. I was texting Maria with that line you fed me. Next thing I knew I was in a big hole and a whole lot of pain."

"Well, I hope that you got the line right after putting yourself to so much trouble."

Karl reached under the bedsheets and pulled out his phone. He handed it to me. "See for yourself."

I searched for his sent items and read aloud: "'My I commiserate with God for creating such a redundant flower as yourself?'" I sighed in disbelief. "You've got it wrong again, Karl," I said.

"I'm just trying to win her back, man. It's the only way: to be romantic, to use big words, to impress her."

"It helps if you get the words right, Karl."

"They were nearly right."

"Karl, you wrote 'commiserate' instead of 'congratulate', and 'redundant' instead of 'radiant', thus giving the sentence completely the wrong meaning, the very opposite of what you were trying to say." I looked over at the pretty young nurse—well, she was younger than me—busying herself around the ward, and I wondered how many times Karl had tried to ingratiate himself with her with big, romantic and impressive words. "Anyway, Karl, you have to be yourself."

"Even when you're trying to be someone else, you're being yourself."

"That was almost profound, Karl."

"Write that word down for me."

"Am I supposed to write down every word I speak with two or more syllables?"

"I'm desperate, man."

"Desperation won't win Maria back. Nor, incidentally, will violence."

Karl acknowledged graciously my allusion to his assault on both Maria's brother's car and her father. It was a sullen acknowledgement, born more of a need to forget that it had ever happened than of genuine contrition.

"I just lost it, man, that's all."

"You should forget about Maria, Karl, and look elsewhere, but don't waste your time on that nurse."

"Nurse Proctor, you mean? She fancies me, man. She keeps bending over to show me her arse. Look, she's doing it again."

I looked over to the bed opposite Karl's. Nurse Proctor was bending over an old man and straightening his pillows. She was indeed making something of an exhibition of her backside, but not for Karl's delectation (or mine), I was sure.

"*You* fancy *her*, you mean," I said. "Every time she walks past, your eyes light up like Blackpool Illuminations."

"She fancies me, man, all day long. But, you know, I wouldn't. Maria's my girl. A man has to fight for his girl."

"That's just the trouble, Karl. You've done enough fighting. It's time you put your head down and moved on."

"There will never be anyone like Maria."

"When you say that, are you responding to the prompt-ings of your heart, or are you heeding the urgings of your loins?"

"What?"

"Do you love her, Karl?" I was humouring the boy: at his age, his experience of love was even more untested than was my own.

Karl put his hand to his heart, rather touchingly, and mut-tered some lovelorn words. He was like the poet wallowing in unrequited love and submitting himself to the perennial anguish of suffering for his art. He was not going to heed my advice, he was not going to meet me on my terrain, so I had to meet him halfway. That was the only way that he would take anything useful from what I was telling him.

"Okay, Karl, do it your way, but I would still urge you to lie low for a while, don't contact her, and then approach her, if you must, but only when the moment's right and not a moment sooner."

"How will I know when the moment's right?"

"It's like my Marmite jar at home…"

"What?"

"For days, I'd tried to open it. Then, one morning, I saw it standing there, teasing me, and I knew that I *could* open it. I did exactly what I'd done many times before—took the lid in one hand, the jar in the other, and twisted—and it yielded. The lid turned. The jar was open. I sensed that I could do it, and I seized the moment. You'll feel the same about making overtures to Maria."

Though he looked bemused as a sociologist at a conference of nuclear physicists, Karl spoke of his wish to be wise as he thought I was.

"Who says I'm wise?"

"I do."

"Wisdom, Karl, consists in knowing the extent of one's ignorance."

"But you're *somebody*, man. What am I?"

"Enlightenment comes with the knowledge that one does not exist. As Rimbaud said, 'Je est un autre'."

"I've watched all the Rambo films. I never heard him say that."

Karl's unwitting witticisms were something to cherish.

"Do you think I could use Rimbaud's dictum for arguing that I'm not liable to pay my credit-card bill? I is someone else, so how can I—more to the point, why should I—pay this bill?"

As Karl strained his every mental sinew to work out what in God's name I was talking about, I gave some of my senses licence to roam my surroundings and to report back to a brain that was overflowing with data relating to the cases I was embarked on solving. The place smelt of old flesh and incontinence, with a bit of disinfectant thrown in to temper the rancid odour, which only made the smell worse. I heard a scream from somewhere in the distance, as if someone were being tortured with something very sharp and deadly. This place had to be downright spooky at night, because it was spooky enough during the day.

Nurse Proctor bustled over towards us. She took the clipboard hanging on the end of Karl's bed and studied it with a professional's competent indifference. I wondered whether Karl would have been quite so enamoured with the woman had she not been wearing her uniform, and concluded that, if he'd seen her in regular attire walking in the street, he would not have given her a second look. She looked at me—not entirely approvingly, though what I'd done to warrant such censure, I could not think—before she glared at Karl and rebuked him for having been out of bed last time she came by to update his chart.

"I was in the bog."

"We're all in the bog, my boy."

With quips like that, I thought I'd get on well with Nurse Proctor.

Karl spread his arms out wide as if to embrace the unsuspecting nurse. "May I congratulate God on creating such a radiant flower as yourself?" His words rang around the ward like something terribly inappropriate said at a funeral; they had the effect of a loud belch emitted during a wedding ceremony; and they were received as a vicar would receive a sex toy given as a Christmas present.

"I beg your pardon!" Nurse Proctor exclaimed amid the confusion and embarrassment.

"I was just rehearsing my lines."

"You won't be taking part in any play with your leg in that state." The nurse was looking down at the stricken Karl as if he were a beggar in the street and she were debating with herself whether to give him any money.

"The line is for Maria, my girl," Karl replied like a whimpering dog. "I'm trying to win her back."

"You won't win her back with lines like that."

"Daniel fed me the line."

The nurse looked at me with contempt. "This one?" she asked.

"Yeah…"

"*You* put those ridiculous words into this boy's mouth?" She put the question to me with a sight more indignation than the situation demanded, but I made allowances for the fact that she was doing a stressful job.

"Don't blame me," I protested defiantly. "I got the words from Chekhov."

"I'll give you Chekhov!"

Nurse Proctor was becoming more charming by the second.

"Young man, your private life is none of my business, I'm sure," she said to Karl, "but I'll give you one piece of advice."

"I'm listening…"

"Don't take any relationship advice from your friend here."

With that, Nurse Proctor went off to spread her charm elsewhere.

"You're right," Karl said as he contemplated the considerable void left by Nurse Proctor's charisma. "She's not my type."

"I doubt that she's *anyone's* type, Karl," I replied. "Genghis Khan's, perhaps," I added. "Now you can see quite how deceptive physical beauty can be."

There was a sudden movement from the bed next to Karl's as a man in his sixties rolled onto his side, leaned on his elbow, and addressed Karl. "I say, young man, what are you in for?" he asked, oblivious, apparently, to the plastered leg that was hoisted practically to the ceiling.

"Armed robbery," Karl replied.

"Oh, well, I came in with a broken arm," the man said. "They put it in plaster. They did some tests and told me they had some bad news. I feared the worst. They told me I had lung cancer. 'Thank God for that,' I said. 'I thought it was something serious.'" He laughed like a madman. "My arm's healing. But what's the bloody point?" He laughed again in similar fashion and then rolled back onto his back.

"I'm sorry to hear of your troubles," I said to the man.

"He yaps away all day long," Karl said. "He even talks in his bloody sleep."

"Have a heart, Karl," I said, "and remember that there is always someone worse off—a lot worse off—than yourself."

As Nurse Proctor bustled past Karl's bed, he seized the moment to attempt another charm offensive, though the nurse had seen it coming and stopped in her tracks.

"Hey, Nurse Proctor, did you know that I have the same name as an exquisite pie-thrower?"

The nurse regarded Karl impatiently.

Karl looked at me pleadingly. "Or is it an essential philanderer?"

I took my head out of my hands. "For what it's worth, Karl, it's an existential philosopher."

Nurse Proctor glared at me, wholly convinced that I was the author of all of Karl's misfortunes, right down to the broken leg. Then she left the ward like a burglar fleeing the scene of the crime.

All of a sudden, spending the afternoon at the offices of Greetwell Housing Trust seemed like an attractive proposition.

NINETEEN

After visiting Karl, I walked down to the Cowley Road, via Divinity Road, and again found myself in the Hobgoblin. A young lady served me a pint of bitter and, as I sat by the window, sipping my beer, I thought about the people that had been part of my life, way back in the past and more recently, about what, if anything, I owed them, and about my ability to repay them.

There were people connected with the Miranda Ward-Homer case whom I felt I owed something, though I wasn't sure what.

For a start, there was Philip Haygreen, my best friend from childhood, the fallen angel, the man who'd lost the woman we'd both loved—the girl we'd both loved as boys: Sylvia Blackman—the man who, in his grief, as grief had turned to a thirst for vengeance against womankind, had founded two brothels, one near home, in Portslade, the other in the city of his alma mater, Oxford.

What did I owe him?

I owed him the cherishing of the memory of our friendship, a friendship that had never died, and never would die,
for we were united by more than the phenomenon that was
and is Sylvia Blackman, and we would not be divided either
by what he became or by his grotesquely premature death at
the hands of his nemesis, Dane Goldman, also known as the
Great Dane. Perhaps I owed Philip my prayers; and if my
prayers were not good enough for the Almighty then, perhaps, I owed him somebody else's.

By extension, I owed Benjamin and Cynthia Haygreen,
my friend's parents, the same as I owed Philip.

Then there was Sylvia Blackman herself, the girl who had
enchanted mine and Philip's shared childhood, the girl who
had beguiled and tormented us, the woman who had ruined
herself and destroyed Philip, the woman who haunted me
now with her lingering presence, with her spectral promises
and threats, with her sheer fragility of mind and her brokenness of heart, a heart that I dared not attempt to put back
together.

If I owed Sylvia anything then it was not to intrude upon
her life again, to keep my distance, notwithstanding the vicis-
situdes that had thrown us back together. For her sake, and
for mine, her aura of mystery had to be preserved, she had to
remain the figure of romantic vulnerability of my imagination, for she was a woman of mystique or she was nothing.

There was Miranda Ward-Homer, also known as Dana,
subject of my previous investigation, erstwhile employee of
Philip's at Oxford Suzie's and Philip's one-time lover, whom
Philip had poached from the gangster masquerading as legit-
imate businessman (as most gangsters do), Dane Goldman,
the man who now wanted my head on a platter and who

was waiting patiently, like a snake in the grass, for the most opportune moment to strike.

What did I owe her?

Absurdly, once I'd tracked her down, she'd invited me to join her in Paris, for a holiday, though her sojourn in that fair city was to have been more than a few days' vacation. She had desired my company simply because she had looked at me and seen Philip, and I still marvelled at how his defection to the dark side had sent his charisma levels into the stratosphere and turned him into some kind of sex god. I was seriously thinking about defecting myself. Anyway, I'd fulfilled my obligation to my client by finding his daughter, and I'd fulfilled my obligation to her by telling her father, through his representative, that she was alive and well and without divulging her whereabouts.

That I had no more need to think about Miranda Ward-Homer had not stopped me from doing so.

Then there was Carey Seymour, another of Philip's Oxford courtesans. Her contribution to the solving of the Miranda Ward-Homer case had been invaluable. She had spent time on her back to pay off the considerable gambling debts of her ex-husband, and she had more time to spend in that supremely compromising position before the debts were discharged, though, given what she had told me five months before, her period of supreme self-sacrifice was almost at an end. I looked forward to taking her to see Lou Reed in concert, a few weeks hence, at London's palatial Royal Albert Hall, and I hoped that the outing would help redeem a small portion of what I owed her.

Carey Seymour was a woman wholly able to look after herself—there was not so much as a hint of vulnerability about her, even in her stricken circumstances—and to stand or fall by her own decisions. Her erstwhile counterpart, at Portslade Suzie's, was at the other end of the scale where durability and confidence were concerned. She was beaten and ravaged, physically and mentally; her body, a bag of broken bones, was no kind of temple for her desolate spirit. With her, it was not so much a matter of what I owed her—for what she had done, so bravely, in helping me to track down Miranda—but what I was able to do to help her, for she was owned by a man who treated her like a chattel, who starved her of everything on God's earth but physical and psychological abuse. I knew that I would have to go back to Brighton, and soon, to face down her oppressor, for doing nothing, given her situation, was not an option. I could only hope that I would not be too late.

Gabriel Tolpuddle sprang to mind. I hadn't seen him for a while, not even in the Dew Drop. I wondered if he'd gone away. He'd been involved, albeit obliquely, in the Miranda Ward-Homer case. I supposed that I owed him nothing. His lifestyle was of little consequence to me. He was the son of a rich businessman and property tycoon, so privileged and carefree that he could afford to spend his days acting as eco-warrior and indulging his addiction to sex, or at least his addiction to paying for it. I cared little for his way of life, but I cared somehow about his life. He was no overentitled brat. He had expressed to me his wish to change, for the better, and the least I could do was care enough to wish to help him become that better man.

Even Maureen, my next-door neighbour—who was away visiting her mother in Devon—encroached on my thoughts as my pint glass became more than half-empty. All that I owed her, according to the lady herself, was to do her the honour of partaking of her shepherd's pie one evening; and all I had done to accrue such a trifling debt was each day to receive her read and digested copy of the *Oxford Mail*, a favour for which I had never asked, but had accepted simply to avoid seeming rude. Even as I indulged such frivolous thoughts, I was mindful that the copy of the *Oxford Mail*, bequeathed to me by Maureen on August the first, of the previous year, had led me towards Philip, who, even in death, had pointed me towards Miranda.

That I should do Maureen the honour of dining at her place: she called that my repaying the debt that I owed her. I called it compounding my debt to her. *She* would come to *my* place to partake of *my* shepherd's pie. If I made only one worthwhile decision that day, it would be that.

Kendal and Rosie, of course, were bound up together. Since Kendal insisted on squatting at my flat, and showing no inclination to leave, I owed her a duty of care. I was, unofficially, with Rosie's tacit permission, Kendal's guardian. Kendal had become, effectively, my sidekick, the Robin to my Batman, and at the tender age of sixteen, an age that no more fitted her than teetotalism fitted me. Though my relationship with Kendal had become somewhat strained recently—we had become like a bickering married couple—I owed her more than a duty of care. I was trying to be a bridge to the freedom that she craved, the actual, physical independence that still lagged some way behind her independence of mind and spirit. The role that had been thrust upon me was proving to be not without its challenges. In Rosie's eyes, I was irresponsible and was leading her daughter astray; I was an adult who ought to have known better than to encourage an errant teenager to drift further from the straight and narrow by involving her in my madcap ventures. When all was said and done, Rosie had the power to take Kendal back any time she wished—and how often I wished she would—but, all the time that Kendal was in my care—albeit only with Rosie's grudging approval—I had the responsibility to manage the girl like a mature and sensible adult. That, as I was discovering, was much easier said than done.

Apparently, I owed Laura, my sister, a visit to Roseanne, our mother, whose whereabouts I'd discovered during my investigation into the whereabouts of Miranda Ward-Homer. I could not use distance as an excuse for my continuing reluctance to make an appearance at the convent where Roseanne now resided, for it was situated, with gut-wrenching irony, just a few miles up the road from my North Oxford home. How was I to tell Laura that I had a vision of Roseanne as she had been when I was but a boy in ill-fitting shorts, and that I did not wish to spoil the purity of that vision, that beatific vision, by seeing Roseanne as she was now? How was I to tell Laura that I had no idea what to say to Roseanne, more than thirty-two years after she'd gone to our school for a parents' evening, and not come home?

If I would go to see Roseanne, I would go for Albert, my father. His death, a few weeks before Roseanne's disappearance, had been—and still was—shrouded in mystery. Why had he crashed his car into that tree? Had he chosen to die? Or had some invisible hand steered him to his death? Albert was more of a stranger to me than was Roseanne, but it was for him that I might go to see Roseanne. I would allow his spirit to guide me. That much I owed him.

There were more people to ponder—people connected with my current investigation—and more debts to consider, but there was no time, for my pint glass was now empty and I had to eat something before making my way down Iffley Pass to the offices of Greetwell Housing Trust, to discuss my compensation package with the chief executive, Ida McSweeney, a woman with a fearsome reputation for driving a hard bargain, but a woman who, according to Matt, recognised her debt to me and was more than prepared to pay it.

TWENTY

Of all the *Big Issue* vendors in Oxford, Allen (that is his first name, despite the spelling) must be the most cheerful. Inclement weather and tight-fisted would-be punters put no obstacles between him and his joviality. If his pitch suffered a major earthquake, his voice would be heard above the rumbling and the carnage, his next sale only a boyish smile away. He was forever upbeat, a jocular figure with a nice line in sales patter. He was also well-groomed, neat and tidy, almost smart, and always smelling of roses. People doubted that he was homeless at all. That might have been why he shifted so few copies of his magazines.

In the drizzle, as I ate a ham-and-mustard sandwich that tasted like rubber doused in axle-grease, I chatted with Allen, who interspersed his chatter with overtures to potential customers.

"Join the longest queue in the world!" he proclaimed. "Come and get my last *Big Issue*!"

"If you're going to say that," I interjected, "at least cover up the magazines in your backpack."

"Come and get your *Big Issue* and win a dogging weekend in Scarborough for two!"

"That's your best line yet."

"Listen, you couldn't cover for me, could you?" Allen asked shiftily. "I need to pay someone a quick visit."

"I'd love to," I lied, "but I need to visit someone myself."

"Oh, yes? A bird by any chance?"

"Yes, but not of the cute and cuddly type…"

"Well, that's too bad, but at least buy a copy of the *Issue* before you go."

I gave him a fiver and told him to keep the change. I also gave him my bottle of water—which was the size of a reservoir: it had come with the sandwiches and a packet of crisps—and urged him not to drink it all at once or he would drown. The crisps were ham-and-mustard flavoured, and I'd had more than enough of rubber and axle-grease, so I gave him those as well.

"Are you on a promise then?" he wondered.

"Yes, but not the kind of promise that you're hinting at."

Allen frowned as if to protest that dirty thoughts had been far from his mind.

"I've an appointment with the chief executive of Greetwell Housing Trust," I said. "She owes me."

Allen sniggered at the mention of the housing association.

"What's so funny?" I asked.

"Some friends and I have a cosy little arrangement with Greetwell Housing Trust."

"What kind of arrangement?"

"We squat in their empty properties."

"How do you manage that?"

"One of the housing officers there—who shall remain nameless—tips us off whenever a property becomes empty. We break in. We live there for a month or two. When Greetwell want the place back, we leave. Everyone's a winner."

"How do Greetwell gain from this arrangement of yours?"

"They gain a lot, because we leave the properties in a better state than we found them. You wouldn't believe the state we find some of their places."

"Believe me, I would."

***

Eventually, I crossed the Cowley Road and made for Iffley Pass. Allen was in full battle cry again. "Roll up, roll up, you know you want it!" he intoned. "Come and get your *Big Issue!*" Apparently, he'd sold about as many copies of the magazine as Oxford United were likely to garner points that month, and that was excluding the copy I'd bought.

A police car, siren wailing, burst up the road towards Cowley in flashes of blue. Another police car was behind it, but it was stopped in its noisy tracks by the hip-hop laden Porsche that had chosen an inopportune moment to reverse into the road. I cast my mind back to days when car chases were my daily lot, when we pursued villains in motors driven by police officers who had attended the Evel Knievel School of Motoring. How I missed the comradeship and camaraderie of my days in the Met, especially the month when I was seconded to the Sweeney and I used up at least six of my nine lives. Life was more sedentary working as a private detective amid the Dreaming Spires of Oxford, though, as I'd discovered, not without danger.

Iffley Pass was a road of two-up-two-down modest dwellings linking the Iffley and Cowley Roads, and, as such, like many another street between the Plain and Between Towns Road. Befitting the part of Oxford in which it was situated, it was bohemian in its outlook and appearance, it was a place for students and people seeking "alternative" paths to enlightenment, a place where ostentation was eschewed in the name of that same pursuit of Nirvana. I looked down the street and smelt Arabian coffee laced with saffron, and beheld imitation Oriental rugs draped across windows as makeshift curtains, and wondered what else I might encounter as I approached the offices of Greetwell Housing Trust. The answer was not long in coming.

I'd not progressed more than thirty yards down the street when, competing with the rumbling and the screeching of the traffic behind me, a strange noise reached me from further down the road. It sounded like the impassioned tones of a woman arguing loudly with herself. As I stepped closer and closer towards it, the noise grew louder, until I reached the source of the noise and stopped in my tracks and gazed in wonderment at the spectacle before me.

Outside The Golden Age, the house converted into an office—and now condemned—was balanced precariously upon a soapbox, wearing traditional African dress (Nigerian, I guessed), a corpulent, yet voluptuous, black woman. Her indignation was booming from an ample chest. She was conducting her performance from the middle of the road, blocking it thereby, and I thought I was her only witness until I looked left and upwards and saw several faces at the windows of the upper floor of The Golden Age. I was studiously curious and enthralled. The faces looked down with a mixture of resignation and horror.

"I tell you, this place does the work of Satan! It stands here so humble, and so full of its own good works, and yet inside its heart is hard and its mind closed! Do not be deceived! The Devil has claimed its soul! When my boiler breaks down, on a cold January morning, 'Twenty-four hours, Miss Djemba Djemba,' they say! Three days later, I am still wrapped in a blanket, like baby Jesus in the manger, shivering from the cold! When my neighbour's boiler breaks down, on that same January morning, 'Twenty-four hours, Mrs Candy,' they say! And what do you know? Before her lunch has been digested, she has shed the blankets and is warming her tender white arse, in the heat of her lovely white home, while the black witch next door warms herself in the love of God!"

The woman was oblivious to my presence, which was hard to fathom since I was the only person in the otherwise empty street.

The big African lady stopped orating when she heard a man shouting at her. A large African man came out of nowhere, he, too, seemingly oblivious to my presence.

"Lola! Lola! What in God's name are you doing, woman?"

"People have to hear what I'm saying, Eric!"

Eric looked around him and saw nobody, not even me. "What people?"

I took my leave with much trepidation as the two Africans continued to argue behind me.

"Someone has to make a stand, Eric!"

"Make a stand if you have to, Lola, but don't do it on a soapbox!"

"I'll do what I must to get the boot of the white man off the black man's throat!"

"Don't be so melodramatic, woman!"

As I entered The Golden Age by the front door, I saw the sign announcing Greetwell Housing Trust. The sign was shiny and made of brass. It was the only thing new and polished about the place. I knew that much even before I crossed the threshold. I strode into reception and beheld a young lady sitting with a straight back behind a protective glass screen. I was struck by her poise. She looked most elegant in a pink roll-neck sweater. When she looked up and revealed two rows of gleaming white teeth, I marvelled at her radiance.

"It's all happening out there," I said.

"It's all happening in here too," the young lady replied.

I looked around and saw exactly what she meant.

"Who's the orator outside?" I asked.

"That's Miss Djemba Djemba," the young lady replied with a sweet smile. "She's out there most days throwing mud at Greetwell Housing Trust."

"Is she one of your tenants?"

The young lady nodded. "She belongs in the loony bin."

"My name's Daniel Winter," I said. "I've come to see Ida McSweeney."

"Oh, you mean the Invisible Woman."

"I have heard that she's somewhat elusive."

"I'll let her know you're here, as soon as I've dealt with this little circus."

"I'm early, so I'm happy to wait."

"The two ladies squabbling are Scarlet Creamer and Bertha Garlick. The lady in the ridiculous outfit is Bertha."

I looked left at the two late-middle-aged women scream-ing obscenities at each other. Bertha was draped in a multi-coloured oversized tweed overcoat; on her head was affixed what looked like a tea-cosy, and she was shod in a pair of red Wellington boots. Though classily dressed and well-spoken (the profanities notwithstanding), Scarlet bore all the hall-marks of someone completely detached from anything that might be described as reality.

"The man standing beside you in a trench coat several sizes too big for him is Lenny Fawcett-Dawson."

The coat of the man would, indeed, have fitted a man much taller and stockier than himself, as the garment seemed to billow like a parachute in the air and the hem practically skimmed the carpet. He was enjoying the spectacle of the two ladies arguing, all but swinging their handbags at each other as they were.

"Lenny was sacked today by the council. He was a car-park attendant. He fell asleep on the job. Or, rather, he got drunk first thing in the morning, and passed out. Too much vodka on his cornflakes. He was in here earlier, pretending to be deaf and dumb, passing silly messages to me under the counter. So, I passed one back to him, saying: 'Speak up! I can't hear you.' At that, he gave me a startled look and ran away. Now he's back. God knows what he wants now."

The man grinned at me. He was like a miniature version of Jaws from the James Bond movies.

"The man in the corner is Francis Burns. He's come to see Louise Duffy, his housing officer, but I've told him a hun-dred times that she's not here. The other chap is Morrison Tonypandy. My name is Maya and I'm the only sane person in the building."

"I can well believe that."

Having observed Francis Burns, and registered no emotion other than wondering if he were the same Francis Burns who had once played for Manchester United, I turned my attention to Morrison Tonypandy. He was holding a leaflet—plucked from the display of leaflets in the window, I presumed—and he appeared to be reflecting mournfully on the passage of his seventy or so years. He wore a moth-eaten tweed suit, a starched shirt, and a tie covered in bits of dried egg. His beaten-up brogues were as brown as his suit. A mane of grey hair was swept back over his head so fulsomely that clumps stuck out by the ears. His face was blotched by too much booze. Though he looked straight ahead, at Maya, his head twitched like an excised body organ on a stick.

"I can see why you sit behind a protective screen, Maya."

"More than the threat of violence," Maya replied, "I'm more worried about Bertha Garlick's spit."

We both beheld the drama unfolding in the cramped little reception area of a condemned building that might well have come crashing down had somebody dared to sneeze.

"I'm here on important business, I'll have you know!" Bertha sprayed saliva as she spoke.

Scarlet took a step back as the saliva was getting closer. "You're always in here, pestering this poor girl!"

Maya watched the quarrelsome twosome with a wry smile. "Word for word, it's the same every day between these two," she sighed.

"My poor Horlicks is stuck up a sixty-foot-high tree!" Bertha lamented. "He went up after a squirrel! Now he's swinging precariously on the end of a branch!"

"That horrible Siamese cat of yours should be put down! It shits in my garden!"

Lenny's voice might have gone, as had most of his teeth, but his grotesque laugh, hoarse and wheezy, was just about intact.

"It's no ordinary tree, neither!" Bertha declared defiantly. "It's a *Juglans Regia*!"

"A what?"

"A walnut tree!" Bertha replied proudly.

"That scrawny bush of yours? If that's a walnut tree then I'm Judy Garland!"

Lenny laughed again. He sounded like a cat being strangled.

Maya frowned in resignation. She shook her head. Then she activated the intercom. It crackled and fizzed and whistled into action.

"Last time, you were the Queen of Sheba!" Bertha retorted.

"Today, if that's all right with you, I'm Judy Garland!"

"You'll probably go the same way as her as well!"

"Living next door to you, I dare say I will!"

The intercom was ailing and Lenny's laugh threatened to break it for good.

Maya put her mouth to the microphone. "See what I have to put up with," she said, calmly and with a self-righteous spikiness that rent the air like arrows heading mercilessly for their targets.

"Where's that pathetic poodle of yours?" Bertha asked Scarlet. "I thought he was an extension of your arm!"

"Stop spitting, you horrid, beastly woman!"

"I'll spit if I want to!"

"Gordon is outside, if you must know, tied to a lamp-post! Do you seriously think I'd bring him in here?" Scarlet regarded Lenny with disgust. "He'd catch something!"

Lenny's face dropped. It was in desperate need of a lift before it dropped. He staggered towards the chairs and took a seat next to Morrison Tonypandy, who was still looking straight ahead, his head still twitching.

"When Bertha's gone, will someone come and hose down the glass screen and steam-clean the carpet?" Maya pleaded via the intercom. "Over and out!" The device screeched and whistled into slumber.

Bertha stepped towards the screen. "What are you going to do about my poor Horlicks?" she sprayed.

"I've told you, Mrs Garlick—"

"*Miss* Garlick, if you please! No man has interfered with my chastity!"

Scarlet was emphatic: "No man would want to!"

"*Miss* Garlick," the harassed receptionist persisted, "the Rapid Reaction Team will be round as … as soon as … as soon as we've found them."

"Those three clowns!" came the next shower of words. "There's not one of them under seventy! What are they doing? Looking for their Zimmer frames?"

Morrison looked at Lenny and proffered a queer smile. Engrossed as he was in the bout of verbal wrestling before him, Lenny took a while to register Morrison's attention. He looked at Morrison, who smiled again. Alarmed, Lenny recoiled with a start.

"I'll have you know," Maya protested, "Ronald Blythe's only fifty-eight."

Bertha was not impressed. "You'll find the other two in the day centre, playing dominoes!" Bertha's tirade was nearly over. "If those geriatric fools haven't reacted within the hour then I'm going up the tree myself!"

Maya gave up being polite. "Be my guest," she returned.

"And mine!" Scarlet added.

Bertha left the building in a strop. As she went, her boots squeaked. The six remaining occupants of the room watched her go. They heard a dog barking and squealing. Scarlet pursued Bertha in haste. That left five of us in reception. We listened as Bertha and Scarlet continued their argument outside.

"You leave Gordon alone!"

"I tripped over the stupid animal!"

Maya reactivated the intercom. It sounded like a runaway train crashing into a railway terminus. "Sheryl, you're the duty housing officer, so get yourself in here now, please, and put an end to this chaos!" When the instrument was deactivated, it sounded like several greenhouses being smashed into pieces.

"Can I tell you something?" Morrison Tonypandy was addressing Lenny Fawcett-Dawson.

Lenny looked on in horror as Morrison's head twitched.

"When I was a lad, my dad had a sex change," Morrison continued. "My mum, too, had a sex change. So, my dad became my mum and my mum became my dad. How amazing is that?"

His face white as a ghost, and his emaciated features looking thoroughly haunted, Lenny stood up. His eyes on Morrison all the way, he crept towards the door. He bumped into it and bounced off it. Still looking at Morrison, he opened the door and scurried away.

There were now four of us remaining in the room.

A woman entered the room from the door to the side of Maya's little reinforced cabin. Her demeanour was one of terrified bravado.

"Not before time, Sheryl!" Maya declaimed.

"Where is he?"

"Who?"

"Lenny Fawcett-Dawson ..."

"He's gone."

As I stood by the glass screen wondering whether Sheryl had ever properly seen me before, other than the time when she thought she'd seen me with Dominic, and as I stood there wondering whether she would recognise me, she looked around the room unconvinced that her nemesis wasn't there.

"I feel cheated," she said. "How dare he not be here when I've psyched myself up to tackle him? But he's here, isn't he, somewhere? It's all part of the charade. He's here. I just can't see him. Any second now, he will emerge from the ether to harass me. Or is he really wasting space somewhere else, bothering someone else?"

"I told you, Sheryl, he's gone."

"How come?"

"Something Mr Tonypany said ..."

Sheryl saw that Morrison was looking pleased with himself. "Mr Tonypandy, I could kiss you," she said.

His head twitching, Morrison pursed his lips invitingly, saliva oozing from between them.

"But I won't," Sheryl added before leaving the room like someone fleeing from a pack of ravenous hyenas.

"Welcome to the madhouse," Maya said, sounding like someone who'd uttered the same words a thousand times before to disbelieving visitors and newcomers to the scene.

"I was prepared for a certain level of madness," I replied, "but not for this."

The madness was far from over.

Francis Burns approached me from my left. I was tempted to step aside, but I stood my ground.

"Come away from him, Thelma!" the man cried.

I looked down at my feet and saw nothing but a threadbare carpet. "Who's Thelma?" I asked Maya.

"His dog..."

I looked at the floor again and then, puzzled, made a face at Maya.

"It's not a real dog," Maya added.

"Dogs hate me," I said. "A dog will cross the road to bark at me, but this is the first time that I've been barked at by an *imaginary* dog."

"It's par for the course in this place."

"Where's Louise?" the man barked at Maya.

"Louise is at the vet's," Maya replied. "You told me when you came in."

I presumed that Louise was his other imaginary dog.

The man thought for a second. "Why am I 'ere?" he asked.

"You came to see your housing officer."

"Who's that then?"

"Louise Duffy..."

The man jolted as if he'd been struck by lightning. "Louise!"

"Not *your* Louise, Mr Burns..."

"Where the 'ell is Louise Duffy then?"

"She'll be with you shortly."

The man groaned like he'd just been punched by a heavyweight boxer and flattened. He slipped into thought again. "Why'd I come 'ere?" he mumbled to himself. He looked at me as if he were trying to make out a figure in the fog. "And who the 'ell are you?" he exclaimed. He turned back to Maya. "Tell 'er to call me, will yer?" he demanded.

"Will do, Mr Burns…"

The man made for the door. He stopped in his unsteady tracks. He looked down at the floor. "Come on, Thelma," he said. "There's nowt for us 'ere." He watched as the imaginary dog walked ahead of him and out onto the street. "That's a good girl," he said before leaving the building.

And then there were three.

"Poor dog, imaginary or not," I said.

Maya smiled again. Smiling came as naturally to her as spraying saliva came to Bertha Garlick. She dialled a number on her phone and put it down when there was no answer.

"There's no answer on Ida McSweeney's number, which should be answered by her secretary, so I suggest you go to the back door, ring the bell, and somebody will meet you there."

"The *back* door?"

"In through the back door and out the front is a company rule."

"Why doesn't that surprise me?"

Maya's phone rang. She answered it. "Good afternoon, Greetwell Housing Trust…" When she saw me stepping into the street, she asked the caller to hold the line for a moment. "If you see Miss Djemba Djemba," she called, "just ignore her!"

I looked around and then turned back to Maya. "She's gone!" I called back.

Maya raised a thumb in approbation.

As I headed for the back door, eager to get my direct encounter with Greetwell Housing Trust over and done with,

I had to skirt around the disputatious Eric and Lola. They had moved to a position at the back end of The Golden Age.

"This petty discrimination is racism of the worst sort, Eric," the big lady with the big hair was telling her bewildered friend, or husband, or whatever he was to her, "the sort that hides behind walls and a corporate name!"

I rang the bell of the back door. I couldn't help but notice how large the door was, as if the builders had found themselves with a surplus of materials and so had decided not to waste them. For being so big and sturdy, the door looked out of place attached to a building that looked as if it were about to crumble. The back of the building was every bit as ramshackle as the front. The brickwork was worn and pocked with little craters. The paint on the frames of the windows and on the frame of the door was peeling as if it were trying to escape before the building tumbled to the ground. A drain-pipe seemed to hang from the wall by a thread. At the bottom of the pipe, the drain was blocked with leaves and dirt and what looked like a used condom. The drain smelt like raw sewage. To the left of the door was a sign that announced The Golden Age. On the cherry-red portal was pinned a hand-written notice. "DRY PAINT," it declaimed.

Eventually, the door was opened by a man of around thirty who was a dead ringer for Tintin, the Belgian comic-book character. Such was the likeness that I looked down at the ground to see if his dog Snowy was at his feet. I was tempted to visualise the creature, to complete the picture, as it were, but one imaginary dog in the vicinity was quite enough for one day.

"Oh, hello, Jocelyn," the man said. "We weren't expecting you until Monday."

I was confused enough without that opening salvo.

"You *are* Jocelyn Dare, our new maintenance surveyor, I trust?" the man asked.

To my disbelief, I'd been handed an alias on a plate and I saw no virtue in wasting it.

"I am he," I said in a jocular tone. "I've just dropped by to tie up some loose ends with Ida McSweeney."

"Oh, well, you'll have to find her first."

"I found her easily enough when I came for my interview." I'd taken a chance with that comment, for I'd no idea who had interviewed the new maintenance surveyor.

"Yes, Harry Fletcher—that's Harriet, our boss in the maintenance department, also known as the customer-service centre—was rather miffed that she didn't get to interview you."

"Office politics…" I ventured.

"The politics in this place are reminiscent of Weimar Germany."

I chided myself for having judged the book by its cover.

The man waved me into the building and introduced himself as Neil Givens, from Leeds, to which I replied that his origins had been betrayed by his accent. The argument went on behind us.

"We have to beat racism, Eric! It's the darkest stain on the human soul!"

"There are ways and means, Lola!"

"Your way is to do nothing, Eric!"

Neil looked over my shoulder at the argumentative pair and shook his head in despair. He then invited me in.

I followed him into the building and shuddered when the door shut behind me. Suddenly, I felt imprisoned, stuck in a place from which I might never escape.

"Welcome to The Golden Age," Neil said. "Nobody has the first idea how the building got the name."

"I think I know."

"Really?"

"It's the large door."

"I don't follow."

"Phonetically, 'large door', in French, is rendered 'l'age d'or'—that is l-apostrophe-a-g-e-space-d-apostrophe-o-r—which means 'the golden age'."

Neil narrowed his eyes in thought. "I'll have to think about that."

"I've met Miss Djemba Djemba," I said.

"She's just background noise now," Neil replied.

"Is she often out there on her soapbox?"

"Upstairs, we have two lever-arch files of complaints made by Miss Djemba Djemba and one file for all the other tenants put together."

"She feels aggrieved today."

"Every complaint she's ever made has been based on a charge of racism."

"Are any of her charges justified?"

Neil frowned. "I doubt it," he said. "Greetwell Housing Trust couldn't organise a tea party, never mind a conspiracy of racism." He smiled to himself, content that he had defended his employer's honour with aplomb. "Follow me."

With one step each we found ourselves in the kitchen. The sink was full of dirty mugs. The water looked cold and a film of scum lay on the top. The bin was overflowing with rubbish and gave off a revolting smell. There were dirty mugs and plates everywhere. At the far end of the room were a table and six chairs. In one of the chairs, facing us, sat a woman, her hands wrapped around a cup of coffee, reading a magazine.

"This is the social hub of our little enterprise," Neil said with a mocking smile.

I looked around the place and tried hard not to vomit.

"This is Sheryl Henry, one of our best housing officers."

Sheryl looked up from her magazine at both of us and her gaze lingered on me. A bluebottle that had been buzzing around the kitchen, feasting on the detritus, circled Sheryl and then hovered before her eyes. She swiped at it with her magazine. The magazine was *Smash Hits*. It had lived up to its name.

"This must be the only place in the country that has flies in January," she said.

"This is Jocelyn Dare," Neil declared, "our new surveyor."

Sheryl studied me closely for some time. Again, I tried to recall whether she had ever seen me before, other than from a distance. She knew my name, my real name, and my outline, but did she know my face? She seemed to be asking herself the same question.

"Good luck, Jocelyn," she said. "It's not too late to change your mind."

Neil and I turned to leave with sugar crunching under our feet.

I was inside The Golden Age, and I had an alias, and there was every chance that I would have cause to use it.

TWENTY-ONE

At the foot of a dark and narrow staircase, Neil and I peered down a dark and narrow corridor.

"This place is like a rabbit warren," I submitted.

Though I tried to resist the surging recollection, it beat me, for The Golden Age, unaccountably, took me back several years to a night at a fairground, a glorious night, a night that, now that I remembered it, stood as a beacon in my mind. The flame that burned that night called to me now in a mesh of sound and light. The night was aflame with romance. The woman in my mind was serene as a somnolent lioness as she floated amid the rides and the stalls of the fair, flashing lights illuminating every blade of grass upon which she trod and the intoxicating cocktail of sounds serving as a herald of her glory. The various smells—the sickly sweetness of toffee-apples and candyfloss, the acrid scent of axle-grease, and the throat-catching aroma of high summer—served only to emphasise her balmy fragrance. The gypsies of the fair to whom she chatted—among them, the man with the wart on his nose and the woman with the beard—magnified her light and caused her to glitter and twinkle like a star in the night sky.

With me too that night was a girl, my love for whom rivalled my love for the woman. My mind was telling me that it had been so, reminding me that fate had contrived to bring both the girl and the woman back to me, and that I should not spurn the gifts of providence.

Then I recalled the painting of mine, from which Philip had fled so dreadfully upon seeing it: the painting of Roseanne Mary Wordsworth, that was the painting of Sylvia Blackman, that was the painting of Kendal Waterhouse. Were Roseanne and Sylvia and Kendal really three persons of some personal trinity? And was that trinity a blessed trinity? Or was it a curse, a perpetual haunting of my every dream, of my every wakeful moment?

Then I realised that The Golden Age was a throwback to the Haunted House of that fateful night, that night when seeds of faith had been planted in my heart, when intimations of hope and charity had caressed my soul.

I wiped away a tear.

"Are you all right?"

"Yes, thank you, Neil, I'm fine."

Neil nodded in the direction of the gloom. "At the end of the corridor is the fire escape," he said. "The staircase there is wider and better lit. We're not supposed to use it, but we do, because it's the only part of the building not in danger of imminent collapse."

The aged intercom squeaked and crackled again. Maya's voice was heard through the whistling. "Listen to that," she said. "Silence is golden." The device sounded like a plane crashing as it was disengaged.

We climbed the staircase and entered a room that a sign on the door told me was the Customer Service Centre. I noted the absence of the hyphen disapprovingly. The room was a morass of dust and decay. The first thing I saw, some six feet from the wall to my right, was a large bookcase stuffed with lever-arch files, ring-binders and books of a technical nature. At the other end of the room, two shelves laden with office flotsam were attached to the wall, though they looked as if they might soon become *de*tached from it. Desks were packed so tightly together that it was a wonder that anyone in the room could breathe, never mind move.

"We have been rebranded the customer-service centre," Neil told me, "though we still think of ourselves as the maintenance department."

I nodded with interest.

Several faces looked up at me, the newcomer, the outsider, the imposter.

"Harry, our new surveyor has arrived," Neil declared.

Harry walked over to me as Neil went back to his desk and sat down. Quickly, so as not to appear lecherous, I ran my eyes over her large bones, extravagant curves and shock of black hair.

"You're as early as Mr Kipling's cakes are good," Harry said.

"Exceedingly?" I replied.

"Exactly," Harry returned. "And don't spoil my punchline again."

"I was at a loose end," I said, "so I thought I would drop by to complete some contractual formalities with Ida."

"What time is your appointment with her?"

"Two o'clock…"

Harry looked at her watch. "It's gone two now," she said. "Ida's out somewhere, but she should be back soon. In the meantime, you can wait in here and watch the team at work. You'll be based in here for the first month, anyway, as it's a Greetwell Housing Trust tradition that all new staff work in the maintenance department for one month as a sort of apprenticeship. Did Ida mention that?"

"Er, yes, I believe she did."

"Well, she should have made it clear during the interview. *I* was supposed to have interviewed you, but Ida insisted that *she* should interview you, just because you're Cornish, as she is. Which part of Cornwall are you from?"

"Er, Polzeath," I mumbled, suddenly remembering my holiday there of some ten years before, and momentarily grateful that I'd once spent a week as an undercover police officer inside a gang of football hooligans that was plotting carnage before, during and after a game between Millwall and West Ham United.

"That's nice," Harry said vaguely. "Let me introduce you to the team." She turned to face her charges. "Listen up, people!" she yelled. "This is Jocelyn, our new maintenance surveyor!" She pointed at the man in the yellow shirt. "Neil, you've met. He's from Leeds, as I'm sure he's told you." She pointed at a young lady who had the look of a parson's daughter. "This is Nicole Sheldon. She's from Doncaster. *I'm* from the posh part of Yorkshire: Harrogate."

"They're all poofs in Harrogate!"

Nicole gave the author of those words a filthy look, before forcing herself to smile at me. "Hello," she said.

I said hello back.

Harry pointed at the man with a full head of thick grey hair that looked like a silver acrylic wig. "The gobshite sitting opposite Nicole is Lester Bloodworm. As you just heard, he's from Liverpool."

I thought Lester's surname most interesting and rather funny, in the same way that a poodle without hair at Crufts is most interesting and rather funny.

"It's rude to point," Lester reminded Harry.

"Ignore him," Harry said to me. "We do."

"Sorry, Jocelyn," Lester said, "but you'll be working with a northern mafia."

"Excuse me, but I'm from the south!" came a Scottish voice from just to the right of Harry and me.

"Yes, well, I suppose that Edinburgh *is* south of the Outer Hebrides," Lester said with a laugh and then a grotesque cackle that had Nicole wincing in terror and grimacing in disgust.

Harry nodded at the Scottish woman, who was sporting a mass of purple hair that was supported with some trepidation by a frayed orange bandana. "This is Jean Fleming."

We exchanged pleasantries with nods of our heads and awkward smiles, before Jean's phone rang and she had to answer it.

Harry pointed at the empty chair opposite Jean. "And that's where—"

Rachel Bannerman breezed into the room and stood by her seat as if she needed permission before sitting down.

"This is Rachel Bannerman." She gave Rachel a look of reproach. "She comes and goes as she pleases."

Rachel smiled sarcastically at Harry. She looked at me with a mixture of surprise and knowingness. She could not have expected me, so I could not account for the knowingness. Rachel did not have much of a cleavage, but she made sure that I saw what she did have by undoing a couple of buttons of her red blouse. I could not account for that gesture either. I tried not to look at the white flesh that Rachel seemed wilfully to have exposed to me. This was our second encounter. Our next—and final—encounter would be decisive.

"When you two have finished gazing into each other's eyes, I will introduce you to Doug," Harry said. "He was bitten by a dog yesterday—a Rottweiler, no less—and he's feeling rather sore, so he won't be coming out from behind the bookcase. Doug, say hello to Jocelyn!"

"Hello, Jocelyn," came a whimper from behind the said bookcase, a huge edifice behind Rachel's desk that served as a partition and cut off Doug from his colleagues.

Doug sounded local, from somewhere in the wilds of Oxfordshire. Of course, I knew more than his colleagues knew about his encounter with the Rottweiler.

"Come this way," Harry bade me.

I followed her to a desk at the back of the room, behind Nicole, who was glaring at Lester as if trying to split his head open with an act of wonton psychokinesis. The desk stood beneath two shelves and some dusty old ledgers that looked like they were about to acquaint themselves with the floor.

Lester cackled again. "What did I tell you all?" he chuckled. "A new man arrives, and it takes Rachel all of ten seconds to show her tits."

"That's longer than you last, Lester," Harry retuned, "so I've heard."

"You should watch what you say, Harry," Lester retorted, meaning his tone to carry a threat.

"And you should learn to take a joke."

"Had Harry meant to sounded worried?" I asked myself. The opportunity to watch these people at work was a godsend, for it promised to offer me clues about the death of Laura Hart. At the very least, it would give me a front-row seat in the study of utter madness. I was enjoying the banter, especially as there was an edge to it.

"As I said earlier, everyone who comes to work here starts here in this room," Harry said. "It gives them a good grounding. So, on Monday—in the new office, of course—you will start taking phone calls and recording jobs on the system. But, while you're waiting to see Ida, please just sit here and watch my staff in action. Hopefully, it won't put you off joining Greetwell."

I nodded at the shelves. "You want me to sit under *those?*"

"That's where the chair is."

"The shelves don't look safe to me."

"They only have to last until Friday."

"By the look of them, they won't last *that* long."

"The *building* won't last that long!" Lester giggled. "Have you seen the cracks in the wall by the staircase?"

"Some of the stairs are more than creaky," Neil put in. "I put my foot through one this morning, and there are holes in several others."

"The building should have been pulled down ages ago," Nicole said.

"It's an accident waiting to happen," Neil added.

"It's a *disaster* waiting to happen." Lester said.

"This time next week, the building will be a pile of rubble," Harry said.

"This time *tomorrow*, you mean," Lester laughed, "with us underneath it all."

"I wouldn't want to be buried under a pile of rubble with you, Lester, dead or alive," Harry said.

"Me dead would suit you, wouldn't it, Harry?"

"Not if I was dead with you."

The continuing banter was fascinating, not to mention suggestive.

"Who normally sits here?" I asked Harry.

"A young lad named Karl," Harry replied, "who seems to have gone AWOL."

"I haven't seen him all week," Lester said.

"Neither have I," said Neil.

"That boy moves in mysterious ways," Harry said. "He'll be back."

"He went to the kitchen to make us all drinks, sometime last week," Rachel interjected, "and we haven't seen him since."

If only they knew the truth, I thought.

Jean slammed down her phone. "God help me!" she exclaimed.

"Difficult call?" Harry asked.

"These people are impossible!" Jean replied as she tipped back her head and adjusted her bandana, her purple hair flowing down her back and over the chair.

"Well, you dealt with it perfectly," Harry crowed. "I hope the others were watching and learning."

"Teacher's pet!"

"No, Lester, just good at her job..."

"Who were you talking to, Jean?" Neil asked.

"Ada Littlemore..."

"What did she want?"

"I never found out. She insisted on speaking to Steve Miles. I told her a hundred times that he's gone."

"He's gone metric!" Lester expressed his mirth at his own witticism with another of his trademark cackles.

"I guess it was another broken boiler," Neil said.

"It will be a long time broken if she won't speak to anyone but Steve Miles," Harry said.

"Isn't Ada Littlemore the old dear who had a run-in with you, Lester?" Neil ventured to ask.

"Who hasn't had a run-in with Lester?" Rachel snapped.

By now, I was sitting under the precarious-looking shelves and enjoying the entertainment enormously.

Rachel winked at me. I felt a strange but genuine sense of kinship with her.

"A 'chippy little Scouser', she called him," Rachel added.

"She was spot on there," Jean said. She reached for her newspaper, *The Guardian*, and turned to the crossword.

"I've been called worse," Lester replied, "and by better people than Ada bloody Littlemore."

"I bet you have," Jean said under her breath.

Harry sighed and told her charges that she was leaving them all to it because she had a meeting to attend, whereupon Lester opined that all Harry ever did was attend meetings, and that her desk was merely ornamental. The desk in question, as Lester had indicated with a pointing finger, lest anyone had been unsure as to its whereabouts, was situated to the side of Doug, in the corner by the door. Harry marched out of the room like a sergeant-major on parade, and the room fell silent for about three seconds.

Lester's phone rang. After Lester had made the introductions with a calm professionalism, there was a hush in the room as he groaned and sighed at the receiver, from which issued volleys of invective. Lester slammed his handset onto his desk.

"This character's priceless!" he exclaimed.

"What's up?" Neil asked.

"It's that idiot Patterson again!"

"What's he done now?"

"He's been bitten by Gwendoline Casper's dog and he wants to sue Greetwell!"

"What for?"

"For allowing tenants to keep dangerous dogs!"

"Your phone's not on hold," Nicole told Lester.

"I don't care!" Lester yelled at the phone.

"Tell him to sue Gwendoline Caspar," Neil continued. "He must know that he can't sue Greetwell for what Gwendoline Caspar's dog has done."

"'Do you want to see the bite marks on my arse?' he asked me!" Lester bellowed at the receiver: "No, I don't want to see the bite marks on your arse!"

"Isn't that the same dog that bit you, Doug?" Neil asked the bookcase.

"I don't want to talk about it," came the voice of rural Oxfordshire from behind the rampart.

"I can't reason with the man!" Lester went on. "I can't get rid of him!" He glared at the handset. "He keeps bloody swearing!"

"Then you're entitled to hang up," Neil said.

"Like Harry keeps telling us, we're not here to be sworn at," Nicole said, "though you swear all the time, Lester, especially at me."

Lester was so wound up that Nicole's jibe all but eluded him. He calmed down enough to permit a moment's reflection. He was delighted to hear another round of expletives coming from the handset. He picked up the phone. "I'm sorry, Mr Patterson," he said in his best supercilious voice, "but I refuse to discuss the matter further whilst you continue to swear at me." He listened. "No, I do not wish to see photographic evidence." The profanities that followed were heard by everyone in the room, for Lester had put his phone on loudspeaker. "I suggest that you call back when you can talk in a civilised manner." Then he had to raise his voice to be heard. "Mr Patterson, this conversation is terminated! Goodbye!"

"He will only call back," Jean said.

Even Lester's groan came with a strong Liverpool accent. "I'm dying for a fag," he said. Overcome by nervous tension, and unable to sit still, he went to the window. "There's Selena Wilcox, soliciting for business again."

I had to restrain myself from going to the window, for I was desperate to see what Selena Wilcox looked like. Lester's observation also had the effect of reminding me that I had to do a job on Stephen Waugh, who might have been conducting some sort of illicit liaison with Selena, hard though that was to believe.

"Congratulations, Lester, on yet another constructive comment." Jean did not raise her head from her crossword as she spoke.

"My sentiments exactly…" Whereas Jean's words had been spoken with an air of nonchalance, almost of indifference, Nicole's were hissed with a coiled malevolence.

Lester groaned again. "I could murder a coffee," he said.

"Don't mind if I do," Neil said.

"Do the honours, would you, then, mate?" Lester said.

Neil sighed in a show of exasperation. "Okay, I'll make some drinks."

Lester stood up. "Will you cover me while I have a fag, Nicole?" He might as well have thrown a lit match onto a sky-high pile of rags soaked in paraffin.

"No, I won't!"

"Why not?"

"Because you're always asking people to cover you when you're on telephone duty!"

"So are you."

"When?"

"When you go to the bog…"

"I need to go to the toilet!"

"And I need a fag!"

"Calm down, will you, guys?" Neil pleaded.

"We're a team, Nicole," Lester went on. "We cover each other. You should pull your weight."

Though Nicole's face had turned from an angry red to an enraged crimson, she seemed determined to maintain her dignity. "*I* should pull *my* weight?" she said, cool as a cucumber in a bucket of ice. "For some ten minutes before you go out to smoke the fag, you sit there rolling it, with your phone switched off. Then you go out and take ten minutes to smoke it."

"Then he takes another ten minutes getting back to his desk."

Nicole was grateful for the support. "Thank you, Rachel," she said.

Lester nodded backwards to indicate Rachel. "Says the woman who comes and goes as she pleases."

"I was ill this morning."

"Nothing that a shrink wouldn't cure."

"Go to hell!"

Nicole was on a roll and would not be stopped. "You spend your time here either rolling a fag or smoking one."

Lester held out his hands. "Do you see me rolling a fag?" He turned aside. "Lend us a fag, would you, Neil? I've run out of tobacco."

Neil sighed, reluctant to be seen to be colluding in Lester's provocation. He took a packet of Benson & Hedges from his shirt pocket. He took a cigarette from the packet and offered it to Lester. "Take it easy, mate," he said. "We all have to work together."

"Cheers, Neil, you're a real team player." Lester put the cigarette behind his right ear. He fumbled in his pockets for his lighter. Then he lifted some bits of paper from his desk and passed them to Neil. "Here are some jobs that I need to book on the system. Give them to Nicole, would you? She can deal with them while we're out. Mine's a black coffee with two sugars." He put his head up and swung his arms as he marched out of the room.

All eyes turned towards the parson's daughter.

Nicole looked both beaten and defiant. "That's it," she said. "I'm leaving."

"You've only been here a month," Jean said.

"Friday will be my last day."

"You have to come to the new office," Jean implored.

"No, I don't."

"Try not to take Lester too seriously," Neil said in a tone that was almost fatherly.

"I cannot work with that man."

"Give it time, Nicole," Neil persisted.

"I've had it with him."

"We can't allow Lester to drive another person out," Neil said.

"If Nicole goes, perhaps Harry will take some action," Rachel suggested.

"Lester's got something on Harry," Jean submitted. "That's why she does nothing."

"Given what I told the police about Lester the other day," Nicole went on, "I'm surprised they haven't arrested him."

"What did you tell him?" Neil asked.

"I told them what I thought of him … and I dropped a few hints, like."

"What kind of hints?" wondered Neil.

"Oh, well, I told them how he likes to use the word 'murder', as in 'I could *murder* a coffee', and how he utters the word with such relish. It makes you wonder, doesn't it? It certainly made the police wonder."

Nicole had a point there. It was a most interesting observation.

Rachel spoke up again and in doing so opened another avenue of exploration. "Me, Donna, Sheryl, and, of course, our dearly departed Laura: we've all filed complaints of sexual harassment against Lester, but Harry did nothing about any one of them. Whatever Lester's got on Harry, it must be something explosive. Why else do you think he can get away with *murder*?"

It was that word again: murder. Rachel was bound to tell me that evening all that I needed to know about the murder of Laura Hart, but she seemed to be dropping hints in advance. Given what I'd come to know about Greetwell Housing Trust, and about my prospective informant, I refused to believe that it was as simple as Rachel was suggesting it was. Such simplicity was impossible where Greetwell and Rachel were concerned.

Ordinarily, I hated being winked at, but in Rachel's case I made an honourable exception.

TWENTY-TWO

The fire-door creaked shut behind me as I looked down the long, dark tunnel that was the principal thoroughfare on the ground floor of The Golden Age. I'd accepted Ida McSweeney's offer of a substantial compensation package. The chief executive had informed me that she was quite happy for me to redirect tenants' calls to the Trust. I told her that I would be changing my number and I'd given her assurances of my own: that I would leave the old number active for long enough for the Trust to inform tenants of the mix-up; and that the old number would cut straight to the answerphone with a message informing tenants of the correct number to call.

The meeting had begun some twenty minutes late, but it had been a productive session with a woman who, contrary to what I'd been hearing, was very much in existence. I was effecting my escape from The Golden Age, at about three o'clock, pondering whether I should pop into the Mother and Baby Unit to see Rosie, when I passed an office in which were standing, rather conspiratorially, a familiar-looking woman and a ginger-haired man wearing trousers and a shirt and a tie that were united in their lime-green hideousness. What had the man been thinking when he dressed himself that morning? For a moment, I felt sick.

"You look lost," the man said to me.

"I'm just leaving," I replied, standing in the doorway, the lemon to the man's lime.

"Are you new here?" the man asked.

"This is Jocelyn Dare," the woman put in, "our new maintenance surveyor."

"Oh, yes, of course, Jocelyn, welcome to the team," the man said excitedly. "When do you start?"

"On Monday," I said, almost believing it myself now.

"As you know, I'm Sheryl Henry, one of Greetwell Housing Trust's best housing officers," the lady announced, mimicking Neil's earlier introduction. Seeing her at close quarters, as I was now, I noticed that her green mohair sweater was a couple of sizes too big for her, and that her skirt displayed a hypnotically elaborate New Age pattern. If she knew who I really was—and there was a chance that she did know—she was hiding it well.

"Sheryl's a housing-services advisor, to be precise," the man said cheekily.

"Ignore this officious pedant," Sheryl said playfully, "and he might go away."

"This officious pedant is Patrick Salamander," the man said, having stepped towards me with an outstretched arm, "the *other* maintenance surveyor."

I shook his hand and said that I was pleased to meet him. The reality was that I could not have got out of that place fast enough.

Patrick told me that he worked in the tower, where it was horrendously hot in summer and hideously cold in winter.

"Patrick's more pleased than anyone that we're moving to a modern office with central-heating and air-conditioning," Sheryl said. "The new office couldn't be more different to this place. Wait till you see it."

"I have joined the company at an opportune time," I said lamely.

"We're all going over there on Friday afternoon," Peter said.

"Just to view it," Sheryl added.

"There'll be a lot of packing to do then." Again, my words were offered in supine manner, uttered for the sake of saying something, anything, that would make of me less of a self-conscious spectator and more of a participant in this theatre of the absurd.

"We'll be packing it in!" With that bizarre ejaculation Patrick punched the air as if he had just scored the winning goal in the last minute of the European Cup final.

Sheryl was as baffled as I was by Patrick's circus-like show of enthusiasm, and she changed tack skilfully by indicating just how thin on the ground they were in the building on that Wednesday afternoon.

"Allow us to introduce the absentees," Patrick said with a theatrical sweep of his hand.

"There sits Donna Tamsin," Sheryl said, pointing at a desk adjoining her own lengthways, "a *housing-services advisor*." She emphasised the job title for Patrick's sake.

Patrick aimed a finger at the desk the length of which juxtaposed Sheryl's and Donna's. "And there sits Matt Prior, a maintenance *inspector*," he said. He spoke that last word as if the rank of inspector was somehow lower than that of surveyor.

I'd worked in the police force for some fifteen years, so I was used to rank and hierarchy, and it seemed that the corporate world had a similar—more subtle, perhaps—attachment to status and authority. Anyway, I was delighted to know that I outranked Matt in the alternative reality to which I had become party.

Sheryl indicated a desk in the corner of the room. "Over there sits Gerard Barnsley, a business manager, though none of us quite knows what business he is supposed to manage."

"Gerard's in Amsterdam," Patrick said.

"Window shopping," Sheryl added with a laugh.

"He's wasting his time," Patrick said.

"Why do you say that?" Sheryl asked, warming to her role as provocateur in this ridiculous comedy double-act.

"Because I've heard that the Dutch sex industry is absolutely flat on its back." Patrick fell into laughter that was borderline parodic, as if mirth were striving for hysteria, reinforcing my impression that I was witnessing some elaborate circus act, an act that had begun the moment I crossed the threshold of The Golden Age. "I like that," he giggled when the fit had passed. "I *do* like that." He chuckled like wee Jimmy Krankie on laughing gas. "I really *do* like that." Then he made a strange noise that was more of a sigh than a laugh, like a balloon being slowly deflated.

The spectacle of these two comedians was such a festival of the bizarre that for a moment I would have given anything to be back upstairs with Lester Bloodworm and his crew.

"It's good to laugh," Sheryl said, "even at Patrick's terrible jokes." She looked ahead, at the desk positioned in another corner of the room, and her colleague joined her in a moment's silence. "We haven't had a laugh here since…"

She stopped herself, or something stopped her, some ghostly presence in the room, I shouldn't have wondered.

"That's where Laura sat?" I knew full well the answer to my question.

There was no reply, only a silence and a stillness that belonged to a graveyard. One of the room's sash windows rattled ominously. We were rescued by Maya's activating the intercom: the hissing and whistling put me in mind of a dust-cart being filled.

"Snow is forecast for this afternoon," the receptionist announced once the din had subsided to a persistent crackling. "So do wrap up warm."

The intercom wailed its displeasure as it was disengaged.

Patrick was nearing the end of a protracted grimace. "God Almighty!" he exclaimed. "I wish that girl would learn to use that bloody thing!"

"What's she talking about, snow?" Sheryl said. "It's thirteen bloody degrees out there!"

To our disbelief, the intercom was soon back in action, and the usual mayhem accompanied this latest shambolic irruption.

"Sorry, people," came Maya's voice. "I got it wrong. I was looking at the weather forecast for Oxford, Mississippi, USA."

Patrick and Sheryl stood there shaking their heads as the sound of a runaway train crashing into a railway terminus rang around them.

Then, incredibly, the intercom crackled and wheezed back into action.

"Sheryl!" came the voice again. "Mr Fawcett-Dawson is back in reception wishing to speak with you!"

Then there was an explosion. Then there was silence.

Though Sheryl's hands covered her face, Patrick and I could hear her muffled groan and the words that were emitted with it.

"There's no privacy in this place, is there? Not even in the bog."

The hospitalised Karl's moment of philosophical inspiration came to my mind, but this was neither the time nor the place to echo it.

"You're not in the bog," Patrick replied.

"Maya doesn't know that, does she?"

Patrick thought about that for a moment, his look of bafflement mirroring my own; but he had the answer, the answer to every problem and to every crisis, five short words that served always to take the despair out of the most desperate of situations.

"I'll put the kettle on."

***

I'd progressed as far as reception when yet another commotion reached my ears. I peered through the little square window of the door giving onto the reception area and beheld Maya and Lenny Fawcett-Dawson going at each other like two belligerents on the Jerry Springer Show. I had no choice but to enter the fray and to attempt to step around it. It was the only way to make my escape complete. I couldn't wait to be back in the real world.

"What do you want now, you fucked-up little weasel?" Maya was yelling at Mr Fawcett-Dawson.

"You can't speak to me like that!" came the blistering retort.

"I just did!"

As I gave Mr Fawcett-Dawson a wide berth, I waved good-bye to Maya.

"You came at a bad time," she said miserably.

"Is there ever a *good* time in this place?" I asked.

Maya shook her head and told me that she felt another tannoy announcement coming on.

With that news ringing in my ears, I was gone.

Outside, I skirted the building, curiously, and I was soon joined by Mr Fawcett-Dawson, who came towards me to see what I was looking at.

"Can you see a tower?" I was talking as much to myself as to him.

"What?"

"One of the maintenance surveyors in that crazy place said that he worked in the tower. But I see no tower. Do you see one?"

Lenny didn't see a tower, any more than I did, and he didn't stick around to interrogate the building, either, for he trotted off towards the Iffley Road like a middle-distance runner trying to break the world record for slowness, dragging his trench coat behind him as he went.

When I heard the rumble of Miss Djemba Djemba's voice again, my first instinct was to follow in the wake of Mr Fawcett-Dawson, but I couldn't, because I'd decided to go and see Rosie, and to do that I had to bypass the woman and the soapbox she'd remounted.

"Those with eyes must see, and those with ears must hear, that this here housing association does the work of Satan, for it perpetrates great evil in the sight of men! But the Lord is not so blind that He cannot see, nor is He so deaf that He cannot hear, and never, ever, will He be so dumb that He cannot speak! He will cast judgement upon this place! He will send it the way of all flesh! He will cast it, and all who work in it, into the burning pit that is hell!"

Again, the audience consisted of me, the desperate-looking Eric, and anybody within earshot, which would have been most people in East Oxford. I was the sole passer-by. I tried not to make eye contact with the lady, though I did exchange worried looks with the hapless Eric.

"This here housing association thinks it can reinvent itself simply by moving to plush new offices on the other side of town! But, let me tell you, the soul of this place is so stained by sin that it could take itself to the very gates of heaven and still carry the whiff of Satan!"

The window of the customer-service centre was open, and through it I heard the voices of members of staff.

"Oh, God!" Lester groaned. "She's off again!"

"I'd rather listen to her than listen to you, Lester," Rachel said.

"I'd rather listen to neither of them," Jean added.

"The Lord will deliver His almighty judgement upon this place and bring it crashing down, like the walls of Jericho!" Miss Djemba Djemba went on.

Lester put his head outside the window. "Belt up, you old hag!" he shouted.

The orator neither saw Lester nor heard him.

"This place will become like so much dust, it will tumble to the ground with one sweep of the Lord's hand! His judgement will fall upon the old! It will pass over to the new! They can run from the Lord's retribution, but they cannot hide!"

I heard Lester's voice again. "Neil, give me that cricket ball, will you?"

"It's not a *real* cricket ball," Neil protested.

"Just give it here!"

"What are you going to do with it?"

"I'm going to knock that singing canary off its perch."

"We have been living in the last days, we have moved between the times—through the time when the Lord's victory was assured, but not complete—and now we have reached the last day, the day when final judgement is delivered, when the wicked are banished to life everlasting in hellfire and damnation!"

Rachel's dulcet tones floated out of the window like the scent of honeysuckle on a summer's day. "She's lost the bloody plot now!"

"I agree!" Jean replied. "She's nuts!"

"Who will flee from the wrath to come? The very foundations of this place are shaking with the Lord's anger as I speak!"

"They're shaking with something," I told Eric across the woman, "but not with the Lord's anger."

Eric shrugged his shoulders despairingly.

Then the imitation cricket ball came flying through the open window.

"The people who work within these walls do the work of the Prince of Darkness!"

The missile knocked the elaborately cushioned hat off the capacious head of Miss Djemba Djemba; the woman rocked on the soapbox and then tumbled to the ground with a thud; she lay on her right side, clutching her back and wailing for the Lord's vengeance.

Several faces appeared at the open window.

"You idiot, Lester!" Rachel cried.

"It wasn't me! It was Neil!"

"That's right, blame me!"

"You threw the ball!"

"You were supposed to catch it!"

"Typical bloody Yorkshire, never could throw straight!"

"Typical bloody Lancashire, never could catch!"

"Where's her hat?" Lester wondered.

"There it is," Neil replied, "on the other side of the road."

"What a ridiculous thing to wear," Lester opined cynically. "You could sit a family of four on that, and still have room for the dog."

"Who's the bloke with her?" Neil asked.

"He's the poor sod who has to give her one twice a week," answered Lester. "It must be like having sex with a bouncy castle."

"Shut up!" Rachel snapped.

Eric was flapping around like a man trying to scatter pigeons.

"Lola! Lola! What in God's name are you doing, woman?"

"Oh, Eric, Eric, look what they've done to me!" Flat on her back now, the woman wailed like a constipated diva. "My back! My poor back!"

"Never mind your back," Eric dared to say, "I reckon the pavement came off a lot worse."

"Help me up, Eric, please!"

Eric held out an arm for Lola to take; in taking it he was pulled down so that he fell on top of her. The couple writhed frantically as man and woman endeavoured to disentangle arms and legs. A passing man, walking his dog, looked on in astonishment, and the dog wasn't entirely unmoved by proceedings either.

"Did anyone see that nature documentary the other night?" Lester enquired. "It showed two hippos in sexual congress. This must be the repeat."

Finally, Eric and Lola were decoupled, and bodies became upright and were straightened.

"Come on, girl," Eric said. "I'm taking you to see a doctor."

"Don't be stupid, man! My back's perfectly all right!"

"It's not your back I'm worried about."

Eric had been propping up Lola, he'd been leading her away from The Golden Age, until Lola, like the woman possessed that she was, began to charge towards the building, taking the helpless Eric with her.

"They are going to pay!" the woman intoned. "They are going to pay!"

"Oh, God, she's coming in!" Lester exclaimed. "Hey, Jocelyn, throw me the ball back, will you?"

Having retrieved the ball, I examined it. It was an imitation cricket ball commemorating the previous summer's Ashes series. I launched it upwards and Lester caught it like a competent slip fielder. Then the window was slammed shut.

It was high time that I paid Rosie a visit at the Mother and Baby Unit. She was bound to give me a hard time. But at least she didn't work in a circus.

TWENTY-THREE

Greetwell Housing Trust's Mother and Baby Unit consisted of an office, wherein worked Rosie and her colleague Grace Helm, and flatlets for young single mothers and their babies. The building, nothing like the precarious wreck that was The Golden Age, was modern and well-equipped. I'd been there before, one lunchtime, when Rosie and I were friends, and I'd been impressed—though not surprised—by Rosie's efficiency in doing a difficult job in which not only did the demands of the girls have to be met but also the problems created by the feckless fathers taken on. Then there was the near-permanent absence of her colleague, the aforesaid Grace, poetess, socialite and lover of wine, fine or otherwise.

By the video-entry panel, I pressed the button for the office and waited to be told to get lost.

"Hello…"

"It's Daniel."

"What do *you* want?"

"I just dropped by for a chat."

"I'm busy."

"And I'm busy looking after your daughter, but I still find time to come and talk with you."

"Looking after her? Is that what you call it? Getting her involved in your capers, and … and … whatever else you two get up to together."

I groaned. "Don't start that again, Rosie. It's not fair, and I resent it."

Rosie was silent for so long that I thought she'd cut me off.

"Rosie?"

"What?"

"It's raining. I'm getting wet."

"I'll give you five minutes."

The door having buzzed and clicked, I pushed it open. The door clicked shut behind me. Ahead of me was a room, full of toys, inside which played three teenaged girls and their offspring. Next to the playroom was a kitchen displaying the wreckage of several lunches. To my left coiled a stairway that would take me to a fraught reunion with a woman who might have become my partner in life if only she hadn't considered me an alcoholic, a keeper of bad company, and a man too scarred by past events to be able to hold down a meaningful relationship. Apart from that little catalogue of inadequacies, she regarded me as the perfect consort for her impeccable self. With heavy footsteps, I climbed the stairs and found Rosie's door open and her sitting at her desk looking like she was in no mood for what she'd always called my "frivolities". That just made me more determined to be frivolous.

Rosie looked around the room and seemed somehow to be inviting me to join her in the impromptu panorama.

"What am I supposed to be looking at?" I said.

"Oh, how about the sink with the dripping tap? Or the cupboard doors hanging by threads? Or the desk covered with paperwork that never gets done? Or the computer screen that's on the blink? Or the door behind me, behind which you will find a cupboard-sized bathroom with a broken toilet and a basin with a leaking tap?"

I did say that the place was well-equipped. The trouble was that the equipment seemed not to work.

The light above Rosie's head clinked into darkness.

"And a lightbulb that needs changing," I said.

"This place has enough bloody damages and breakages without you adding to them."

"I've just been to The Golden Age," I announced. "It's a laugh a minute over there."

"Don't talk to me about The Golden Age. I don't step foot in the place unless I have to. I don't even phone anyone over there unless it's a matter of life or death. I don't know who are the more screwed up, the staff or the tenants."

"That's a decision that would definitely have to go to a stewards' enquiry," I replied.

Rosie shot me with a look of scornful derision. "You always did have a warped sense of humour, Daniel," she said. "That must be why you took up with me."

Rosie was trying to steer the conversation onto the subject of our separation, when I could have argued, with some justification, that we'd never got together in the first place. How could we ever have hoped to discuss a relationship that was impossible to define? For a time, we had been more than friends, but less than lovers, and, arguably, not even on the spectrum somewhere between the two, but somewhere a safe distance from both, a place too nebulous to be described by recourse to line and length, or by rhyme or anything approaching reason.

"Working here was bad enough before we had a murderer in our midst."

That was much more my type of subject for conversation.

"You think that someone from Greetwell killed Laura Hart?"

"I don't doubt it. The police are getting nowhere because the people here are covering for someone, or they are covering for themselves. Perhaps we should put *you* on the case."

As I was about to sidestep Rosie's last suggestion with some wisecrack or other, she asked me why I'd been to The Golden Age, to which I replied that there had been a mix-up involving mine and Greetwell's telephone numbers that needed to be sorted out.

Rosie narrowed her eyes and looked pained for a moment, as if she were trying to make sense of my words, and failing, because she lacked the mental energy even to begin to ponder them.

"I'm too tired," she said with a dismissive wave of her hand at both me and my words.

"You look cold."

"That's because this place is a bloody fridge, and that's because those two idiots from the Rapid Reaction Team, Ivor Bagshot and Hugh Windlesham, spent last Saturday here installing a smoke-detector when they should have been fitting a new heater." Rosie shook her head in despair. "They haven't a brain cell between them. I mean, why do we need a smoke-detector in here?"

Perhaps smoke had begun to issue from Rosie, for the device in question began to bleep hysterically. We both looked at it, she on the verge of apoplexy and I in admiration of its impeccably timed audacity.

Rosie shouted something but I couldn't hear what she was saying. She opened one of the drawers under the sink and pulled out a mallet. She placed her chair under the smoke-detector, stood on it, then, with the mallet, dealt the screaming device a volley of heavy blows. The covering panel having fallen to the floor in pieces, several times she struck the censor and the wires until fizzing and sparkling usurped the bleeping. In a state of frenzy now, she continued to thresh the device until it blew up in her face, causing her to tumble off the chair with a scream.

"Well," I said, looking down at the prostrate Rosie, "you have smoke now."

The remaining light and the computer went off.

Rosie regarded her blank screen in horror. "That's marvellous!" she moaned. "I hadn't saved that file! That's an hour's work down the drain!"

"Up in smoke, don't you mean?"

That comment went down like a lead balloon weighed down by a hundredweight of gold bullion.

Rosie took my outstretched hand and hauled herself to her feet. "It's that force field of yours again," she said. "I make that nine lightbulbs, one microwave oven, and one computer at my place, and now two lightbulbs, a computer, and a smoke-detector here."

"I suppose that your savage assault with the mallet had nothing to do with it."

"*You* set the smoke-detector off."

"How?"

"Just by being here."

At that moment, a bewildered-looking woman in her sixties entered the room; she wore a black mackintosh and matching boots, and she was crowned by a scarlet beret that sat aslant a mass of tangled hair. She was Grace Helm, Rosie's sidekick—the Cagney to Rosie's Lacey, or was it the other way around?—the woman who focussed on the pastoral side of the duo's work whilst Rosie dealt with the paperwork; the woman who, inbetween counselling and ministering to the vulnerable girls at the Mother and Baby Unit, wrote poems and walked her dog, often at the same time.

"Is something wrong?"

"No, Grace, everything's fine." Rosie's characteristic sarcasm put even mine to shame.

"Oh, hello, Daniel…"

"Grace…"

"As usual, whenever Daniel's around me, everything goes tits up."

"Oh, I see."

"Where have you been, Grace? You've been gone two hours."

"I was walking Lulu, over at South Park, as usual."

"Walking your bloody dog won't get all this paperwork done, will it?"

"Since when have I done paperwork?"

"Since I became snowed under!"

Rosie was sweating now, and her shoulder-length black hair had become even more stringy than usual. Her lack of vanity was one of her more endearing traits, she was natural-looking, in a dishevelled kind of way, but somehow immaculate for all that. She ran fingers through her hair, and then touched her denim-clad thighs with her palms, as if to signal the beginning of some haka-type war dance. Fearful, I took a step back, but all that Rosie did in anger was nod at the lead in her colleague's hand and ask if something might not be missing.

Grace lifted the lead so that it dangled before her disbelieving eyes.

"Oh, God," she said forlornly. "Where's the bloody dog?"

I was about to take my leave, but Rosie beat me to it.

"That's it!" she barked. "I'm going out for a fag!"

"You don't smoke!" I called at her back.

"I do now!"

Grace went after Rosie, leaving me standing there, in an abandoned room with a still-fizzing smoke-detector.

Just before I left, I noticed the list of tenants and their respective room numbers. It was pinned to the wall. Selena Wilcox lived in room number thirteen, a number deemed to occasion adverse fortune for anyone who became acquainted with it. I was reluctant to assume that the girl was the victim of perpetual bad luck. I wanted to make my own judgement, having seen her, and my mind rapidly formulated a pretext for paying her a visit on my way out.

It was only when I was leaving Rosie's little control centre that I noticed the sign on the outside of the door. It was Greetwell Housing Trust all over. "Unauthorised Personnel Only," it read.

Well, in Rosie's eyes at least, I was certainly one of those.

***

Room number thirteen was through one set of double-doors, and then another, on the same floor as Rosie's office. I heard movement inside the room—or flatlet, as it turned out to be—so I knew that Selena and child were at home. I knocked on the door.

"Hang on a minute!"

The girl had been invested with a level of mystique that I found disconcerting, and hearing her voice did nothing to make her sound more real, more corporeal, more human. I found myself barely able to contain my curiosity as to what she looked like, how much make-up she put on, what kind of clothes she wore, and how she would react when she opened the door to a stranger.

"Oh, hello," she said in greeting, as if she knew me or recognised me from somewhere.

"Hello, Selena," I said in a familiar tone that was designed to reassure her that I was not a policeman or some other emissary from the land of officialdom. "My name's Jocelyn Dare. I'm Greetwell Housing Trust's new maintenance surveyor."

"Okay!" The girl's tone was jolly and trustful. She was warm and friendly, not in the least suspicious, and she held open the door as if she were quite happy to let me in.

"I've been asked to have a quick look at the window frames in all the rooms at the Mother and Baby Unit," I went on. "It won't take a minute."

"Come in," the girl said, the warmth of her welcome banishing the memory of Rosie's earlier frostiness.

I entered and closed the door behind me. The girl wore orange leggings and a purple sweatshirt, and her long dark hair cascaded down her back like waters of ebony in freefall. She was strikingly pretty, with narrow eyes, full lips, and perfect white teeth. The room was full of the accoutrements of girlhood—and motherhood—though tidy, exceptionally tidy, as if so many belongings had to be arranged with care and more than a modicum of order to be manageable in so confined a space. The main room was twice the size of the adjoining bedroom, and the kitchenette was tucked away in the corner by one of the windows that I hadn't gone to inspect.

"Would you like a cup of tea?"

Although I could have devoured a cup of tea with indecent haste, I declined for the sake of sustaining my deception.

"I'm trying to dress my daughter," Selena said. "She's just had a feed, and a change of nappy, and now we have to go out."

The baby lay on the bed, clad only in a nappy, and it wriggled and fidgeted like a cat lying on its back and having its tummy tickled.

"What's her name?"

"Celia…"

"That's a lovely name."

"*I* chose it."

"Does the father like the name?"

"Don't talk to me about the father."

My question came back not to haunt me but to torment me. Could Rick Mallett really have been the father?

The girl was finding dressing the child akin to putting a wetsuit on an epileptic having a seizure: just as she was about to put the chubby little fist into the sleeve of the baby suit, the arm would jerk away, it would thresh all ways except the way it was meant to thresh; she succeeded in getting the tights on only after a desperate struggle with flailing legs; and the little right shoe was on the point of enclosing the little right foot when the little right foot kicked out, and continued to kick out, until it was restrained by the firm hand of parental ardour. The coat went on the child as if it were a straitjacket stifling a deranged puppet, and the little woollen hat might as well have been a crown of thorns. The gloves, at least, met with little resistance.

"I tell you what, young lady," the not-much-older lady had sung at the child in the heat of battle. "I'll put you in the buggy naked, shall I?"

The child had spluttered and spat out warm milk.

"You'd like that, wouldn't you?" the girl had cooed like a nesting hen.

Now the child looked as if it were about to laugh, then a screaming tantrum seemed likely, so the girl was relieved—and so was I—when only a cherubic smile shot back at her from the semi-darkness of the hooded pushchair. The energy expended in battle had left the child dazed and listless. She needed to collect herself before the next act of combat, before the next test of her mother's patience. When she beheld more warm milk seeping from the child's mouth, then spewing out, the girl seemed to consider throwing a screaming tantrum of her own, but she desisted, mindful that an outburst would only trigger renewed restlessness in the child. To Selena's disgust, the milk refused to be absorbed by the fabric of the coat; instead, like drifts of virgin snow, it gathered resolve and substance, it hardened, promising expansion before it condescended to be assimilated by the material. The girl considered expunging the truculent outpouring with a single sweep of an already-sodden towel, but she realised soon enough how futile that would have been, for the erased substance would only have been replaced by more of the same.

"I have to do this several times every day," the girl said, cheerfully, almost as if she enjoyed wrestling with a stubbornly uncooperative infant.

"You're doing a fine job," I said.

"Do you have children?"

"No…"

"Do you want children?"

"No…"

"You don't say much, do you?"

"You'd be surprised…"

"I reckon you'd be a good dad."

"You can make that startling deduction after five minutes?" I asked with a smile.

"Yes…"

Selena was now ready to leave, so I submitted the window frames to a cursory examination, said they were fine, and made ready to leave myself. As I was leaving, the girl asked me if I wouldn't mind walking with her to Café Arabica, on the Cowley Road, where she was due to meet someone for a coffee and a chat.

"You sound like you need protection," I said after I'd agreed to go with her and we were in the lift descending to the ground floor.

"It's the father," answered Selena. "He didn't want to know when Celia was born, so I had 'father unknown' put on the birth certificate, but now he *does* want to know—or says he does—and he harasses me all the time, waiting outside the MBU and following me around."

"You think he's outside now, waiting for you?"

"He could be."

"You don't want him in your life?"

"He's a drug-dealing, pot-smoking waste of space. He's trying to worm his way back into my life because his girlfriend dumped him, but he would be off again as soon as he took up with someone else."

"How old is he?"

"Nineteen … nearly twenty …"

"If the authorities knew he was the father, he would be prosecuted."

"That's another reason why I don't want him back. I had to say that the father could have been any Tom, Dick or Harry. I had to pretend to be a slag to protect him."

"It sounds like he doesn't deserve your protection."

"He doesn't. He got me in trouble with the law when he put his cannabis plants in my flat, though in the end *he* was the one who got nicked."

"Did he go to jail?"

"They let him off with a caution! Pathetic!"

"Why did you store his cannabis plants?"

"He paid me to look after them for a few days, when I was in temporary crisis accommodation, after I left his place and before I came to the MBU. I needed the cash. The police were watching his place. A social worker came to the flat, saw the plants, and reported me to the police. Bloody social workers! So, I had to grass Jez up. I wasn't going to take the blame. He hasn't let me forget it. He says if I take him back, he'll change, go straight, and look after me and Celia. Like I'm going to believe that load of old flannel. I used to be desperate, but I was never stupid."

"Who else knows that Jez is the father?"

"Only me and Jez know."

"If he owned up to being the father, he would be done for."

"Since he found out I was pregnant, he's been saying that I was sleeping around, so that anyone could be the father, but he knows that's not true."

"Yet now he wants to take care of you and the baby, as the *actual* father, but not the *official* father?"

"That's what he says. But it's bullshit."

We were out on the street now. There was no sign of Jez. There were other callow-looking youths hanging around, but Jez was not among them, so Selena told me. I judged that I had gained enough of her trust to be able to touch on the subject that had become close to my heart. For me, it was not just a matter of compassion for the man in question, it was a matter of justice.

"I've been working at Greetwell for only a few days, but I've been hearing whispers about Rick Mallett, that he might be the father of your child."

When Selena stopped suddenly in her tracks, I feared that I'd offended her, that I'd touched a nerve, that I'd provoked her, and so broken into pieces our fragile understanding, but Selena was proving herself to be a sixteen-year-old every bit as precocious—not to mention, perspicacious—as her peer, one Kendal Waterhouse.

"You *know* Rick?"

"He and I are acquainted."

"You know, Jocelyn, I really wish Rick *was* the father," the girl said gravely, looking mournfully into the distance as she spoke. "He lost his little girl, Melissa, and he's such a good man, so I really wish that I could share Celia with him."

"You do realise how wrong that sounds, don't you, Selena?"

"Yes," the girl sighed. "It's a proper mess."

"Did something happen between you and Rick?"

"We kissed once, one afternoon after the summer school had closed for the day, everyone had gone home, except for me and Rick, and we were putting tables and chairs away."

"What kind of kiss?"

"The kind of kiss that often leads to something else…"

"So, where do these rumours come from, about Rick being the father?"

"Jez has been putting the word about that Rick could be the father."

"Why?"

"Because he wants to embarrass me…"

"Such rumours threaten to do more than embarrass Rick."

"I know. I would happily tell his wife that the rumours aren't true. But that would probably make things worse."

"I'm told that his wife knows nothing about the rumours."

"She must be deaf then."

We carried on walking. A sense of fellowship with the girl stole over me. Like Kendal, she was spirited and blessed with inner strength. I wondered if the two girls would get on. Selena was damaged and yet somehow bolstered by the harm that had been done her; she carried both her innocence and her experience with an effortless facility of mind and body; and, though lost, she was moving towards a destiny that gave her life purpose and meaning. I worried that, through my investigation, I was exploiting her in some way, and I regretted that I had to lie to her in order to get to the truth. I hoped that she would understand, if and when my deception came to light. I wanted her to hold nothing against me.

"Where are your parents, Selena?"

"My dad went AWOL before I was born, and, shortly after I was born, my mother gave me up for adoption. My adoptive parents are nice people, but I gave them nothing but trouble. When I got pregnant, I left them, to save them the embarrassment, the shame, whatever you want to call it. Jez was living with two mates in some dive in Blackbird Leys. When I moved in, he didn't know I was pregnant. When he found out, he kicked me out. That's how I ended up at the Mother and Baby Unit."

"Have you ever met your real mother?"

"No …"

"Do you know who she is?"

"Her name is Amelia. She lives in Melbourne, Australia, now."

"How do you know that?"

"My dad told me."

"Your *real* dad?"

"Yes, I'm going to meet him now."

I thanked God, if not for matching me with *His* hour then certainly for matching me with *this* hour.

"How did you find out about him?"

"It's a long story."

"You can tell me another time."

Selena nodded. "You can meet him now," she said with a blissful calmness, as if nothing in life could ever perturb her. "You can have coffee with us, if you like."

"No, thanks, I'd like to, but I really need to get back to checking those windows."

When we arrived at the café, Selena led me to a table at which sat the mortified-looking figure of somebody I knew all too well. The girl picked up on our mutual recognition, and for a moment, nonplussed, looked at us both with eyes that demanded answers.

"Hello, Daniel," said Detective Inspector Stephen Waugh.

Selena was more than nonplussed now. "His name's Jocelyn," she said.

"I *know*, Daniel," the policeman said, his tone combining defiance and sheepishness, an uneasy alliance that had him squirming in his seat like a captured eel wriggling in a bucket. His eyes were fixed on me.

"You know *what*?" I asked in reply.

"You *know* what."

I shook my head, as if shaking it would have discharged some of the fuzziness that had come upon it.

"I haven't been this confused since I attended the wedding of my friends Will Hoskins and Jill Haskins," I said.

Stephen Waugh regarded me sagaciously, as if he knew that I knew that he knew, or was it as if I knew that he knew that I knew?

"Suffice it to say that you need do nothing," he said at last. "*I* shall tell my wife."

TWENTY-FOUR

There were more than two hours to go before my rendezvous with Rachel when I looked up and down a wet Cowley Road and wondered which way to turn. I thought about turning right and walking the hundred yards or so to the Zodiac Club, but I had no need to do that since I knew the programme there for the next year and I had already bought my ticket for the forthcoming Paul Weller gig. I looked left, down towards The Plain, and considered walking into the city centre and browsing the bookshops, but decided that I would only be lured into one of my favourite watering holes and emerge into the darkness of evening a less sober version of my usual sensible self. There was only one course of action open to me, then, and that was to have a couple of pints in the Hobgoblin and wait for the seconds to tick slowly by until my furtive and portentous meeting with the smouldering Rachel. I was becoming excited just thinking about what Rachel might reveal, in terms of information that would gift me the answer to the question of who killed Laura Hart. I needed a drink to calm me. As I made to enter the Hobgoblin, I reflected that the problem with Oxford was that there were pubs every-where, and that, if I went to one part of the city to put myself out of temptation's way, that part was bound to present me with temptations of its own. There was simply no escape from temptation, and, where pubs and real ale were concerned, I simply could not resist temptation, especially in Oxford.

But first I had to call Kendal for an update.

The first thing she told me was that I had two prospective new cases, that one of them sounded most intriguing, and that she would furnish me with the details upon my return to Summertown. Then I asked her how Dominic was, and she said that he was fine, and that she had cooked him some breakfast and made him some tea. I told her that in a few hours' time the boy would be in the clear, exonerated, off the hook. Kendal asked me if I were heading straight back to the office, so I reminded her about my meeting with Rachel and said that I would likely be late home. I was surprised when she asked me if I wanted her to spend another night with Dominic, to which I replied that, yes, that would be hugely helpful, to which she replied that the living-room floor was bloody uncomfortable, but that, yes, she would do as I wished, and that, consequently, I owed her big time. I told her that I'd got the money from Ida McSweeney and Greetwell Housing Trust.

"How much?"

"Enough to take you clothes shopping on Saturday…"

"I can't wait!"

"Neither can I. It will mean that this surreal nightmare will be over."

"I made all the changes on the telephone lines. It's all set up."

"You're a genius, sweetheart."

"It wasn't difficult. We should have done it sooner."

"I know, but we were being good citizens, looking after the needy and the vulnerable."

"Come off it, Daniel, you were just enjoying the freak show. It goes with your warped sense of humour."

"That's exactly what your mum told me just now."

"You saw Mum?"

"I went to her office after I'd seen Ida. I have to keep her onside, Kendal, for all our sakes."

"How was she?"

"The same as usual: about as friendly as a rattlesnake, and more highly strung than a Jimi Hendrix guitar."

"And how was Karl?"

"He's as spaced-out as ever, and he's trying it on with all the nurses. He'll be in hospital for another week or so, I should think."

"Are you standing on the edge of the M25? Whenever you call me, it's hard to hear you for traffic noise."

"I'm standing outside the Hobgoblin, since you ask."

"And about to go in, I suppose?"

"Well, I do have a couple of hours to kill before I meet Rachel Bannerman."

"Be careful with that woman, won't you?"

"Yes, Mum!"

"She's trouble."

"As I keep saying, trouble is my business."

"Who do you think you are? Philip Marlowe?"

"Well, *he* said it!"

"I'll see you tomorrow then."

"Okay, but one last thing before I go, Kendal…"

"What?"

"Please would you check my tax return?"

"Where is it?"

"It's in an Excel spreadsheet. The file is called 'Tax Return 2004/05'. It has to be submitted to HMRC by the end of the month."

"What am I supposed to be checking?"

"Just check the figures. I made them all up. But they need to *add* up."

"You used to be a policeman, Daniel, but you break all the rules."

"That's why I'm not a policeman anymore."

***

The Hobgoblin beckoned invitingly when my phone rang. I looked at the screen and beheld a new number.

"Hello, Daniel…"

I recognised the voice. "Hello, Rick…"

"Matt gave me your number. Listen, Daniel, can we meet?"

"If you like. Where and when?"

"Friday morning, at eleven, at Botley Cemetery?"

"Okay, but why there?"

"It's where Melissa is buried. I visit her grave every Friday morning."

"Why do you want to meet me, Rick?"

"There's something I want to talk to you about."

"Is it about Selena Wilcox?"

"Yes, how did you know?"

"I'll tell you on Friday."

"I need you to do me a favour."

"Okay, what is it?"

"Tomorrow, at about eleven, please would you go to the big Tesco, in Cowley, to see my wife, Caitlin?"

"I don't know what she looks like."

"She wears a name badge. She walks around the store, stacking shelves. She sometimes helps in the bakery."

"What do you want me to say to her?"

"Just tell her that I'm innocent. There are rumours circulating about me, disgusting rumours, and it's only a matter of time before Caitlin hears them."

"If you're referring to the rumours about you and Selena and her child, I know about them, and I know you're innocent."

"Oh, my God, how do you know all that?"

"Again, I'll tell you on Friday. But I can tell you now, Rick, you have nothing to worry about."

I could have sworn that, all at once, I heard a sigh of relief, a cry of release, and the heaving snivelling of tears.

"Thank you, Daniel, but you will go and see Caitlin, anyway?"

"Yes, of course, but why *me*?"

"Because you're a good man, and your goodness shines through, and you believe me, and you believe *in* me, when not even Matt, one of my best friends, believes me or *in* me."

I'm a good man, I reflected, who fiddles his tax returns and who tells lies for a living.

"I never doubted you, Rick."

"That means a lot to me."

Little did I know then that, by the time I kept my appointment with Rick, I would have much more to tell him than either he or I could have imagined.

***

The Hobgoblin missed out on more of my custom that day owing to Matt's sudden appearance kerbside. He urged me to hop in. We were soon stuck in yet another traffic-jam, so we had plenty of time to catch up on the day's events.

"I've been out with Donna Tamsin," my friend began.

"How nice for you."

"We went out to the Littleworth estate to see Adrian 'Pecker' Poole. He's been bending our ears for months about this, that and the other, making out that his bloody house is falling down."

"Why do you call him 'Pecker'?"

"Because he's said to have tackle the size of a Grand National winner swinging between his legs. And, by 'Grand National winner', I don't mean the jockey."

"Yes, all right, I get the picture."

"Anyway, in spite of his nag-like characteristics, Pecker is recognisably of humanoid provenance, though, by God, he's a bloody wreck of a human being. Thin. Gaunt. Emaciated. He looks like Iggy Pop on hunger strike. And there's bugger all wrong with his house. Apart from the fact that *he* lives in it!"

"How is Ms Tamsin, anyway?"

"I tell you what, my friend, she's on to us. She kept dropping hints. You'd better get some joy with Rachel tonight. Remember, whatever it takes."

"It won't come to that. You underestimate the woman. And you certainly underestimate me."

"Don't tell me you're not tempted. When did you last get your leg over?"

"There's more to life than sex."

"Only people who don't get any say that." Matt sniffed the air for the scent of alcohol. "Are you Brahms and Liszt?"

"Far from it, I'm stone-cold sober and right on top of my game."

"Well, stay that way because you have a tough assignment starting at six."

"Who killed Laura Hart? That will not be the first mystery that I've solved today."

"Really? Do tell."

"Mystery number one: why is the office building of Greetwell Housing Trust called The Golden Age? Solved. Mystery number two: who got Selena Wilcox up the duff? Solved. Mystery number three: who is the father of Selena Wilcox's child? Solved. And I got the spondoolies from your esteemed leader, Ida McSweeney."

"How did you manage to solve all these mysteries?"

"I'll tell you when we get there. Where are we going, by the way?"

"To the Victoria Arms. I'd arranged to meet someone there, but she blew me out."

"You'd arranged to meet a woman in a pub at four o'clock on a Wednesday afternoon? She must be married. Anyone I know?"

"Nobody you know. Much too classy for you, my friend. Anyway, I thought I'd still go to the Victoria Arms. Get some country air in my lungs."

"Old Marston is hardly the countryside. And it's January. And it's dark. What are we going to do? Sit on the terrace and admire the view across the meadows?"

"The view from the snug will be quite good enough for me. That's if we ever get there. What's the hold-up now?"

"It's rush hour."

"It's four o'clock. Is that really when people knock off for the day? Too many part-timers. No wonder we're way behind the Japanese."

"*You're* knocking off at four!"

"For me, finishing work early is an occasional treat, not a custom."

"Your working day seems to consist of one long lunch hour, Matt."

"Says the man who spends most of his working day in the boozer …"

"Boozers are where I get much of my information."

"Well, nice work if you can get it."

"There's nothing to stop you becoming a private detective and frequenting dens of iniquity for a living."

"True, but this city is nowhere near big enough for the both of us; and I would hate to muscle in on your territory and put you out of business."

"Fat chance, sunshine!"

***

No sooner had we entered the Victoria Arms—a riverside public house that is enticing in summer and cosy in winter—than Matt clocked the woman who had spurned his charms sitting in a corner with a man who looked like a nightclub bouncer.

"I don't believe it!" he said. "The barefaced cheek of the woman! She's only gone and come to the same place at the same time with a different bloke!"

"We live and learn, Matt."

"Don't they look cosy? Tell me, what's he got that I haven't got?"

"By the look of him, I would say a certain handiness with his fists, so I wouldn't venture over there, if I were you."

"She's looking over at us." Matt waved at her cheekily, a gesture that did not go down well with her companion. "Some people have no class and no taste. Get them in, will you, while I go and splash my boots."

***

Since I was still in a reflective mood, a carryover from lunchtime, I related the day's events to Matt and then embarked on a dreamlike inventory of the enemies and waifs and strays—and now ghosts—that I'd collected in Oxford alone, leaving aside those that life and work had given me elsewhere, especially in London. I began with my newfound enemies: Sabrina Connor; her taxi-driver boyfriend, Jimmy, who was no Robert De Niro; Dane Goldman, also known as the Great Dane; Donna Tamsin, and possibly several other of her colleagues; and now there was Greg Tinnion, and possibly Detective Inspector Stephen Waugh too. Rosie was perilously close to entering enemy territory. If I acquired any more enemies, I told Matt, I would soon be too dangerous a person to know. He replied that I was that already. Then I described my genius for picking up society's misfits. I mentioned my lowlife snouts scattered around the city. Well, of course, I'd cultivated them deliberately, as I'd done as a detective in London, because such folk saw and heard things that regular citizens were not even aware of. But others I had not nurtured. They had simply appeared. In addition to the people who'd preoccupied me over my lunchtime pint, there was Dominic

Kane, Karl Jaspers, Selena Wilcox and Rick Mallett. Rick's wife, Caitlin, might yet join the club, I said to Matt, as might Belinda Waugh if she reacted badly to what her husband had to tell her, and there was every chance that she would so react. Rachel Bannerman was a sure candidate for the waif-and-stray club: a potential mine of information, and a possible mine of another sort, the sort that, when you stepped on it, blew you up and scattered you over a wide area. Time would tell with her. Though I trusted her, I knew that I would have to handle her with care if I were to extract the information that I wanted from her, and without any disagreeable fallout. The ghost, of course, was Laura Hart. She was not going to stop haunting me anytime soon.

Matt was only half-listening. I suspected that he was too bowled-over by my skill—or luck, as he called it—in solving several mysteries in a single day fully to absorb my words. He looked like a man lost in thought. I say "looked like" because the idea of Matt thinking, never mind being lost in the act of cogitation, was a mite fanciful.

We downed two pints each and, on the way back to The Golden Age, Matt played Paul Weller's *Illumination* album, which had been released in October of the previous year. I reminded him of the review of the album that I'd written for a music magazine, in which I'd claimed that in the record there were intimations of Nico, Lou Reed, The Doors, Elvis Costello, Tom Wait, and even Eastern Mysticism, and that, as such, *Illumination* represented Weller's most eclectic solo album to date. Matt gave me his sceptical look, rolled his eyes, and told me that I read too much, thought too much, and spoke too much. It made a pleasant change from being told that I drank too much.

Matt dropped me off outside The Golden Age a few minutes before six. He wished me luck with Rachel and told me that he wanted a full and frank account first thing the following morning. I felt like a child with his mother just before his first day at school as a four-year-old.

I got out of the car and made a dash for shelter from the pouring rain.

TWENTY-FIVE

In a dark corner of the bicycle shed opposite the back door of The Golden Age I hid and waited for Rachel. The rain bouncing off the tin roof above my head sounded like the playing of a steel drum in a Calypso quartet. As I lingered in the shadow, like a snake awaiting its prey, I hoped that I would not be spotted by any Greetwell Housing Trust employee who might recognise me. I had to wait no more than three minutes for the first person to emerge from the building, and, luckily, that person was Rachel. The rain was no longer torrential, but it remained heavy, as evidenced by the patterns given by the swirl and the spray against the backdrop of the light cast by the headlamps of passing cars. Rachel hoisted over our heads the kind of womanly umbrella that would not have looked out of place embellishing a pina colada. She took me by the arm and squeezed herself against me so as to be fully under the umbrella's protection. Her squeeze was tight as a leech against my skin. My long black coat and Rachel's cream-coloured raincoat both flapped in the wind. Her red tights were getting wet. I was already wet enough to find the rain oppressive, though normally I experienced rain as therapy, something that soothed me and lifted my spirit.

"Where are you taking me?"

"Home…"

"Are you cooking dinner for two?"

"Not exactly…"

We'd not spoken for a while when Rachel asked me whether we were going to walk all the way back to her place in silence. I told her that we were not walking anywhere in that weather. Outside the Hobgoblin, then, I hailed a taxi. Rachel lowered her head and climbed into the car. I followed and took a seat on Rachel's left. I watched as Rachel shook rain from her umbrella. The hem of her skirt rose five or six inches up her thighs as she made herself comfortable, and she decided not to push it back down to her knees when she noticed my eyes giving her legs a discreet, but searching, examination.

"Burgundy Crescent, please," Rachel told the driver.

I looked over my shoulder at The Aquarium as the cab moved away towards Cowley. My head had turned almost a half-circle by the time the place was out of sight.

"Is it following us?" Rachel asked.

"Is what following us?"

"Whatever it is that you're looking at…"

"It was, but I think we've given it the slip."

"You had me worried."

Rachel was acting weirdly. She seemed to be in a kind of trance, and I wondered if she might not be under the influence of something illicit. Her condition was of little consequence to me, other than how it related to her ability to give me the information that I wanted and needed.

"Do you know…" I began.

Rachel looked straight ahead and remained silent.

Then I began a different question. "Have you ever…"

I was met with the same response.

Through the steamed-up window and the rain, I strained to see the street signs. I was able to identify Divinity and Southfield Roads without the aid of signs because I knew people who lived in those avenues of respectability. The likes of Belvedere and Cumberland Roads, however, though their names were announced quite openly, the signs being illuminated by lamps that seemed to have been placed specifically for the purpose, I knew only by reputation. I looked for the ladies of the night, some of them mere girls, that I knew patrolled that stretch of the Cowley Road. I saw none. Perhaps the night, unlike some of their clients, was too young for them.

We two passengers absorbed the sights and sounds of the evening, the loudest sounds coming from the sirens of invisible police cars. I noticed a man turning left into Marsh Road. He was wearing rags and his beard and hair were long and straggly.

"That man has no shoes on his feet," I said.

"We call him Creeping Jesus," the driver replied.

I wondered who he meant by "we".

"It's a shame," the driver went on. "He's a clever man, or he used to be. He was a professor of something or other, you know, at the university. He's got two kids as well. Now he's homeless and shuffles up and down the Cowley Road all day, and in all weathers, wearing nothing but rags."

"What happened to him?"

"God knows, though I bet a woman was behind it."

I looked at Rachel to see if the driver's comment had produced a reaction, but she remained impassive, her gaze fixed on the darkness in the distance and her mind's eye seemingly fastened on the darkness within.

"As David Essex once sang, it's just another winter's tale," the driver added. "They're all too common nowadays, I'm afraid."

The windscreen-wipers droned in the silence until we reached our destination. I paid the driver. I cursed the black cab, every black cab, for being so dreadfully difficult to alight from. I wondered if people who spent much of their time travelling around London in black cabs did not spend as much time consulting chiropractors. I helped Rachel out of the car by extending my right arm and allowing her to take it. Rather than putting up her umbrella and squeezing herself against me, as she had done earlier, Rachel strode ahead and made for the communal entrance of her block of flats. I looked up at the concrete monolith standing before me. It reminded me of the many soulless blocks of flats where I'd spent many of my days as a detective in the Met. Truly, this state-owned monster was every bit as uninspiring and lacking in spirit. The white dishes that decorated the face of the building resembled a rash of acne. I listened to the hum of the traffic on the ring road nearby. I looked left as three boys raced past me on mountain bikes. They were chasing the departing black cab. When we reached the communal entrance, I saw that it was a gaping hole, a forbidding archway daring me to pass and to climb the cold stairwells leading to cold corridors leading to cold dwellings. Something about the place reminded me of Mountbatten Close, the street where I'd spent part of my childhood, the place where I'd loved and mourned Roseanne, and where I'd revered and wept for Albert.

I wondered why the place was called Burgundy Crescent, for there was no trace of burgundy about, and neither the building nor the street was shaped in a crescent. Perhaps the architect of the block had been under the influence of Burgundy when he designed it. The word "burgundy" made me think of Dominic, for the birthmark on his face. Then I started to wonder, which made me think of the book *Hard Times*, by Charles Dickens, in which Mr Thomas Gradgrind, purveyor of facts, and nothing but facts, in grimy Coketown, exhorted his daughter Louisa never to wonder, never to feed her imagination, or let it feed her. The thought of that book made me think of Josiah Bounderby, banker, merchant and manufacturer, friend of Thomas Gradgrind and no less devoted to facts. "Bounderby" sounds like "burgundy", I thought. It occurred to me that the block should have been called Bounderby Crescent, for it was built on the premise that two plus two equals four, not more and not less, whatever possibilities to the contrary might be suggested by the imagination.

One of my feet was on the concrete steps when I heard a door creak open. I looked to my left at the three red doors of a storage area. One of the doors was ajar. The room was too dark for me to be able to see inside it, but I heard groaning coming from within. Someone was inebriated amongst the mops and buckets, it seemed. Somebody needed a wash.

I was halfway up the first flight of steps when I was nearly sent flying by a black cat. I watched as the creature scampered into the wet night, the bell on its collar tinkling as it went.

Realising that I'd lost Rachel, I made my way up the concrete hill. My footsteps echoed loudly. I let them echo to remind Rachel that I was coming. The steps were lit dimly by feeble lamps attached to damp walls. I came to the top of the first flight of stairs. I looked up at one of the lamps. It flickered, and continued to flicker, long after I was gone.

I found myself by an open door. I looked down at the bare, concrete floor and saw a red shadow. I stepped inside the flat, nervously, leaving the door open in case I needed to beat a hasty retreat. From a distant room came the inimitable voice of Edith Piaf and *J'ai Danse Avec L'Amour*. The colour was everywhere. But what colour was it? Was it red? Was it crimson? Was it scarlet? Was it, well, burgundy? I thought of the Red Room in David Lynch's film *Fire Walk With Me*. I thought of seedy hotel rooms in Brighton. I thought of bordellos in Soho. I thought of wine. I thought of blood.

"Rachel?" I called.

The place had an ominous air.

"Rachel?" I called again.

"In here!"

At once, relieved and dismayed that I'd come to the right place, I closed the door behind me and then walked down the small, narrow hallway. On my right, by the entrance to the lounge, was a little table, upon which stood a lamp casting red light. I looked into the lounge and saw two more lamps radiating red light, the one on a wooden coffee table on the left, and the other, by the window, atop a tall wooden shelf.

Rachel came to meet me. "Are you wet?" she asked, caressing my left arm as she spoke.

Rachel's skirt seemed shorter and tighter now. I wondered if it were the same skirt that she'd worn all day. The pattern was the same, a garish yellow tartan, a disposition of colours that looked ghastly in combination with the red tights. I defied Gradgrind again by wondering. Bannerman was a Scottish name, I thought, so could she have been wearing the Bannerman clan's tartan? I thought it unlikely.

"I *am* wet," I replied, "but not too much."

"I'm soaked," Rachel returned, "so I'll just slip into something drier."

"You're the hostess," I said.

"Make yourself at home." Rachel turned on her flat heels. She stepped away from me. She stopped by the doorway. "Someone followed us here," she announced gravely.

"Really?"

"I didn't see him, but I knew he was there."

"Who?"

"He wants *me*, but he'll get *you*."

"You mean Greg?"

"He caused a scene at the office this afternoon. He arrived at reception and reported that his mother's boiler was broken and in urgent need of attention. Sheryl Henry had to deal with him. She warned me that he'd come and that he'd likely be waiting for me outside."

"And was he?"

"Yes, though I didn't see him."

"I've encountered bigger fish than Greg Tinnion in my time," I said. "He doesn't scare me."

"He should."

Rachel sauntered away to the strains of *La Vie En Rose*.

***

I stood by the living-room window. The curtains were still open. There was little point in closing them, for only people in low-flying aircraft and aliens in passing spaceships could have seen inside. There wasn't much to see on the outside, only a black hole and shimmering headlamps on the ring road. I realised that I must have climbed to the third or fourth floor. A streetlight, a luminescent white atop a stalk, peered at me across the dark expanse. The multifarious lights crawled over the distant road like ants on the march. My eyes were drawn from the road ahead, to the solitary streetlight, and back and forth, with Edith Piaf's *Je Ne Regrette Rien* serving as little more than a subliminal acoustic backdrop.

"You *can* take your coat off, you know."

Startled, I turned around to see Rachel standing right behind me. She had been true to her word, for she had indeed slipped into something drier. It was something considerably lighter too. It was debatable whether she was dressed at all.

"Here," she said. As if she were a venerable auntie, regaled in her Sunday best, handing over a cup of tea to an awestruck nephew, she held out a glass of beer.

I tried to stay focussed on the beer as I took the glass and drank thirstily from it.

"Steady on," Rachel purred. "It's going to be a long night."

"I'm not sure I can stay the night."

"We'll see about that, won't we?"

Desperate to change the subject, I searched the room for a prompt. On the uppermost of three shelves was a collection of books: small beer compared with my extensive library, but a respectable display, nonetheless. I strained my eyes to read the titles. I approved of Finn's *Mister God, This Is Anna*, nor was I inclined to sneer at *The Tao Of Pooh*, by Benjamin

Hoff. I was astonished to see *Blasted* and *Phaedra's Love*, for I thought I was the only person on the planet who'd heard of Sarah Kane, the late Sarah Kane, never mind read her work. I thought about raising the subject of the playwright, of her suicide at the tender age of twenty-nine, but I was not in the mood for high-minded conversation, especially with someone masquerading convincingly as a woman consisting of little more than a seething mass of eminently requitable hormones. I couldn't believe my eyes when I saw a volume of Franz Kafka's stories, *Metamorphosis* and all. How tempted I was to broach the subject of those masterpieces among masterpieces, *The Bridge* and *A Country Doctor*. CDs occupied the middle and lower shelves, and, reviewing the titles, I concluded that Rachel's taste in music lagged some way behind her taste in books.

"Have you seen something you like?" Rachel asked in her best feline voice.

The woman's tone jogged my memory and so gave me the pretext for a much-needed diversion. "That black cat on the stairway..."

"What about it?"

"It nearly took my legs away."

"You mean that it nearly swept you off your feet?"

Rachel raised her eyebrows suggestively. She moved closer to me. I could smell her perfume. The smell was familiar. I tried to remember what it was.

"Is the cat yours?"

"Merrylegs?"

"Is that its name?" I thought of the cat in the *Hard Times* of Gradgrind and Bounderby. It had happened again. No longer did I bother being surprised by coincidences.

"It's not mine."

"Whose is it?"

"Nobody knows."

"So how do you know it's called Merrylegs?"

"It has a collar."

"There's no address on the collar?"

"No…"

Rachel was now so close to me that I could smell her breath. It carried a trace of nicotine. She was upon me, a woman past her prime and fading into middle-age, but a woman that men would struggle to resist for at least another ten years. I was desperate to resist her. I wanted her to talk. But she wanted to do anything but talk. I began to wonder if I hadn't overestimated her.

"Take your coat off," my hostess intoned seductively, "and follow me."

I watched her go. She wasn't making a show of being sexy. She was being sexy simply by being herself. She could not have been otherwise. She would have needed to put on an act of Oscar-winning proportions *not* to look sexy. Her languid departure took an age. I waited for the flimsy garment, which hung from her shoulders on lace so thin that I could barely see it, to drop to the floor, but by some miracle it stayed on her back. I was still trying to work out how the garment had defied both gravity and the woman's sinuous movement when she disappeared from sight.

***

I couldn't wait any longer. Rachel, I knew, could and would wait as long as it took. She would wait all night, if waiting all night was what it took to break my resistance. She was waiting, somewhere, and I waited whilst she waited. Without my coat on, I felt naked. I needed all the protection I could get. With my body protected, I felt less inclined to go with the flow. I wondered what I was about to walk into. Would she be in bed, waiting? Given how long we'd been in separate rooms, it was not inconceivable that she would be in bed, asleep. That wouldn't do. I needed to keep her talking.

I walked towards the bedroom. I stopped by the open door and leaned against the jamb. I saw Rachel sitting on the end of the bed, not moving so much as a muscle, not even to smile. I saw her reflection in the mirror that leant against the wall. I saw both sides of her face. Neither side was smiling. She looked as if she were straining for a monumental feat of concentration, intent on business rather than pleasure.

"Are you going to stand there all night?" Her lips had moved, but even they were now still again.

"I can see you," I replied. "Do I need to be standing next to you?"

"If you could be standing in the same room as me at least, that would be polite."

Edith Piaf was singing *L'Étranger*.

"This was a good choice of music," I said.

Rachel nodded and so indicated that she was now in the business of conserving energy.

"Edith Piaf was a tragic figure," I went on, "a doomed chanteuse."

I could see why Rachel was drawn to Edith Piaf. That wasn't all that I could see. Plenty of Rachel's flesh had come into view, and it was all that I could do not to look. She was as quiet and as still as Edith Piaf's next song, *Va Danser*, was full of life and vigour. At last, she turned her eyes towards me.

"He's here, you know, not far away," she said, a note of distress in her voice. "I can sense him."

"Greg?"

"He followed us here."

"Shall I go outside and take a look?"

Slowly, she shook her head. "Come inside," she said. "I'm scared."

***

The bedroom was even redder than the lounge. Only, again, it wasn't red. It was a type of red, in the same way that a good man exhibits types of goodness and a virtuous woman displays types of virtue. I wondered at the apparent obsession with red. I thought of the third colour in Kieslowski's *Three Colours Trilogy*. I thought of Roeg's *Don't Look Now*: of the spilt wine, of the cut finger and the blood on the slide, of the little girl's coat, of the dwarf's coat, and of the blood at the thrilling end to the film. I thought of Laura Hart's coat in the photograph on the desk at The Golden Age: that, too, had been red. I thought of the pool of blood in which she'd been found. I thought of Dominic's birthmark. I wondered whether Rachel's apparent obsession with the colour red was a considered signal to the world that red was part of who she was, or whether the red in her life amounted to nothing more than a multiplicity of decisions and choices based on a preference for the colour red, a preference, moreover, that was never given a second's thought. I doubted that she'd ever made a grand, sweeping statement that she'd fallen in love with the colour red at a young age and remained faithful ever since. I was having these crazy thoughts for the simple reason that

I'd been crazed: under stress, far from going blank, my mind goes into overdrive and takes me where it will.

My hands had turned red. I looked in the mirror and saw that my face, too, had turned red. The siren's body was wrapped around mine, like a snake around a pole, as we danced. It was a strange kind of dance, for she moved in sensuous ripples on the spot, and I moved with her even as I endeavoured not to move at all. I was Wagner's Tannhäuser in the Venusberg, the place where the profane rites of love are celebrated to lascivious music. My head rested on the shoulder of Venus as she told me of her discontent with the life of indolence and abandonment. The Goddess of Love consoled me and asked me to sing to her. "Praise resound to thee," I might have sung. Seductive as ever, she pleaded with me to sing, but my place was not to give anything of myself away, not so much as a note.

"This song's special to me," Rachel whispered in my left ear.

"I quite like the song myself."

"A friend of mine mixed it for me and made an extended version."

What I did not need at that moment was Edith Piaf singing in glorious seductive French. I stilled—or calmed, at least—my stirring loins by trying to work out what the French lyrics meant. Thinking of emerging from this particular Venusberg without giving so much as a note away, I prayed for a miracle.

"So, Daniel, you want to know who killed Laura Hart?"

Rachel held me so tight that I could barely breathe, never mind talk.

"Guess what you have to do to find out who killed Laura Hart?"

"Sing you a song?"

"Yes, that's one way of putting it …"

"I'd like to keep my clothes on, if that's all right with you."

"You're going to sing to me with your clothes on?"

"I've a terrible singing voice. You really don't want to hear it."

For a while longer, we danced, the ever-alluring Venus and the desperate Tannhäuser, tyrannised both by desire, the one eager to indulge it, the other to contain.

Finally, one of us spoke again.

"I've got something to show you," Rachel whispered, this time all but inaudibly, "and, once you've seen it, you'll be singing like a canary."

***

By the time we were interrupted by knocking, furious knocking on the front door, the show was over and the disc safely back in its case and locked away in a drawer. On Christmas Eve last, the film had been made on a handheld digital device. What a film it was. Rachel had viewed it as if she were watching an episode of *Coronation Street*. I'd sat on the sofa and stared at the computer screen as if the Second Coming of Jesus Christ were being broadcast live on television. The sexual content of the hour-long film was almost incidental, because I'd known that the conclusion would be dramatic, explosive, the answer to my question, the fulfilment of my quest, though what I would do with the answer, now that I had it, was another question entirely and one that I could not answer without a nagging sense of foreboding.

The knocking on the door was persistent and becoming louder.

"That's him."

"Greg?"

Rachel nodded almost sadistically.

"Should I expect trouble?" It was a silly question. I was trying to be detached, nonchalant even, but my nerves were refusing to cooperate.

"If I had a backdoor, you could leave by it."

"Do you have a rope? I could leave by the window."

"That would be fitting. You look like the Milk Tray Man."

For the sake of the door's integrity, the knocking could not be ignored for a second longer. Rachel went to the door first. I had little time to lose. I put my coat on. I'd seen where Rachel had placed the key for the drawer. I snatched it up, opened the drawer, retrieved the disc in its case, put the case in my pocket, and then locked the drawer and replaced the key. Then I, too, went to the door, determined not to be a coward. I paced down the hallway with my chest out and my wits addled by fear. Rachel had opened the door. Two uniformed policemen were standing at the door. Rachel took a step back and allowed me to take over the situation.

"Someone reported a disturbance at this address," one of the officers announced.

"That depends on what you mean by a disturbance," I replied.

"We're not philosophers," the policeman returned.

"We know what people mean by a disturbance," the other policeman put in.

"You might want to speak with the lady," I said. I looked down the hallway, halfway down which Rachel was standing, shrouded in a red mist and still on the point of nakedness.

The policemen, too, looked down the hallway, until their looks became stares, and one of them took hold of his truncheon.

"These things are sent to try us," said the officer whose hands were free.

"So is that saying," replied the other, his grip on the weapon tightening.

Though baffled by what was happening, I thanked providence for granting me an opportunity to take my leave. Before they were able to lift a finger to stop me, I told the officers of the law that I was just going. As I left, Edith Piaf's *Jezebel* began to echo from the bedroom.

When I reached ground level, Merrylegs was sniffing at the hand protruding from the storage room. The hand lay on stone-cold ground, but I was so desperate to flee the scene that I suppressed the urge to investigate. I stepped under the archway and into the rain. A man leaning against the wall startled me. He was soaking wet. Water dripped from his nose like melting snow from a ski slope.

"You?" I said.

As if his unshaven face had the slightest bearing on what he was about to say, the man caressed his thick stubble. "Don't you just hate busybody neighbours who call the cops at the slightest hint of a disturbance?" he asked.

"You did me a favour," I said defiantly.

"She still wants me," Greg said.

"I hope you'll both be very happy together," I said.

***

For one feeling apprehensive about the following days, and what they portended, Nico's *The Marble Index* was not the best choice of music, what with the threatening instrumentation and the haunting voice of the Teutonic femme fatale. Every night, I went to sleep to music. Though sleep was starting to claim me, I toyed with the idea of going into the lounge and watching an Eric Rohmer film. My equilibrium was in urgent need of restoration. Alas, I was too tired even for my usual cinematic medicine.

After leaving Rachel, I'd taken a taxi from outside the Roman Catholic church in Hollow Way, and then embarked upon a pub crawl: from the Turf Tavern, I'd gone to the King's Arms and thence, on foot, to the Dew Drop, where I'd learned of the sudden death of my old friend Mandy, he of the gags concerning kangaroos of the western hemisphere. Apparently, a pickled liver was the principal cause of his death, and I'd been duly urged by all the usual suspects present, every one of them a functioning alcoholic, to take heed of the warning given by Mandy's demise. I'd supposed that that was a mind-boggling example of alcoholics' logic. An erstwhile alcoholic friend of mine, now deceased, had once invited me to celebrate one year of his being on the wagon by accompanying him on a bender.

As I pondered Mandy's death, as the German chanteuse droned on irresistibly, I struggled to get the images of Rachel's homemade video out of my head. The film's afterglow was tormenting me. The images would swirl in my head for the rest of my days. They were not the kind of images that one forgot in a hurry. Sex and death were juxtaposed again. The little death, several little deaths, had foreshadowed the big death.

I thought of the women involved. The dead woman haunted me now in more ways than one. I'd very nearly become intimate with another. A third woman among them

I knew as the caring professional who had made Dominic homeless. The fourth woman I guessed was Caitlin Mallett, whom I would see the following day, and who no longer needed a name badge to help me identify her. The three surviving women had nursed a secret for seventeen days. But the secret was out now. One of the women had broken rank. She'd wanted someone, someone who'd not been there when Laura Hart died, to know the truth. That, I'd been told, had been the plan all along, though the women had been prepared in the meantime to let an innocent young man be framed for the murder of Laura Hart, the murder, indeed, that had never been committed.

***

It was not until the middle of the night, when images of writhing female flesh again harassed me, that I'd woken and asked myself the question that I should have asked Rachel several hours before. How had the question eluded me? Perhaps I'd simply been overwhelmed by what I'd witnessed. Perhaps my brain had been as scrambled as my nerves in the threatening ambience given by Rachel Bannerman and her home of shimmering red pervaded by the strains of the doomed Gallic chanteuse. Perhaps it was because my senses had been and remained in tumult, my hearing thinking it was my sense of touch, my eyesight tasting, my sense of touch believing it could smell, my sense of taste hearing, and my sense of smell confusing itself with my eyesight. The film had been *that* graphic. My five senses had fed my brain with sensations that it could barely process. I could have been there, amid the writhing flesh, on Christmas Eve last.

What was that question?

Four women had taken part in the orgy, one of whom had died. But a fifth person had been present, the person with the roaming eye, the person who'd followed every movement, including the final migration to the kitchen and the reaching for the knife. Someone had held the camera.

Now that I knew who killed Laura Hart, another question needed answering.

Who had held the camera?

TWENTY-SIX

Matt and I sat facing each other across the kitchen table, drinking tea. He had looked doubtfully at his cup more than once since I served the tea, and now he asked me what he was drinking and why the liquid had a strange malty flavour. I told him that he was drinking Assam tea, the best tea there was in my or any other house inhabited by people with taste as good as mine.

"Coming to your flat is always a life-affirming experience," Matt declared sarcastically, "and I always learn something."

"I'm always glad to make the rich tapestry that is your life even richer."

"This music's cheerful," he moaned.

"It's *Strange Days*," I replied. "I thought you liked The Doors."

"I do, but not first thing in the morning."

"Tell me something..."

"*You're* supposed to be telling *me* something, Daniel. Or, rather, you're supposed to be *showing* me something."

"I *will* show you something. But first I want to *ask* you something."

Matt sighed his usual sigh of irritation at my beating about the bush. He then rubbed his face and eyes, looking like a man who hadn't slept much the night before.

"How long's this interview going to last?" he asked. "Only I've got an appointment at twelve."

"Before I started looking into the death of Laura Hart, did you have any idea who the killer was?"

"I had some ideas, yes, but I shared them all with you."

"*All* of them?"

"Yes, Daniel, *all* of them."

"It's just that you seem to have kept a lot of relevant information from me."

"All that I *thought* was relevant, I shared with you."

I raised my eyebrows in a show of scepticism.

"Look, I didn't want to crowd you out," he protested. "I wanted you to get on with your enquiries, in your own way. I trusted you."

"Okay, well, all's well that ends well, I suppose. But I remain unconvinced."

"Turn it in, will you, Daniel? I've got a splitting headache."

"You'll have more than a headache after you've watched the video that I'm about to show you. I've seen it twice now, and I'll still be reeling after I've watched it a third time."

"Should I prepare myself for a shock?"

"Put it this way, I'm wondering if I shouldn't call an ambulance and have it on standby outside."

"Whatever you're about to show me, don't worry, I've seen it all before."

"Tell me that in an hour's time."

***

"Say something then."

Matt looked at me with pleading eyes. "What the hell do you expect me to say after watching that little performance?"

"You might ask me how I obtained the disc."

"That's obvious," Matt said, his head now buried in his hands, covering the eyes that had seen it all before. "You got it from Rachel."

"Indeed," I said, "and with an exquisite sleight of hand."

Matt sat up, looked at me, and laughed.

"We know that she wanted someone other than those involved to know the truth," I said.

"Rachel did, yes, but did the others?"

"It's too bad if they didn't."

"So, did Rachel just give you the disc?"

"Not exactly, no ..."

"What do you mean?"

"I reckon that she wanted me to leave the flat, one way or another, with the disc. My simply watching the peep show wasn't enough. She wanted me to have the evidence."

"But she could have taken the disc to the police herself. Or she could have—they *all* could have—gone to the police and told them what happened."

"Apparently, this is the way that she—or they—wanted it done."

"What a palaver!"

"I tell you, Matt, last night at Rachel's flat was too weird, it was like a dream, a *bad* dream, and there was a strange twist at the end of my fraught couple of hours or so with Rachel."

"You say that as if that grotesque circus act caught on camera wasn't strange enough."

"My opportunity to escape from Rachel's clutches came when two coppers arrived at the flat. Somebody had reported a disturbance at the flat. That somebody was Greg Tinnion. I saw him waiting outside as I fled the scene, the disc safely pocketed. He told me that *he'd* called the police. Greg and Rachel, I would wager, are in bed together right now, getting to know each other all over again. I could tell that she wanted him back."

"She didn't want *you* then?"

"Like I said, it was all a bit weird. She said that she would give me the information I wanted if I gave her something in return. But I didn't find out what that something was."

"Isn't it obvious what she wanted?"

"No, it isn't, and it wasn't, because, although she came over a bit seductive, she was holding something back. Whatever it was that she wanted from me, I'm not sure it was sex. Perhaps it was just a cuddle, company, tenderness. I don't know."

"A cuddle? Tenderness? This is Rachel Bannerman we're talking about, not Florence bloody Nightingale!"

"Well, we'll never know, will we? And it doesn't really matter. We know who killed Laura Hart. Job done."

"I have to give you credit, my friend. You did it. You found out who killed Laura Hart. I knew there was something going on between those women, something sexual, and I knew that they knew the truth about Laura's death, but never in a million years did I think that anything like … Well, *that's* beyond even *my* warped imagination."

"The police should be told now."

"Yes, but how?"

"We show them the disc."

"Okay, but we need to be careful about how we go about it."

"The police need to know that Laura Hart's killer is not Dominic Kane."

Matt put his head in his hands again. He then removed his hands from his face and peered up at me from a slumped position. "But Donna, Caitlin, Rachel and Sheryl?" he pleaded. "They are *all* involved."

"Sheryl?"

"She was the one who filmed it all."

"How do you know that?"

"Because she was involved in that little lesbian scene of theirs, and she has a camcorder and has made a few short films. She's a budding little filmmaker."

"Well, she's played a blinder with this little caper."

"The girls could all go down for perverting the course of justice, as could you."

"*I'm* all right."

"Oh, really?"

"I'll be granted immunity from prosecution."

"You harboured the prime suspect!"

"Yes, I did, to avert a miscarriage of justice!"

"Is that how it works? You make a deal with the Old Bill?"

"I'll simply drop the truth into their laps. They don't even have to know that I've been protecting Dominic. Though I *shall* come clean about that."

"*You're* the ex-copper, so you know how these things work."

"I don't understand you, Matt. You wanted me to find out who killed Laura Hart, but, at the same time, you wanted me to hand them Dominic on a plate."

"I was trying to protect you from your own recklessness."

"I did what you wanted me to do, Matt. I did it *my* way."

Matt smiled and tried in vain not to laugh. "Okay, Frank Sinatra," he said. "I can see why your face didn't fit at the Met."

We sat in silence for a minute or so and collected our thoughts.

"Can the girls be done for anything else, Daniel?"

"Manslaughter, possibly…"

"Good God!"

"But a clever defence lawyer might be able to get them off, since none of the women present actually plunged the knife into Laura's chest."

"Yes, but they *made* her do it."

"In a sense, yes, they did."

"What a mess!"

"I wouldn't want to be the police officers picking the bones out of this one."

"It will be like trying to take eggs out of an omelette."

"Okay," I said, suddenly decisive. "Here's the plan."

Matt moved to the edge of his seat and offered me his left ear in an exaggerated show of attentiveness.

"Tomorrow night, at about ten o'clock, during the Goodbye Golden Age Dinner and Dance, Kendal goes to Saint Aldate's nick with the disc. That will give Rachel and company time to enjoy the major part of the evening before the police pick them up. It will suit the police to have all the women in the same place at the same time. Kendal will take Dominic with her."

"You've got it all worked out, haven't you?"

"Justice must run its course, Matt."

"You're going to be popular come midnight tomorrow."

"I've got enemies everywhere. A few more won't make much difference."

"Rather you than me..."

"If you have no enemies then you haven't lived."

"Where is Dominic now?"

"He's at the office with Kendal. He'll stay here tonight, and for a few more nights, whilst I fix him up with somewhere to live."

"Somewhere to live? Where?"

"I was thinking that Greetwell Housing Trust could find him a little flat somewhere in Oxford."

"Greetwell? Are you having a laugh?"

"Greetwell *owe* him."

In sighing, Matt expelled enough hot air to power a steam engine. Though he was a friend of mine, and I'd done what he'd asked me to do, what he'd *paid* me to do, I remained unconvinced that he was wholly on my side and that he didn't have some trick or other up his sleeve, a conjuring act that might yet undo all my good work. I couldn't have imagined what that trick might be, but part of me clung to the thought that Matt had not been fully cooperative during my investigation, that he had wilfully—or, more likely, carelessly—withheld information from me. I was bound to dismiss all such considerations as immaterial now. The job was done. The disc was in the safe in my bedroom. The evidence was incontrovertible, and whether it was damning remained to be seen.

"I don't know about you, but I need a drink."

There remained *some* unfinished business, of course, not the least of which was my impromptu (for her) interview with Caitlin Mallett in the big Tesco store in Cowley. That could wait for another hour or two. Matt needed a drink. He wasn't the only one.

As I changed, I put on David Sylvian's album, *Brilliant Trees*, a choice of which Matt wholeheartedly approved.

*****

In the Dew Drop, as we drank, bits of the film flashed before my eyes in random order, they were replayed in my mind, they were everywhere, on the walls, on the ceiling, in Matt's eyes, even at the bottom of my beer glass. Then the images fused into one amorphous mass of writhing female flesh, a seething profusion of carnality, a twisting, turning, rolling, thrashing abundance of sensuality. Suddenly, I was overcome by the feeling that four women enjoying each other's bodies was a more elegant spectacle than four men doing likewise could ever be. In my mind, I replaced the four women with four men and was condemned to witnessing a thoroughly unedifying vision of thrusting muscularity. The men lacked either tenderness or any sense of art and beauty. They wished only to gratify themselves, the sole purpose of the others being to provide a fitting repository for lustful exuberance. Mutuality, it seemed, was the preserve of woman. It did not so much as occur to man.

Though I struggled to engage with Matt, I was again dragged into contemplating sex between men (not a subject that I was given to dwelling upon overmuch), and to compare that with sex between women (again, not an idea with which I grappled out of habit). Again, then, I couldn't help but appreciate the artfulness of the women's sensuality, as expressed in the film. Once more, I marvelled at the arrangement of the bodies; at their sinuous, synchronised movements; at the pretty patterns they made on the bed. The performance had needed no direction, no orchestration. It was natural, unforced, each woman knowing her part. Even the noises they made, the audible manifestations of their pleasure, evoked the harmony of sublime music. No four men could have performed in such a way. It almost made me ashamed to be a man.

There was nothing sublime about how the beautiful charade came to a sudden end, however, for that was merely brutal, it was sinister and ugly and, ultimately, deadly. I heard the voices now. Once more, the sights and sounds of that momentous Christmas Eve, as captured in some furtive Oxford hideaway, flashed before me and swirled around me. I saw the undulating flesh. I heard the groans of pleasure. I saw Laura Hart take herself off the bed and into the kitchen. I saw three women go after her, their various body parts wobbling and swerving and shaking. I saw Laura Hart take the knife from a drawer and point it at her heart. I heard the incantation. "Do it!" they chanted. "Do it! Do it!" So she did it. As she fell to the floor, blood spilled from her breast and spewed from her mouth. When she hit the floor, blood seeped from her right ear.

I snapped out of my trance when Matt asked me how many copies of the film I thought there were.

"Well, since someone—probably, Sheryl—has the original, an unlimited number, potentially, though I suspect that we have the only current copy, and they are hardly going to mass-produce the video, are they?"

"No, I don't suppose they will. Another beer?"

"I'd better not. I have more work to do."

"Daniel Winter refused a beer. January twelfth, two-thousand-and-six. I think I'll make a note of that in my diary."

TWENTY-SEVEN

It was after lunchtime by the time I arrived at the big Tesco store in Cowley. I parked the Jensen in one of the few available spaces in the vast carpark, narrowly avoiding a demented woman and her out-of-control trolley as I manoeuvred into position. Naturally, the near-collision had been my fault, and I had no answer to the woman's calling me a "blind bastard" other than to claim that being born in wedlock was one of my few accomplishments. To that the woman had decided that, in addition to having questionable eyesight and being of dubious parentage, I indulged in solitary sexual practices. I didn't take it personally.

The weather that day was proving to be as changeable as Oxford United's form: when Matt and I had gone into the Dew Drop, rain was bouncing off the furniture in the beer garden; upon our emergence back onto the streets, the sun was shining; hail had threatened to shatter the windscreen of my pride-and-joy as I navigated the ring road; and rain was again falling, though not so heavily, when I beheld the overflowing supermarket trolley coming at me like a runaway juggernaut.

I was making a dash for the front entrance of the store when I saw Caitlin standing there, by herself, smoking, and looking worried. I wondered how best to approach her. I tried to think of a pretext for talking to her: a request for directions, perhaps, or a question as to whether the shop had any jobs going. Caitlin was already halfway through smoking her cigarette, and I saw the advantage of speaking with her when she was outside, at ease, away from prying eyes and oversensitive ears. As it happened, I was reduced to pretending to speak on my phone, all the time keeping a discreet and watchful eye on proceedings, after a gnome-like fellow had crept up on the woman and drawn her into the most bizarre of conversations.

"Hello!"

"My God, Jake! You scared me half to death!"

"I'm sorry."

Caitlin studied the contrite little gnome. She looked not a little contrite herself. "No, you're all right, Jake. You did me a favour. I was lost in all sorts of disagreeable thoughts."

"About your daughter?"

"Among other thoughts…"

"It must be hard."

"It is."

"How's your son?"

"Weird as ever…"

"How was your morning?"

"It was busy. I spent the morning stacking shelves. A man came up to me by the breakfast cereals and asked me if he was going the right way for the airport. I told him to go to the end of the aisle, turn right, and take the second turning on the right. Later, I found him looking for aeroplanes over by the organic fruit and vegetables. How was your morning?"

Jake winced as if the recollection of that morning's labours were too painful to voice. "I did okay with the buns," he said, "but I burnt the fairy cakes."

Caitlin's reply was vacant but kind. "Oh, well, never mind. These things happen to the best of us."

Jake looked out at the row upon row of parked cars, at the people coming and going like ants, and at the articulated lorry approaching the bottle bank. "Why do you smoke here?" he asked.

The long arms of the lorry reached out and grabbed the bell-shaped steel container, then lifted it like the leading man on the ballroom dancefloor raising his partner over his head in a single motion of grace and poise. The lorry's pulling the bell towards it was neither so graceful nor so poised, and its turning of the bell upside down, to relieve it of its cargo, lacked finesse of any kind. The crashing and smashing of the glass, as it fell into the gaping mouth of the lorry, scattered the dozen or so pigeons that had gathered expecting rich pickings. The ground rumbled underfoot, and somewhere nearby, out of sight, a baby began to cry.

"Why wouldn't I come here to think?" Caitlin replied. "It's such a tranquil spot." She dragged on her cigarette and blew out a tunnel of smoke.

In the corner of my eye, I watched the smoke disperse and fade. I wondered where the smoke went. I toyed with the idea that all the smoke that had ever formed gathered in one place—in outer space, possibly—and either joined an ever-thickening cloud or was consumed by some cosmic black hole.

"Do you know Greg Tinnion, Caitlin?"

"You know I do."

"Of course, he's a friend of Rick's."

"More's the pity."

"And you're friends with Rachel Bannerman."

"You're on the ball today, Jake."

"He's out of prison now, you know."

"I know."

"I fear that Rachel's going to get it."

"Get what exactly, Jake?"

"Greg's an angry man."

"He's a *violent* man."

"Greg's always saying that there's a state of war between the sexes, and that he's a soldier fighting the good fight, keeping woman in her place, not letting her get the upper hand."

Caitlin had put out her cigarette and lit another. She blew smoke at the baker. She looked at him as if she were an anthropologist who, stalking a remote jungle in a distant land, had just stumbled across an exotic member of a hitherto undiscovered tribe.

"Do yourself a favour, Jake, and avoid Greg Tinnion."

"But he's my mate."

"You don't need mates like him."

"People think he started the rumours, but he couldn't have, because he was inside."

"What rumours?"

"About Rick, and that Wilcox girl, and her baby…"

"I know all about those rumours, Jake. They're despicable rumours spread by despicable people. I know my husband."

"Look, I—"

"I don't want to hear it, Jake."

Caitlin gave Jake a look of disgust as she dropped the cigarette on the sodden ground. Looking down, at the embers at the tip, she stamped on the butt and put out the flame. For good measure, she twisted her foot three or four times and listened as the cigarette suffered the throes of extinction.

"Get back to work, Jake!" she hissed. "Playtime's over!"

I was grateful to Jake the baker for saving me the trouble of initiating and sustaining a conversation with Caitlin Mallett on the delicate subject that was her husband's involvement with a girl and her baby girl. As a detective, in London, I'd been involved in cases of all manner of sexual degradation, featuring, among other horrors, rape, incest, grooming, exploitation and trafficking, but Rick Mallett was nothing like the unsavoury characters that I'd encountered during my time fighting crime in the metropolis, for they were people of a different species entirely, they were evil men (and women) who knew they were evil and cared not who knew it. That is not to say that Rick was blameless; only that he was being given the benefit of the doubt by me (for what that was worth) and by his wife (that was worth much more). In any case, the word of Selena Wilcox was worth more than anybody else's in the matter, and she had stated categorically just how far Rick had gone in the indulgence of his fancy in a moment of weakness.

For a minute or so, I stood outside the store and watched and listened as people came and went, many of them carrying heavy bags and pushing loaded trolleys; as cars entered and left the carpark in a cacophony of hooting; and as lorries drove towards the loading bay, doing their level best not to get in the way. An old lady steered her mobility scooter through the chaos. Like single mothers with pushchairs when they get on board a bus, she expected people reverently to make way for her, though she steered the conveyance erratically and with indecent haste. When a boy omitted to show due deference, the scooter screeched to a halt.

"Get that child out of my way!" the old lady cried.

"You might be disabled," the mother of the boy retorted, "but that doesn't mean you can drive around like you own the place!"

"Why isn't he at school?" the old lady demanded.

"None of your business!" the mother returned.

"You nosey old cow!" the boy shouted as the old lady drove her contraption into the store and took out the magazine shelves like a bulldozer driving through a china shop.

The capacity of the public to be richly entertaining never ceased to amaze me, as did my capacity to combine work with alcohol. So it was that I returned to the office to review the prospective new cases of which Kendal had spoken, but not before I'd enjoyed another pint of Courage Best bitter in the Dew Drop, the place where I did most of my most fruitful thinking.

TWENTY-EIGHT

I was glad that Melissa's grave was situated by a hedge, for it served as a shield against the rain that swirled at my back. I looked around me and beheld a thoroughly wintry scene, a landscape ravaged by the harshest elements of the harshest season: the recent frosts had left the grass all around the place pocked and fissured, and the neglected graves in a state of abject and mournful abandonment, like daffodils shocked and awed by an early-spring hailstorm. Though the sound of dripping water was all around me, I saw no water falling, only swirling drizzle moving in riotous clouds, in lawless, billowing swarms, like a plague of insects or sand in a desert storm. Aside from the splashes of colour afforded by the scattering of floral tributes—which, themselves, were in various stages of depredation—three colours abounded: the pale green that was the mottled carpet of grass; the black of the pervasive naked branches, which reached for the heavens like the fingers of desperate, baying supplicants; and the grey shroud given by the all-enveloping cloud and its murky precipitation. Apart from Rick and me, there were no people about. Only the ravens squawking in the trees, like harbingers of death, animated a prospect that was hauntingly silent.

"Thanks for coming, Daniel."

"I'm happy to be here, Rick."

We stood in the rain like two Bedouin in a sandstorm. The wind had got up and I spotted in the distance a row of mighty beeches swaying and bending like majestic pagan gods in some animistic dance. Both Rick and I looked up as a solitary raven emerged from the mist and the rainfall and glided menacingly downwards, maintaining its ominous descent until it came to rest on the war memorial by the obelisk, from which it surveyed the scene before it with sinister, dispassionate eyes. We were standing on the far side of the cemetery, beyond the chapel, over by the war graves.

We regarded the grave of Melissa Mallett sombrely, and I tried to imagine how Rick was feeling. I wondered how many years would pass before the grave was left to rot, before it was abandoned to the elements, before there was nobody left to care for it. Quite a few years, I supposed, though graves had a habit of becoming objects of neglect depressingly soon after a period of well-meaning care and attention from the bereaved. The inscription on the headstone was something of which tears are made. "Here lies Melissa Geraldine Mallett, daughter of Rick and Caitlin, and sister of Jordan. 9th January 1994 to 10th January 2005. Sweet dreams, our precious one." Time might have left Rick's emotions expiated, but mine were at that moment in turmoil. He was calm, collected, focussed, like an actor about to step on the stage and play Hamlet.

"Sorry to get you out on a day like this…"

"It's not a problem, Rick. I like rain."

"So do I. I thought I was the only one."

"There are at least two pluviophiles in this world, Rick."

Rick was standing over the grave with his hands in his jacket pockets and his shoulders slightly hunched. He looked as if he were looking at his reflection in a pool of water, which, in a sense, he was. He had the look of a man who was battered and bruised by the blows meted out to him by life, though not of a man who was beaten. I sensed a certain resilience in him, a durability that would carry him through adversity, a stamina born of a hope that life could and would get better, as if life were a patient with no life save for a weak pulse, but a pulse strong enough to promise recovery, and, beyond that, prosperity.

"You said that you come to the grave every Friday."

"I do, just to be with her," Rick replied, "though, like I told you before, I hear her music, her violin, playing in the house all the time."

"Do your wife and son visit the grave?"

"Caitlin comes two or three times a year, and Jordan hardly ever, as far as I know. They both find it too upsetting. They haven't come to terms with Melissa's death. I doubt they ever will."

"I can understand that."

Rick sighed upwards at the sky as if in supplication. "For me, it's a kind of communion, you know, a *direct* communion."

"I know what you mean." I thought of the few times that I'd visited Albert's grave and chided myself for my negligence.

"Thank you for taking the letter, Daniel. Have you put it somewhere safe?"

"It is safely ensconced *in my safe*, the safest place within my four walls."

"Thanks ever so much. I feel much better knowing that it's not in my house, taunting me, luring me towards it, calling me. It has no power over me now."

"I saw Caitlin yesterday, as you asked."

Rick waited for the inevitable.

"Don't look so worried, Rick. She knows about the rumours, but she doesn't believe them."

"She *doesn't* believe them? Or she *refuses* to believe them?"

"She believes in you, totally, Rick."

Water seeped from Rick's eyes. The drops might have been rainwater running down his face. Or they might have been tears.

"I've really let Caitlin down."

"How?"

"I can't hold down any kind of job. I'm nearly always out of work. And why's that? Because I'm argumentative. I don't like being told what to do."

"Who does? That's one of the reasons why I left the police force."

"Matt said that you left because you refused to become a Freemason."

I smiled my knowing smile, the smile that I smiled whenever I felt vindicated. One might say that the smile is a touch vindictive.

"I was on the verge of being promoted to chief inspector, but I wouldn't have progressed any further without any friends in secretive places."

"Did you want to?"

"No, because, once you go beyond the rank of chief inspector, you are back in uniform and more of a politician—or a diplomat—than a policeman."

"Well, at least you got to be an inspector," Rick said. "I wouldn't have lasted a week in the police force. I haven't lasted more than a week *anywhere*."

"Are you looking for a job?"

"Of course, yes, because we can't live on Caitlin's wages … and, anyway, a man needs to work."

"I might be able to help you there."

"Really?"

"Leave it with me."

"Thanks …"

Rick stepped away from the grave and over to the obelisk and stood under the protection of the cupola. He looked out at the sodden graveyard. I wondered if he were considering my offer to help him find gainful employment. Was he too proud to accept charity from me? Not that he should have seen my offer to help him as charity. I knew someone who would give him a job, a decent job, and who would give him a chance to prove himself. Rick looked to his left at the war memorial. I walked over to it and read the inscription. "THEIR NAME LIVETH FOR EVERMORE." For Rick, it might have read: "HER NAME LIVES FOR EVERMORE." Rick was again on the verge of tears. He was trying to hold himself together. I wanted to tell him to let himself go, and that there was no shame in doing so. I joined him at the obelisk and stood with him, shoulder-to-shoulder almost, taking in the silence that was permeated by ambient sounds and punctuated by the barbed cries of the ravens that swooped here and dived there, and soared back to the trees with worms in their beaks to feed their young.

"Then there's Jordan," he said at last. "He's not a conventional kid. He's downright weird, in fact. But Caitlin connects with him all right, she has no problems, whereas I can't get anywhere near him. God knows I've tried. But he's lost to me. He mocks me all the time. He taunts me. I don't know why he does it. It only widens the gulf between us. As for Melissa…well, she's gone, and why wouldn't she be gone when she had such a weak father?"

"Your daughter's death had nothing to do with you, Rick."

"She was fragile, Daniel, like a China doll. She got that from me."

"Okay, so she got her sensitivity of soul from you. That is nothing to be ashamed of. Quite the contrary."

"Then there's Selena."

"Stop tormenting yourself, Rick."

"I *kissed* her."

"In a moment of weakness, you acted foolishly. Forget what happened. Selena actually thinks very highly of you."

"Caitlin and I should never have married."

"Come on, Rick, give it a rest."

"We're from different worlds. Her father's a lawyer. My parents are factory workers. Her parents told her a thousand times not to marry me. They said I wasn't their sort. I've proved them right, haven't I?"

"All you need to concern yourself with is Caitlin, Rick, and she loves you for who you are, not for where you come from."

"I've dragged her down to my level."

"Are you listening to me, Rick?"

"We've never had a single holiday as a family, not a proper one, if you discount a wet week in Bognor Regis a few summers back. Thankfully, Jordan was too young to remember that shambles of a holiday. It's a wonder we didn't all return home with pneumonia."

"You'll find that it's *Caitlin* who's let *you* down, Rick."

"What do you mean?"

"You'll find out tomorrow."

"Has something happened?"

"Something happened on Christmas Eve."

Rick looked at me as if I'd just uttered the unthinkable. "Laura Hart?"

I nodded.

"Caitlin knows who killed Laura?"

I nodded again. My neck was starting to ache with all the nodding.

"Was Caitlin involved?"

"You'll find out tomorrow, Rick."

"Caitlin was out with friends on Christmas Eve."

"Indeed, she was, Rick."

"Is she in trouble?"

"Not yet, but you need to brace yourself for trouble ahead."

Rick lost himself in thought for a few minutes. I hated seeing him look so worried and alone, but at least he'd stopped wallowing in self-pity.

"I went out with Greg the other night, Tuesday, the day he came out. Well, I met him in town."

"I know," I replied. "I was with him on the night he called you. I was in the Round House. He came in, looking for Rachel."

"Yes, he said. Don't get on the wrong side of Greg, Daniel."

"I'm already on the wrong side of him."

"Caitlin was upset that I'd met Greg in town, but she said nothing to me about it. That is typical of her. She suffers in silence. More often than not, her suffering is caused by *me*."

"Well, the suffering that she's about to endure had nothing to do with you."

"You uncovered something, didn't you?"

"Yes, I did."

"Matt said you were clever."

"That's praise, indeed, coming from him."

"What was it like working for the Met?"

"It had its moments. I was seconded to the Sweeney for a time. I once infiltrated a gang of football hooligans, a firm of Top Boys."

"Which club?"

"West Ham," I said. "I was rumbled just before a rumble with a Spurs firm was about to kick off. We got the ringleaders of both firms, but it changed nothing, it never does, you take out the leader of a gang, any kind of gang, and he'll be replaced by someone else, and, if you take out an entire gang, another gang will take its place."

"Did you investigate any murders?"

"I was involved with a lot of murder cases, but murderers in real life are nothing like the glamorised genius serial killers that you read about in novels and see on television. The real world is altogether more prosaic, more banal, and grubbier. Most of the killers that I encountered were desperate in one way or another. That's why I felt sorry for them. I always felt as sorry for the killers as I did for the victims. That wasn't allowed. I never wanted to see *anyone* put away. I'm not sure that banging people up solves much."

"What's the alternative?"

"Depending on the severity of the offence, some sort of rehabilitation or capital punishment, and the former seems inadequate and the latter utterly barbaric."

"I'm all for rehabilitation, and totally against capital punishment."

"I agree with you. Capital punishment is judicial murder."

"Whatever someone has done, they should be given the chance to reflect and repent."

"Crime and punishment, Rick. These ideas dogged humanity long before Dostoevsky."

"I bet you had fun in the Met."

"I did, of course, but policing changed so much during my time in the force, and the new ways of policing were not for me."

"I imagine that policing is all very scientific and technical now."

"I didn't mind that so much. It was more the type of cases that I was becoming involved in. One of the last cases that I worked on was the apprehension of a gang of cigarette-smugglers from the Balkans. Months of work that took, working with the Drugs Squad—there was heroin involved, too—just to arrest a bunch of shaven-headed Serbs that were operating on our patch. That's not why I joined the force. I didn't give a damn about smuggled fags. All we achieved was taking out a few blokes at the end of the supply chain. As I speak, cigarettes are being smuggled into every port in the land. No, I preferred the human touch. Solving crime by working out people and what makes them tick."

"Perhaps you should have just left London and joined another police force."

"I was offered an inspector's job in Newcastle, but I don't really understand the north-east, and I was offered another inspector's job in Anglesey, but I didn't fancy spending all my days going after delinquent sheep."

"What was the last job that you worked on in London?"

"The last *big* job—there were always lots of smaller jobs to work on—was the Hatton Garden jewellery heist. It was almost reassuring to bust a bunch of middle-aged geezers from the East End. George Fitchett, Tommy Carter, Dennis Wragg and Harry Goodman: proper old-school tealeafs, they were."

"And now you're a private detective."

"Yes, it's much more my scene. It's more personal. I get to solve puzzles, and the longer it takes me to solve the puzzles the more I get paid."

Rick shot me with a smirk, and I winked at him.

"And I don't even have to arrest people."

"Will Caitlin be arrested?"

"Possibly…"

The wind had stiffened so we retreated inside the obelisk and sat down on the curved bench. Rick's hands were in his jacket pockets. His hair was untidy and he had not shaved for a day or two. He was a handsome chap, solemn, and wrapped up in himself, a man entombed inside several shells, like a Russian doll. He was a man whose inner self was desperate to say something but whose many shells were keeping the words contained within. I tried to coax the words from him.

"You said you wanted to talk to me about something, Rick."

"I just wanted to talk to you…about something, about everything, about nothing in particular. You're a good man, Daniel, someone who *knows*, someone who *cares*. There are not many men—not many *people*—like you about. I can relate to you, if that makes any sort of sense."

"I'm just a regular guy, Rick."

"I don't think so."

"I'm just like everyone else, Rick. I'm caught up in this calamitous sea, clinging onto the life raft. With any luck, we'll all reach the port of eternal bliss in one piece."

"That's a noble sentiment, Daniel, but my life raft has capsized and I'm drowning."

"Hang on a little while longer and the storm will pass. You'll see."

"You're a man I can trust, Daniel, so thanks, thanks for everything. I feel better now. I'll just say goodbye to Mel. Then we can go. I reckon I can face the world with a bit more strength in me now. I just wanted somebody to understand. I just wanted a friend."

"What about Matt?"

"He's a friend, yes, but he doesn't understand, not really."

"After this past week, I'm not sure that I know Matt at all."

"Now, Matt *is* your regular kind of guy. Okay to have a beer with, but there's no side to him, either good or bad."

"Oh, I wouldn't say that. I've discovered that he can be devious and cunning. He's certainly given me the runaround these last few days."

"I think you're crediting him with too much depth of character."

"You're probably right, Rick, but don't ever tell him that, will you?"

Rick smiled. Then we got up to go. The rain was coming at us from all directions now, but we didn't mind that. He looked like a man reborn. I was simply enjoying the rain.

TWENTY-NINE

My meeting with Rick had turned into a bout of mutual soul-searching, and I had the sense that we'd recognised each other as kindred spirits. We'd seen innocence reflected in each other; innocence educated by experience rather than blighted by it. Rick was a man of my age whose course of life had been nothing like my own, save, perhaps, for similar tastes in music and a single mutual friend. Our lives had converged in a moment, in Oxford, and, doubtless, would thenceforth diverge, though I hoped that we would remain friends. If we were to have remained friends of the spirit, rather than actual friends, I would not have been at all unhappy with that. The two of us had touched base, we had put down a marker for the sensibility that we shared. We had established kinship. It remained only to see what fate had in store for him once his wife's collar had been felt by the long arm of the law. For Rick, I hoped for the best, but I feared the worst. Caitlin Mallett was up to her neck in trouble; and to think that the finger of suspicion had been pointed at *him*.

***

I was back in the King's Head, drinking Tribute in the snug, meditating on all the loose ends that needed tying up in the case of Laura Hart. At the time, I gave little thought to the power that rested in my hands, courtesy of the disc that languished ominously in my safe. I was concerned more with the sheer joy of being able to wallow in the prospect of tidying up the collateral fruits of my labours.

I felt like a man who had built a house with his bare hands and had only the dusting and polishing to do to make the place fit for habitation. The hard work had been done, and I felt that I'd earned the good luck that had come my way during the course of the investigation.

Halfway through my pint, it occurred to me how many burdens I'd saddled myself with during the previous few days. To Kendal, then, had been added Dominic and Karl, two young men who needed guidance, the former far more than the latter. I even felt a little bit responsible for Rick. Thanks to me, his life would change irrevocably, for better or for worse. Selena, I reckoned, was strong enough not to need any further ministrations from me, and I hoped that she would find someone to take care of her, someone who would nurture and even feed off her strength of mind and spirit.

The barman approached me—he was young, a student, I was sure of that—and smiled. He was fresh-faced and curly-haired, and he spoke with a Home Counties accent.

"Last call for lunch, sir," he said. "Have you decided if you want to eat?"

I looked at the clock on the wall over the bar. The time was nearly two o'clock.

"It's a bit late for lunch," I replied.

"Not just yet," the barman said.

I looked over the young man and wondered what life had in store for him. Would he have a successful career? Would he be a doctor, or a lawyer, or a politician? A stockbroker, I guessed, oiling the wheels of capitalism, working in the City, beginning his professional life sharing a house in the East End with people of his own age, background, and tastes. Such would be a somewhat predictable rite of passage before the equally foreseeable retreat to Surrey with his new wife to make house and home for themselves and their children. Or was I doing the young man a disservice by stereotyping him? For all I knew, he was a potential artist or writer or philosopher or sculptor or any other kind of creative soul uninterested in embarking on what Forster called the longest journey.

"Go on then," I said. "Scampi and chips, please. Oh, and one more pint."

"Coming right up, sir."

The previous evening, I'd gone to Mass at the Oratory, sitting at the back, as usual, and observing proceedings with interest. I'd gone to the altar rail for a blessing during Holy Communion. After Mass, I'd chatted with Helena. I'd invited her to dine with me, on the Tuesday of the following week, at Gino's, a fine Italian restaurant down by Gloucester Green bus station, a setting much more romantic than it sounds. To my relief, Helena had accepted, and she had concurred with my claim that Gino's made the best spaghetti carbonara outside Italy. I'd warned her that I would regale her with chapter and verse of the case of Laura Hart, and I'd promised that I would see her the following day, the Friday about which now I write, at the Oratory, again, for the Mass.

It wasn't that I needed divine fortification for that Friday evening, which I knew would be eventful and a tad fraught, but I thought that a bit of help from the Almighty would not go amiss.

Seeing Helena, too, would help me. Each time I saw her, I drew from her a sense of consolation, something soothing and ennobling, as if she represented in her distinguished and beautiful form an inexhaustible reservoir of goodness to offset the myriad horrors of the world. Our relationship was analogous to something poised exquisitely on the cusp between literature and philosophy, or between prose and poetry, or between the blissful indulgence that was pure thought and the sublime possibilities of expression.

There was no goddess in the pantheon of Ancient Greece as glorious as Helena Johnson-Roffey. What in the name of Zeus, I wondered, did I have to offer *her*? As my lunch and beer arrived, I pondered that it would take a God infinitely greater than even Zeus himself to bring Helena and me together and to keep us together until death did us part. I was poking my chips, rearranging them on my plate, when I considered the Annunciation and the Archangel Gabriel's telling Mary that her aged cousin Elizabeth was with child, and that she was so for the simple reason that nothing was impossible with God.

Another pint did nothing to keep my dreams and related meditations on the omnipotence of the Godhead in check.

THIRTY

When I arrived at the Wolvercote Hotel (by taxi), the dinner was over and the dance about to start. A band prepared to begin its cabaret, its two vocalists and three musicians looking intense, as if their lives depended on the quality of their performances. The band members regarded each other furtively, each fearful that they might be the one to sabotage the show, each suspecting that one of the others would supply the wrong note or prove to lack the requisite vocal range. I wondered how such an apparently disharmonious collection of individuals could possibly produce harmony in their music.

"What time do you call this?" Matt demanded as I entered the dining area.

"I needed a couple of drinks."

"The dinner's over."

I surveyed the scene of devastation before me. The dinner had not been eaten so much as demolished. Images raced through my mind. A gang of Mafia hoods had stormed the building and sprayed bullets everywhere, causing blood and glass and china, and meat and vegetables, to scatter in all directions. A fleet of bulldozers had driven through the party and flattened everything before it. A brawl had broken out in which not only fists were thrown. I was put in mind of the scene in *Carry On Up The Khyber*, when native insurgents dropped bombs on the British officers at dinner, who carried on dining, regardless, passing the port around the table, and the band played on as the ceiling and other parts of the shattered building rained down upon them.

"So I see." My tone was sardonic, as well as a tad nervous, for there was potential for my plans for the evening to go horribly wrong.

"On the way in, we drew names from a hat to see who we would sit with. On my table of six, as luck would have it, were both Donna and Sheryl, so you can imagine what an uncomfortable couple of hours I've just had."

"Who was on my table?"

"Rachel Bannerman was one…"

"It's a good job I missed the dinner then."

Around us people stood in groups, at the bar, at the wrecked tables, and on the outskirts of the dance floor.

"So, what happens now?" I asked.

"We dance."

"No, thanks, you're not my type."

***

I went to the bar to buy a round of drinks. The band, The Vignettes, was in full swing. People were recognising their musical facsimiles.

"That's a Duke Ellington number!"

"That's a Miles Davis!"

To my left, as I waited to be served, the group of women that I was trying to avoid was chatting semi-drunkenly over cocktails. There was one woman in the group whom I did not recognise, but I'd just heard her referred to as Louise, so I assumed her to be Louise Duffy. I listened to their conversation.

"What is your funniest memory of The Golden Age?"

The question had been put by Donna, and I eagerly awaited the answers.

"For me," Jean said, "it has to be the time when Somerset Pheasant locked himself out of his house, smashed a window to get in, and then realised he was at the wrong address."

There followed an outbreak of laughter, followed by a synchronised drinking from glasses.

"For me," Rachel began, "it was when Tucker Plumlee proposed to Victoria Carnegie-Arbutnott in reception, when, unbeknownst to him, the intercom was switched on."

"That's right," Sheryl said, "and she replied, in her posh voice, 'I regret that I have to inhabit the same planet as you, you malodorous guttersnipe, so your proposal of marriage can only be viewed with utter disdain.'"

Sheryl's mimicking of the said accent sent the company into raptures.

"What about you, Louise?" Donna asked.

"It has to be the time when Archie Buffkins went onto his roof to replace a slate, and his ladder was blown away by the wind."

"That's right, I remember," Donna said. "He had his mobile with him, and he called you frantic with worry."

Harry said that she was not surprised, and that she wouldn't want to be on a roof without a ladder on a windy day.

"Yes, but what was funnier," Louise went on, "was that Brian Boobyear, Archie's next-door neighbour, was standing in his garden throwing apples at Archie, trying to knock him off the roof."

The women laughed and drank from their glasses.

"Archie Buffkins could have been seriously injured, or even killed, but you can see the funny side," Louise concluded.

"It's your turn, Sheryl," Donna said.

"I'd say it was the time when I went to see Tristram Featherstone-Grundy about his rent arrears, and, during a break in our interview, he fell down his toilet."

Louise was so overcome with laughter that it was all she could do to ask what happened next.

"I heard him screaming, calling for help, so I ran up the stairs to see what was happening. He was in hysterics. I thought he'd set himself alight or something."

Harry was desperate to know how the lavatorial impasse was resolved.

"Well, I was all set to kick the toilet door in, when I saw that it was unlocked. When I entered the lavatory, I saw that Tristram—posh, but seriously confused, Tristram—had his arse and legs stuck in the toilet. He'd sat on it without putting the seat down, and had fallen in."

Amid the hilarity, Rachel begged to be told what transpired next.

"I gave him my hand and helped him out," Sheryl returned. "He's a big guy, so it wasn't easy, and he was in the middle of parking his breakfast, so it wasn't pleasant."

"It's a good job you told us that *after* dinner and not *before*," Jean said.

"You next, Harry…"

"Well, for me, there can be only one answer."

"What's that?"

"It has to be the time, on my first day, when I took a call from Dingleby Scroop."

"What happened?"

"I can't remember what the issue was, but what was funny, what cracked me up at the time, was the bloody name, Dingleby Scroop. I mean, it's like something out of a Dickens novel."

"We've had some laughs," Louise said.

"And long may the laughs continue," Donna added.

"Do you think things will change at the new office?" Louise asked.

"If you mean our corporate culture," Donna replied, "then, no, why should it?"

"We're moving into a pristine new office."

"That's just window-dressing," Donna said. "Believe me, nothing will change. I'm not sure that any of us want change."

"Things had *better* change," Harry said. "We can't carry on being a total shambles."

"Does it matter?" Donna said. "We're in the not-for-profit sector."

"Right now," Harry said, "we're in the going-bust-very-fast sector."

"How do you figure that?" Louise said.

"The small matter of overspending our maintenance budget last year by one-hundred-per-cent..."

"That's because we're not strict enough with the tenants," Jean put in. "They phone, say they want this, and they want that, and we give it them. We're a soft touch."

"Don't tell me," Harry rejoined. "Tell senior management. They're always telling me to keep maintenance spending down, but, whenever we refuse to give a tenant what they want, the suits overrule us. They will the end, but they don't will the means."

"Talking of senior management," Donna said, "they were all standing at the other end of the bar just now, but they seem to have left us."

Rachel opined that the chief executive's speech had been crushingly dull, and that she had never heard so many platitudes in one speech.

"Don't they live in Australia?" Donna asked.

"What?"

"Those duck-billed platitudes ..."

"You mean the duck-billed platypus?"

"Oh, yes ..."

Jean asked why Rosie Waterhouse was not in attendance.

"Why, indeed?" I said to myself.

"Of course, Matt Prior is here, the Lone Ranger, though what his trusty sidekick, Tonto, is doing here is anyone's guess."

"They are Batman and Robin," Jean added.

"Holmes and Watson," Donna snarled.

"Hey, Donna," Louise said. "You haven't told us about *your* funniest moment."

"That's easy."

"Do tell."

"The time when Matt Prior was attacked by Gwendoline Caspar's Rottweiler ..."

"That must have been well funny," Jean said.

"Unfortunately, Matt spoiled the fun by getting away."

***

"This band's just gone up in my estimation," Matt declared. "This is *The Paris Match*, by the Style Council…and that bird's got a great voice."

I could not help but notice that a great voice was not her only attribute.

"They've just done *Have You Ever Had It Blue?*," I replied.

"How did I miss that?"

"You were too busy having a slanging match with Donna Tamsin."

"Well, I was on my way back from the gent's, and she accosted me."

"What did she want?"

"She knows."

"Knows what?"

"She knows that something's going down tonight. She knows that because you're here, and you would not be here otherwise."

"I assumed that the purpose of my presence here tonight was to send them a signal, to unnerve them."

"Donna asked me what the hell you were doing here. She called you my boyfriend."

"Well, she would know all about that sort of thing, wouldn't she?"

About five yards from us, but still within earshot amid the din, stood Neil and Lester.

"It's a shame that Karl couldn't come tonight," Lester said. "He owes me some blow." The man from Liverpool drained his glass of lager.

Neil looked around the dining area at the wreckage. He watched as the waiting staff worked tirelessly to clear up the mess. They were having to step over streamers and spent crackers as they dashed to and from the kitchen in their black outfits. His eyes followed a particularly attractive blonde girl whose dash was more of a skip. She was graceful and feline, sinuous in her movements.

"Do you think she would purr if I stroked her?" Neil asked.

"There's only one way to find out," answered Lester.

Out of nowhere, Harry appeared on the scene. "All right, are we, lads?" she said in a tone that was to sobriety what Her Majesty the Queen was to a bacon butty.

"Couldn't be better, Miss Arroyo," Lester replied.

"Miss who?" Neil enquired, his features compressed in half-drunken bafflement and his hair spiked like a virgin toilet brush.

Harry looked angrily at Lester. Her face turned bright red. Hers was the kind of pale Celtic complexion, accentuated as it was by a mass of black hair, that flushed easily.

"Isn't she a porn star?"

Harry flushed a deeper shade of red. "Isn't it your round, Neil?" she ventured to ask.

Sensing that Lester and Harry needed a private moment together, Neil took his leave awkwardly.

"What are you playing at, Lester?"

"Leave it out," Lester returned. "As if Neil's going to work it out…"

"You do *not* use my…my…nom de guerre in public! Do you understand?"

"It was a slip of the tongue."

"Like hell it was. What's your game, Lester?"

"Well, now that you come to mention it, there is the small matter of the appointment to the post of supervisor that you're in the process of creating."

"How do you know about that?"

"You forget that my girlfriend is a business manager and, as such, is party to such discussions."

Harry shook her head. "How very cosy."

"Look, I hate to exploit the situation, but there are photos in my possession which could easily—accidentally on purpose, like—slip into the public domain."

"You hate to exploit the situation, my arse. You're loving it."

"Why are you so ready to assume that I have an ulterior motive?"

"Because you *do* have an ulterior motive…"

"I'm just protecting my interests."

"You have as much to lose by showing those photos as I do."

"How do you work that out?"

"You want people to see photos of you at an orgy?"

"My reputation would be enhanced. Yours, on the other hand…"

"You've got it all worked out, haven't you?"

"One photo would be particularly damaging to your reputation."

"Which one's that then?"

"The one in which I'm asking you what a nice girl like you is doing so intimately acquainted with my manhood."

"I wouldn't even think about doing that with you again, now that I know you."

"I agree. The anonymity is half the thrill."

"And I wouldn't have joined Greetwell at all, never mind the customer-service centre, had I known that you worked here."

"Well, unluckily for you, I *do* work here."

"You know what, Lester?"

"What?"

"You wouldn't dare show that photo."

"Wouldn't I?"

"I dare you."

"Okay," Lester said. "If you haven't given me a 'yes' to the job by lunchtime on Monday, that photo—and, perhaps, other photos too—will turn up somewhere most embarrassing for you."

"Where?"

"Do you really want to find out?"

Matt and I exchanged knowing glances, for the overheard conversation had answered questions that had long been circulating at Greetwell Housing Trust. Matt wanted Lester and Harry to know that their careless talk had reached our ears, so that we were now party to the confidence, and that their long-kept secret was out.

"Hey, keep the noise down over there, will you?" Matt said in a sadistic tone that shocked me, for I'd never seen that side of his nature before; in fact, I'd never seen any side of him other than the straightforward and transparent one that my hitherto one-dimensional friend had ever shown to the world.

"Go to hell, Matt!"

***

Although people were letting their hair down and enjoying themselves, they were doing so in clusters. I looked around me and saw groups of people huddled together, a group here and another there, like sheep scattered across a field in pockets of unity. Matt and I watched as people shifted self-consciously on the dancefloor, looking about as comfortable as vampires at a laser show.

"Look at Jim McBride and Sue Carter," Matt said. "There's definitely something going on between those two."

"They're just dancing ... and not very well."

"Sue's in danger of knocking herself out, jumping around with Bristols like hers."

"It looks like she's trying to knock *Jim* out."

"*You* would knock *me* out if you got a round in."

"I got the last round in."

"Trust you to quibble over minor details."

"Is it fair to say that Greetwell Housing Trust is ridden with cliques?"

"Looking around at the huddled groups of people, I think it's fair to say that we're not one big happy family."

"This venue doesn't help."

"Too right, it's vast, and we're—what?—sixty people."

"That dancefloor's practically a bus ride away."

"When you finally go to the bar to get the drinks, I'll give you the cab fare."

"Look at the drummer."

"I'm looking at him."

"He hasn't taken his eyes off the singer's backside since they started playing."

"What, Nina Simone over there?"

"She's prettier than Nina Simone."

"Yes, she's rather cute." Matt looked over his shoulder at the gathering of women by the bar. "Unlike that lot over there," he added.

"They're looking at us."

"Have you ever seen such a harem?"

"A coven, more like…"

"So, what's your strategy, you know, with the disc?"

"I've told you what it is."

"So, Kendal and Dominic, they're both at Saint Aldate's nick now, are they?"

"As we speak…"

"There's going to be some drama in this place later then."

"Perhaps we could be elsewhere when it all kicks off."

"You must be joking! I wouldn't miss this hour of reckoning for the world!"

"You're not going to be Mister Popular at work on Monday morning."

"I don't care. The people who have done wrong will be out of the company."

"And Rick? How do you think he'll cope without Caitlin?"

"Well, I doubt that anything will happen to Caitlin. And her employer need never know about her involvement with Laura Hart's death, so she needn't lose her job either."

"Rick will know."

"He'll forgive her."

"I dare say he will, but will Caitlin forgive herself?"

"She'll have to, or she and Rick are finished."

"I suppose I'd better get the drinks in then."

"Not before time…"

"Are you going to stand here like a spare one at a wedding?"

"No, while you're at the bar, I'll go for a walk." Matt ran his eyes over the various coalitions. "I'm sure there's a group out there somewhere that will take me in. I'm not a complete outcast just yet."

"This song sounds familiar, but I can't place it," I said.

"It's *Black Friday*, by Steely Dan."

"How apt," I said. "Same again?"

"Same again..."

***

The police arrived before the evening degenerated into outright drunken acrimony. Tensions were running high, and fingers of suspicion were being pointed, most of them at me. I was right in the firing line, and in those heated circumstances the ability of the accusers to aim straight was not affected by the amount of alcohol consumed, except to make the aim more likely to hit the target. I was reeling and eager to make myself scarce and make last orders at the Dew Drop, my sanctuary.

The arrival of a posse of soberly dressed detectives would put the dampeners on any party, and this one ended with a splash. One minute the music was playing, and people dancing, the next minute the band had fallen silent and people were being led away by uniformed officers. The band didn't even finish the Nina Simone number they were playing.

Donna Tamsin was the last person to be escorted off the premises. I couldn't let her go without saying something to her.

"Why, Donna?" I asked.

"Each time we met, we became more daring," Donna began earnestly. "By Christmas Eve last, sexually, there was nothing left for us to do. We were in a trance, induced by sexual pleasure. We were in a strange place, all of us. And we knew that Laura wished to die. She was so unhappy. She'd tried to take her own life several times before. In our collective trance, with the threat of violence in the air, we became hysterical. We made sure that our friend died happy."

"What about Dominic? You were prepared to see him go down for the 'murder' of Laura."

Donna dropped her head in shame.

"No, we weren't." The voice was Rachel's. She was shackled to a tall muscular detective who was impatient to frogmarch her away. "Not all of us." She smiled wanly as she was taken away to an uncertain future.

My phone rang. It was Rick calling. He told me that Caitlin had just been taken away by the police. I told him that I knew. I reminded him of the need to be strong. He told me that, having lost his daughter, he couldn't bear to lose his wife. I'd made an omelette, all right, and eggs had been well and truly broken.

***

Matt stopped the car outside The Golden Age, erstwhile home of Greetwell Housing Trust. The Mother and Baby Unit was still there and would stay there. Rain was falling, so Kendal, behind me on the passenger side, wiped condensation from the window in order to see outside. Dominic leaned forward to look too.

"It's sad to see the old place in such a sorry state," Matt said. "It'll be pulled down on Monday, if it hasn't *fallen* down by then."

"What's that written on the front door?" Kendal asked.

Words had been sprayed on the door.

"That, no doubt, is Lola Djemba Djemba's handiwork," Matt said.

We all marvelled at the four words.

"SATAN'S WORK IS DONE."

www.ingramcontent.com/pod-product-compliance
Lightning Source LLC
Chambersburg PA
CBHW030801200726
48285CB00013B/363